THE WOMAN IN ROOM 9

TIM ADLER

INKUBATOR
BOOKS

Published by Inkubator Books
www.inkubatorbooks.com

Copyright © 2025 by Tim Adler

Tim Adler has asserted his right to be identified as the author of this work.

ISBN (eBook): 978-1-83756-617-4
ISBN (Paperback): 978-1-83756-618-1
ISBN (Hardback): 978-1-83756-619-8

CHAPTER ONE

Blood.

My hands and arms are covered in blood.

I don't know where it's come from. All I know is that it's all over me, right up my arms with an awful, cloying smell. They're slathered with it and it's drying already. I'm about to wipe this ghastly mess down the front of my nightdress but that's stiff with blood too, like a butcher's apron.

Where's this blood come from?

Why am I covered with it?

I have absolutely no idea where I am or how I got here. I am standing in a hallway I don't recognise in a bloody white nightdress. Got to get out. My bloody fingers scrabble with the brass door latch, only I can't open it. Something terrible has happened—that I do know—right behind me.

Finally, the latch gives and I'm out the front door, clattering down stone steps, out into the street. Swerve left. I'm not wearing any shoes and the pavement is icy cold.

This London street is empty. Pale Belgravia white-stucco houses behind railings face each other. It's the dead of night and nobody is around to see what's happening. No one is awake. Just the moon above the cold winter street.

Suddenly, I do remember something.

A man's head pooled in gore, his blood edging towards me along the grouting in between floor tiles. The blood I am now covered in. He's staring at me, a question on his dead lips, asking, "Why did you do this to me?"

The shock of what's happened sends me into convulsions. My whole body is shaking and there's nothing I can do about it.

That's when I remember to scream.

My scream is loud enough to penetrate the brickwork. A dog barks. Up ahead, a third-floor bedroom light snaps on. Thank God, they've heard me. If I scream again, they will call the police.

"Help!" I scream. "Murder, murder!"

I'm running along the pavement, my bare feet slapping stone. It's cold enough to split paving slabs and my nightdress feels like tissue paper. The air is so sharp, it's painful to breathe. But I need to scream. Somebody help me. For God's sake, somebody help me.

This time when I howl, my guts feel as if they're being pulled out through my mouth.

The front door slams behind me. Heavy boots. He's coming after me, the man I must get away from; I know that. *Faster. You must run faster.* He's gaining. I sense him coming up behind me and I trip over my legs, feel myself going, but no, I'm back up on my feet again.

The houses jangle as I run towards them, breathing hard, trying to reach the end of the road. Something tells me there's more people there. The more I run towards it, the street stretches farther away.

That's when I hear it. The reassuring grumble of a London taxi coming towards me. Thank God. I yell for it to stop, flagging it down. But the driver switches off his for-hire light once he spots me, shaking his head. For a moment I can see what he sees, a hysterical woman in a bloody white nightdress, trying to flag down a taxi.

Turn left at the junction. That way leads to Victoria Station. There are always people around a railway station, aren't there? Find the police. Tell them I didn't do it. Throw myself on their mercy. They'll believe me. They have to.

I turn left into Upper Belgrave Street. Only this street is empty too. I stand in the middle of the road, my bloody arms outstretched, as if pleading for witnesses.

For a moment, I glance back and glimpse *him*, the man coming after me. He's stopped, winded, hands-on-knees as he gets his breath back. Why's he stopped? What's he seen that I haven't?

I hear it before I see it. Behind me. Another lone taxi in the dead of night coming straight at me. Yellow for-hire sign on. Time slows and stretches out, as if everything has gone into slow motion. I stare into its headlights. Can't move. Then I push my arms out as if I can repel two tonnes of metal.

Then the taxi hits and I glimpse the driver's terrified face. The street windmills upside down as I somersault over its bonnet. A descent into something I don't understand but is inevitable. This is going to hurt.

In that moment, I see his beautiful face again, blood pooled around him like a spreading halo, a question on his lips, asking me why, why have I done this to him, and I have no answer. Then, looking up at a woman in a wheelchair, rigid with shock at the top of the stairs when she spots the two of us, and a man placing his hand over mine in a theatre box, and his grin as he hands me a glass of champagne, and this woman again, catching me wearing one of her dresses, our eyes meeting in the wardrobe mirror. Then pushing her along in a wheelchair, and the very first time I walked up those front steps into that house and went through the front door—

All these images flash through my head in an instant, before the hard tarmac rushes up towards me and I think, this is it, the moment of my death—

Something black explodes in my head and that's the last thing I feel.

Oblivion.

CHAPTER TWO

Silence.

The black slowly, so very slowly, begins to lighten.

Open your eyes. Everything's blurry as my eyes adjust to wherever I am. Sudden focus. This must be Heaven. Only it can't be Heaven because the ceiling I'm staring up at is covered in dirty polystyrene tiles. God wouldn't allow a grubby ceiling, would he?

I have no idea what this place is. All I know is that I have a pounding, throbbing headache and I want to swallow. Only I can't. Through my brain fog, I realise I've got some kind of hose shoved down my throat, taped over my mouth, gagging me. It's so invasive and my throat feels raw, as if I've been strangled. I just want it off me, all of it.

Somebody has placed an iron band around my head, and they're tightening the screws, one by one.. I've got a neck brace on too—I can feel it—so I can't move my head. A fly edges across my cheek, its tiny legs padding up my skin, and I'm desperate to shake it off, shoo it away. The fly edges towards my open eye and it's unbearable. Suddenly, it buzzes off. Only I can still hear it, flying around, tormenting me just beyond where I can see it.

Where is this place? What am I doing here?

I flash on those images. They felt so real. *Looking down at my arms slathered in gore, wiping them down the front of my nightdress. The sweet smell of dried blood, not my own. Knowing that I've got to get out of there. A man lurching forward, trying to block me. Bolting for the front door, my fingers scrabbling with the bloody entry lock. Throwing myself down those front steps and out into the street. The taxi accelerating towards me.*

Then nothing.

A yawning chasm opens up beneath me as I realise...

I have absolutely no idea who I am.

What my name is, how I came to be here, any of it. It's all a complete blank. Rising panic. To my right, some kind of monitor, where I can't see it, starts beeping. Keep calm. Only the beeps get more insistent.

This place must be a hospital. I must be in hospital. I want to cry out for help, but this ribbed tube is rammed down my throat, connected to the machine helping me to breathe. In, out, in, out.

Keep calm, whoever you are. Fight the rising claustrophobia. At the same time, everything hurts, with deep throbbing pain. Somebody tried to kill me. Yes, that's it. *Those images, the only things I remember, they weren't a dream, they were real.*

That's when the itching begins, a maddening itch which I just can't get to. I cannot scratch my scalp through my dirty hair. I smell rank and my hair feels so greasy. I am fully awake now and I just want somebody to come into this room and find me. Please, before I go insane.

Fractionally, I turn my head and notice a grey bulb that's been looped around my iron bedhead. Some kind of alarm. If I could just reach that alarm with my fingers, I could call for help.

But when I look down at both arms lying over the hospital blanket, I'm shocked. They're so terribly thin, almost skeletal, marked with bruises. Cannulas are taped over my elbows with tubes coming out of them. I can't move either arm. They won't do what my brain tells them to.

Please, somebody help me. A tear edges into the corner of my eye. *For God's sake, someone please find me.*

Finally, someone does run into the room. She's bustling around my bed, and I blink my eyes wider to show that I'm awake. She stands over me, peering closer. She's a nurse. So I was right. This is a hospital.

Suddenly, she turns on her heels and runs out. *Wait! Don't leave! Come back. Water, I need water.* But I can't speak because I've got this alien thing rammed down my throat.

I want all of this off me.

There's two of them now standing over my bed. The first nurse takes my hand, and I feel its warmth.

"Can you hear me?"

Slight nod, more of a grimace with this neck brace on. Even that takes all my effort.

"Well done. Can you squeeze my hand, please?"

I squeeze her large brown hand.

The one thing I can do is make a feeble scissor motion with my fingers. I want these lines and tubes and catheters ripped out of me, so I can breathe again, on my own. Understanding, the nurse nods and moves away. *No, don't leave me. I didn't mean that. Don't leave me like this.*

Things move quickly after that. A penlight is shone into my eyes, momentarily blinding me. Intense white light. I flinch.

"You have a tube in your mouth. We're going to try and remove it. Is that okay?" She gives me a blue-gloved thumb-up. "Nurse, can you please extubate?"

"I've turned off the ventilator."

"I'm going to count from one to three and then I want you to cough, okay?"

On the count of three, I cough. Slowly, the ribbed plastic hose is pulled out through my mouth. It hurts even through what I'm guessing is a fog of painkillers. There seems to be yards of it, and I just want it out of me. Finally, the plastic hose is prised away, and I can breathe again.

Thank God. I take in my first gasp of real air. Reborn.

"Well done. Just breathe for me, okay? I'm going to give you some oxygen through your nose." She plugs some kind of plastic clip into my nostrils, and I can feel clean air. "Are you okay? Just breathe for me, okay?"

The first thing I need to do is ask questions. *Where am I? What am I doing here? What happened to me?* Most importantly, *who am I?*

But when I open my mouth, nothing happens. I can form words in my head, in my mouth, but nothing comes out.

"You're in hospital. You're in safe hands. We will explain what happened to you later, okay?"

Whatever it was that I saw or did, my bloody hands, someone coming after me, being knocked down by that taxi, I can't tell them, can't say what I witnessed.

Because I can't get the words out.

I cannot speak.

CHAPTER THREE

They keep the blinds closed to help my eyes. I don't even know whether it's day or night. The strange thing is that nobody says a word to me. Not really. They haven't said who I am or how I came to be here. Surely, they must know I have so many questions. And I still can't say a word. The best I can do is grunt.

What I do know is that they've got me on strong medication, as if my brain is wrapped in coarse blanket wool, making it difficult to think.

The nurses make sympathetic faces while they change my bedpan. My scratchy nightgown is covered with diagonals spelling out the word Hallam in tiny brown letters. Some part of me thinks I should recognise this name. Maybe it's my surname but I don't think so.

The Asian nurse—Linh, I think her name is—comes to give me a bed bath. Seeing my naked body stretched out before me for the first time, I am shocked. I am painfully thin. All joints and angles with my bones jutting out of me. My breasts have shrunk, and I touch my ladder of ribs.. Like somebody you see on a TV documentary about starvation. Or behind barbed wire in a prison camp. My God, what have they done to me?

Worst of all, I can still smell myself, sour and rank. Nurse Linh twitters on, telling me that she's just got back from holiday seeing her family in Vietnam as she wipes me down with a flannel. Because I can't reply, I am her unwilling audience of one.

Later, the other nurse, Birgita, runs a wand up and down the soles of my feet and, understanding, I nod. She tests my pathetic grip strength and reflexes, telling me to track her finger with my eyes. She massages my arms and legs, as if rubbing my dead flesh is somehow going to bring it back to life.

Together, they talk over me, as if I'm not even here, while they remake the bed. Neither of them will meet my eye, almost as if they're afraid of me. This heavy presence hangs over us, glowering, like the moment before a thunderstorm when the first raindrops tap at the window.

All I can do is lie here, neither alive nor dead, like in one of those zombie films we used to watch—wait, that was a memory. A memory of what? Who's the *we* I'm thinking of? Then a woman's voice, as clear as a bell, says sharply, "Everybody betrays each other in the end."

That woman's voice wakes me. I must have fallen asleep because the blinds are drawn back for the very first time. But there's nobody in my room. Yet that voice was inside my head. Even though the venetian blinds have been opened, there are still iron bars on the windows, flecked from where the paint has gone, as if somebody has gnawed at them with their teeth.

Is this a hospital or a prison?

Beyond the window is a porridgey grey sky and what looks like marshland stretching into the distance. Wherever I am, this is an eerily desolate place, with nothing on the horizon. It's the gloom of a mid-winter English afternoon.

Nurse Birgita fusses around me, pulling me farther up my bed. Everything throbs. I feel like an old sofa with busted springs as she manhandles me into position.

"Doctor Quane is coming to see you," the nurse says briskly.

Doctor Quane, when he finally arrives, has a kindly face like a Victorian cleric, and his round gold wireframe glasses remind me of John Lennon. At least I remember The Beatles.

I want to sit up but it's too much of an effort and, in any case, he raises his hand to stop me. I slowly lift my own hand towards my parched lips.

"Speak? You're asking when will you be able to speak?" I nod as hard as I can. "Your vocal cords are the same as your muscles. They've wasted away. Don't try to speak. You haven't used them in a long time. I just want you to blink once for yes and twice for no. Can you do that for me?"

I give him an exaggerated blink.

"Do you know where you are?"

Double blink.

"Do you know why you're here?"

Two more rapid blinks.

He scrutinises me carefully. Frowns. Then he says, "Do you know what your name is?"

This time I manage an almost imperceptible shake of my head. It's the first time I have actually moved my neck in what feels like years.

Who are these people and why have I woken up in this

place? It's like I'm Sleeping Beauty but this isn't a children's fairy story, it's a nightmare.

"You really have no idea who you are," he marvels, shaking his head.

I make a writing motion with my bruised hand, like pushing a planchette on a Ouija board, the dead sending a message to the living. Doctor Quane takes a moment before he understands and unclips my medical notes from my footboard. He turns the paper over and fishes around for a pen.

My writing is childish, as if I'm back in primary school, still learning to form words. I can just about scrawl "Where am I?" before the effort wears me out.

I have been away for a very long time; that I do know. All I want is a mirror to see how many years I have lost and how old I have become. Because I get the feeling I must be a wizened old woman. I must be at least one hundred years old.

"You're in a hospital in Suffolk. A place called Orford Ness. You've been asleep for a long time."

How long? Weeks, months, years? Self-pity wells up inside me. *Stop it. That's not going to help. It's not going to get you out of here.*

I grip the pen tighter and scrawl another word.

"Why?"

I'm so tired through whatever pills they've got me on that even writing this one word exhausts me. I let the Biro drop.

"You were knocked down by a car. You've been in a coma. I've been in charge of your care ever since you came here. I'm a consultant psychiatrist. Nurse Birgita and I have been looking after you."

Nurse Birgita, the one who's been pulling me about, changing my dressings and emptying my bedpan, nods but it's more like a frown. She touches the crucifix on her neck, as if I'm somebody to be afraid of.

She's wary around me, disapproving. I get the feeling she doesn't like me very much. Or worse, she's frightened of me. Why? What have I done to hurt her? The way she treats me, it's as if I'm a wild animal. Or something unclean to be kept at arm's length. Doctor Quane smiles. "This is a psychiatric hospital specialising in brain injury trauma. You're our only patient. This entire facility has been kept open just for you."

What kind of hospital only has one patient?

I tap my Biro-ed scrawl again.

"Why?"

This time, Doctor Quane shakes his head. "No, you're not ready yet. Listen, my hobby is scuba diving. You've been down further than anybody else has, probably ever, and we've got to take things slowly, like a diver coming up too fast that gets the bends. Let's get your motor actions working first, and then we'll talk."

No, this won't do. I need answers and I need them now. I tap the word "Why" impatiently with the Biro before under-lining it twice.

"You see—" He pauses, weighing up just how much to tell me. "Your name is Susan Gummer and you're probably the most famous coma victim in the world. You've been asleep for ten years."

CHAPTER FOUR

Ten years?

I have been asleep in a hospital bed, this white coffin, for ten years. I was knocked down by a car and then I woke up in this place. A whole decade missing. But it's worse than that. Because they don't know that I don't remember anything about who I am or how I came to be here either.

Blood on my arms. Running down the street. That taxi accelerating towards me.

That's all I know.

One thing I can do is see what I look like. There's a washbasin over in the corner with those long-handled chrome taps and a mirror above the basin, only it's oddly made of polished tin, not glass.

My toes gingerly touch the cold hospital floor. Pushing with my elbows, I bounce on the mattress edge, hoping to get some momentum. That's it, I'm up. I teeter for a moment, afraid I'm going to crash to the floor, unsure of how to take my first step.

Suddenly, I feel myself going. It's inevitable. The floor rears up and there's nothing I can do about it as my head crashes into the cold linoleum. Thudding pain. Blue dots circling my head. The room canted at ninety degrees and everything spinning in figures of eight.

There, that'll knock some sense into you, I think, sniffing hard to get rid of the bulb of blood perched on my nostril.

And that's how the nurse finds me, sprawled on the floor with my scratchy nightgown hitched up to my bum, showing off my humiliatingly soggy paper knickers.

"Look here, what's going on?" she says, running into the room.

You tell me.

You're the ones keeping things secret from me, who won't tell me who I am or what I'm doing in this place.

We try again that afternoon.

I grip the bars of the walking frame with all my strength, which isn't much, terrified I might fall a second time. My nurse watches me as closely as an unforgiving ballet teacher.

"Look here, you're doing fine," she says. "Don't look down. Keep your eyes on me."

I still cannot speak. My vocal cords are raw from ten years of being intubated.

As far as I can work out, Nurse Birgita—whom Doctor Quane calls Bunny—is one of only two nurses working here. Nurse Linh, the nurse who also helped me wake up, is the other one. Apparently, there's a gardener and handyman called Hussein but I've yet to meet him.

It is Nurse Bunny who prepares my food and changes my sheets. Prepares my food—whom am I kidding? My throat is still so raw, all I can do is sip baby food she literally spoon-feeds me. Or suck in tepid soup through a straw. Being so helpless is humiliating.

I grunt, determined to take my first step, only my brain has forgotten how to move my legs.

The object of today's exercise is to make it as far as the commode beside my bed. That toilet seat might as well be on the dark side of the moon, as far as I'm concerned. I want to cry with frustration.

Move, damn you.

Finally, my foot scrapes along the floor and I take my very first step in ten years. Then my other foot. My face gets hot with the effort. I shuffle forward in an ungainly, rolling stagger.. I just want this all to stop. It's too much.

"Can't," I grunt.

Bunny's eyes widen and we both realise what's just happened.

I have spoken my very first word.

I'm so surprised, I nearly topple over, and Nurse Bunny grabs hold and steadies the frame.

"All right, girl. You done good today. Now, let's get you over to the potty."

Once I'm done, it's a relief to crawl back under the sheet and cellular blanket. I am totally wiped out. I smile weakly up at her.

"Now, you deserve something good to eat." She tells me I have been fed gloop through my nose and into my stomach for years. "I'm going to make you something in the kitchen. What do you want? You liked that spinach soup, didn't you?"

She talks to me in a cheerful singsong voice, as if I'm a child. I might not be able to speak yet, but I am a grown woman.

I shake my head. No more pureed pap. I have an overwhelming urge for protein — the most delicious, soft buttery goodness I can think of... scrambled eggs.

I manage to say "eggs" but it comes out more like a she-gorilla beating her chest.

"You're getting your appetite back, girl," Bunny says approvingly.

Waiting for Bunny to come back from the kitchen, I feel a creeping sense of guilt take hold. It's been getting worse. I can't seem to shake it. I must have done something very bad to wake up in this place, to be kept apart from the rest of the world. Because this isn't just a hospital, it's a high-security psychiatric unit.

An entire hospital being kept open for just one person, me, and they won't tell me why. What is it that I've done that makes those nurses so frightened of me?

My next goal is to shuffle on my walking frame out of my hospital room for the very first time. The shower is down the corridor. The idea of washing this rank grease off me seems like unimaginable luxury.

The top-floor corridor is drab and sagging, with buckets collecting rainwater from holes in the roof. I heard water coming in during the night. Dirty linoleum floor tiles. Chemical smell. It all seems in a very poor state for a private hospital.

There's a nursing station between us and the far-end security door, which acts like an airlock. I clock the beige desktop computer half-hidden behind the counter. A computer would give me all the answers I need. If only I could get to it.

My progress is painfully slow along the corridor.

Eventually, Bunny lifts off my hateful hospital gown and I see myself in the bathroom mirror.

A death's head stares back at me.

Dark smudges of exhaustion under my eyes. My cheeks are hollowed out as I bare my yellow teeth. My shaved head has grown back in tufts and a thick scar with ugly staples runs along my scalp.

I look like I have been in a car accident, and then I remember that I really have.

For the first time, a salty tear runs down my cheek as I realise the sorry state I'm in.

"That's not going to help," Bunny says brusquely, guiding me towards the shower seat. Why's she so mean to me? As if I'm a dangerous animal trapped in a cage. Do not put your fingers through the bars. Do not feed. Nil by mouth. It's the same thing.

Bunny sniffs and pulls a face when she smells me, guiding me towards the fold-down stool. I move like a crabbed old woman, and she can't hide her distaste.

The hot water massaging what's left of my hair and running down my face and shoulders feels wonderful. Turning my head in the water needles, I stick out my tongue to rinse my parched mouth. Never mind the embarrassment of squatting naked on a bench.

Sitting there as Nurse Bunny kneads shampoo into my hair, watching sudsy water drain away, the questions start building again. Why keep a hospital open for just one patient? Those bars on the windows. Is this a hospital or a prison?

Am I some sort of experiment, and if so, what?

There's something they're not telling me, and I am going to find out what it is, so help me God.

Bunny helps me stand again, rubbing me down with a towel. Funny then that I was thinking about God, because that's when she says it. I think it's a Bible reference.

"Wash me thoroughly and cleanse me from my sin," she mutters. Then she looks me straight at me. "Some sins can't be washed away though, can they?"

CHAPTER FIVE

I must have been awake for a week or so. You lose track of time in this place. What I do know is that my head was pretty messed up from all those drugs they gave me.

It's Doctor Quane ("Call me Max") who teaches me how to speak again. He sits beside my bed, pointing at cardboard picture books, the kind they use in kindergarten to teach little ones to read.

"My daughter's." He shrugs. "She's in secondary school now."

If he has a daughter, that means he has a wife and, deep down, I feel a twinge of jealousy. Because while I've been asleep, the world has carried on. All the happy chaos of family life has been snatched away from me. Then another thought—maybe I do have a husband and child somewhere out there, and that's something else they're not telling me. But if I had a husband or a child, they'd have visited me, wouldn't they?

I am no closer to finding out who I really am. They keep

telling me that I'm the victim of a hit-and-run accident, but that's not the whole truth. There's more to it than that. Much more.

Impatiently, I make the writing gesture with my right hand. Max hands me the notepad from my bedside table.

"Tell me who I really am."

Max shakes his head. "It's still too soon. Right now, your memory is as fragile as a cobweb. Susan, you have to trust me on this."

If I really am the most famous coma victim ever, then I could just Google myself and find out everything I need to know. A plan starts to form in my mind. Softly, softly, catch the monkey. Somebody told me that once and then, with a pang, I realise I have absolutely no idea who.

Everything else is like looking in a black mirror. I can see myself but nobody else.

During a break, Max tells me what's been going on in the world for the past ten years. Britain is no longer part of the European Union. Donald Trump was elected President of the United States. Twice. (I am not sure who Donald Trump is, but I dimly remember seeing him on TV.) And, worst of all, a terrible virus has killed millions of people all over the world.

If that's what's been going on, perhaps it is better that I have been asleep.

"You've been in the most socially distanced place on Earth... considering." Max smiles. "Just you and the three of us."

It's strange but I can remember things on the periphery. Past world events. History. That's all coming back to me now in the developing bath of my mind. But the more I try to remember about myself, the more the fingers in my mind's eye stretch into the past, the darker those shadows become.

"Memory = bad. Why?"

Max ignores me and picks up another picture book. The message is clear. If they're not going to tell me, I'm going to find out for myself.

There's a knock on my hospital room door and Nurse Birgita steers the wheelchair into the room. She's taking me downstairs for my first physiotherapy session.

"Ah, is it that time already?" asks Max, closing the book. "You're going to love Bunny. She's the best."

I do not love Bunny.

And I get the feeling she doesn't like me very much either.

However, being alone with my nurse without the chance of Doctor Max interrupting us makes me think she could be the one who will answer my questions. Maybe she can give me just one piece of the jigsaw puzzle.

It's my first session in what looks like an old-fashioned school gymnasium. There are stationary bicycles and a mini trampoline and Swiss balls you use for doing sit-ups. All sorts of racks and torture devices line the walls.

I grit my teeth as Bunny helps me up onto the treadmill. Because this is what I am going to do. I am literally going to get better, one step at a time.

"Where you from?"

It's the longest sentence I've spoken so far, only the words come out mushy, as if I've had a massive stroke.

"Australia?"

Nurse Bunny frowns and shakes her head. "South Africa. I came over here to work for the NHS, then I saw a job ad for this place. Just looking after one patient, shame. All very hush-hush."

"Where. Here."

Bunny forms an answer in her mouth, then shakes her head; she likely can see where I'm going and wants to head me off.

"That's not for me to say. We're under strict instructions. Doctor Max will explain everything."

Instead, she starts the treadmill at a barely moving walking speed. Bunny watches every painful step but she's hardly encouraging.

"More," I grunt. I am determined to start walking by myself, even if it kills me.

"It's too early for this."

"More."

No matter how much this hurts, I am going to get through it. Bunny leans across and picks up the speed. The black treadmill grinds away at a slow walking pace—honestly, you've seen faster tortoises.

It's agony.

Grey sweat pops on my face as I put one foot down in front of another. That's all I have to do. Stabbing pain in both my calves.

Ten seconds.

I grunt and grimace but keep on walking. Black tadpoles of pain swim across my vision. But if I walk, that means I can run, and if I can run, I can get away from this place.

Thirty agonising seconds.

Forty.

Fifty-seven.

"Enough," I gasp just as the digital clock hits one minute.

Bunny jabs the off button. Exalted, I want to raise my arms above my head like a boxer, only I can't let go. Even the *Rocky* theme is playing in my head. Because if I can walk for one minute today, I can walk for two minutes tomorrow.

Bunny helps me off the treadmill and, taking my arm, now it's her turn to ask me a question. Do I have any memory of what happened before I woke up in this place?

"Can't remember," I confess.

Is that a look of satisfaction on her face? Are they all in it together, keeping the truth from me?

"How convenient," she mutters, adjusting the weight on her next instrument of torture.

"What do you mean?" I persevere. She's going to be the one who tells me the truth, who finally tells me who I really am.

"It's a shame that you ever woke up," she says abruptly, turning to me. "Vengeance is mine, saith the Lord. I shall repay."

I am genuinely dumbfounded. I have no idea what she's talking about. What have I done to make her hate me so much? Another question forms in my mouth but the double doors bang behind us and the moment is gone.

Doctor Max stands in front of the gymnasium double door beside the parked wheelchair. Dressed in his doctor's white coat, he looks confident and trustworthy. Without his piggy NHS spectacles, he'd be handsome.

"Come on, Sleeping Beauty," says Doctor Max, steering the chair towards me. "Session over for today."

That afternoon, I am allowed into the first-floor day room. It smells musty and unused, crammed with sagging, uncomfortable armchairs and tired sofas. Nobody has been in this room for a very long time.

Best of all is the picture window that faces the marsh. The horizon is dotted with eerie buildings, weird concrete pagodas. The landscape is utterly flat and peppered with strange lagoons like cysts. A squadron of birds flies overhead in V formation. There's something military about this place but I can't put my finger on it.

Increasingly, I get the feeling this hospital was used for experiments. Is that what's happened to me? I was a guinea pig for a drug experiment which went wrong? They dosed me with some drug, and I had a psychotic episode? *Those bloody fingers grappling with the door latch, being chased down the street by a security guard.* Is that what this is all about?

Leaning on my walker, I search for clues. There's one sepia photograph on the wall with nurses in stiff uniforms, standing beside patients seated in bath chairs. There's another photograph of this very room in its heyday, crammed with pot plants on occasional tables. "Taylor's Hotel, 1927" reads the brown handwritten inscription. So, this Art Deco hospital was a hotel once.

One thing I do discover is a pile of old copies of *The Week*. Frustratingly, they only go back five years. If they ask, I'll tell them I want to learn as much as I can about the decade I've missed.

And yes, it's fascinating to see how the world has changed over the years I have been asleep.

Only they've been one step ahead of me. Pieces have been scissored out of magazines, whole pages missing. There's one headline that they've missed: "*SLEEPING BEAUTY SUSPECT MAY NEVER WAKE UP.*"

I trace the headline with my finger and snap the magazine shut guiltily when Bunny coughs behind me. She must have clocked what I was doing. That headline has something to do with me. I know it.

"You've got a visitor," my nurse says. "They're waiting downstairs."

A visitor?

This is the first time anybody has been to see me. Then, is this my husband, a man I have no memory of? Whoever they are, the moment we're left alone, they can tell me who I really am and what this place is.

Bunny stands in the dayroom doorway with my wheel-chair, but I shake my head. Yes, I may look like a deep-sea diver clomping along in heavy lead boots, but I am determined to walk on my own. Use it or lose it, that's what Bunny says. Well, I am going to get better again.

It takes a good ten minutes of crab-like shuffling for me to drag myself to the lift with Bunny scrutinising every step. She's both my nurse and my warder.

The woman waiting downstairs in the hall must be in her sixties. I have no idea who she is. She's tiny like a bird, with features as delicate as sparrow bones. Her skin is dried up from what I guess is too much smoking. Whoever said that suffering ennobles the soul was lying—this woman, whoever she is, has been hollowed out and is grey with worry. Her eyes are grey-blue like mine but they're cloudy with cataracts. She gets tearful the moment she spots me.

"I can't believe it," she says.

This total stranger tries to hug me and, alarmed, I stand immobile. I have no idea who this person is or what she wants. Realising that I'm as rigid as a stone carving, she steps back.

"Susan, it's me. Don't you know who I am?"

I can only shake my head and glance at Nurse Bunny for

a clue. Even Bunny looks embarrassed. It's heartbreaking because I feel sorry for this woman and I do want to help, really, I do.

Bunny looks down at the ground and the three of us stand there in awkward silence.

"I'm your mother," the woman says finally.

CHAPTER SIX

To: █
From: Doctor Max Quane
Subject: Susan Gummer recovery
Dear █

I wanted to put down in an email what we discussed
in our phone call this morning and reiterate my
reasons for not involving the authorities for as long as
is permissible.

Given the extraordinary nature of this case, I kindly
request that we maintain strict confidentiality
regarding Ms Gummer's awakening for the time
being. This will allow us to conduct thorough evalu-
ations and protect the patient's privacy during this
sensitive period.

Of course, I understand your nervousness about not
alerting the authorities immediately, especially the

Metropolitan Police, because of the reputational damage this might have on the Hallam Group. The optics are difficult, I admit. However, my first duty must always be to my patient, and I strongly feel, as clinical director of this hospital, that subjecting Ms Gummer to questioning this early will undo the progress she has made so far.

As of now, only four people know that Ms Gummer is awake: you, myself and nurses Mbalula and Nguyen.
To recap: after ten years in a persistent vegetative state, Ms Gummer has unexpectedly regained consciousness. This event occurred on January 3 at approximately 5:53 a.m.

Ms Gummer, now 35 years old, has emerged from her comatose state with significant memory impairment. She exhibits no recollection of the accident that precipitated her condition. Her long-term memories from childhood and early adulthood appear largely intact, but there is a clear gradient of memory loss leading up to the night of the accident.

Our recovery plan for Ms Gummer includes gradual physical rehabilitation, speech and language therapy, occupational therapy, and continual neuropsychological evaluation.

We anticipate a prolonged recovery period, given the duration of Ms Gummer's vegetative state. However, with intensive rehabilitation, we hope to

see significant improvements in Ms Gummer's retrograde amnesia.

I have conducted standard post-coma language and
reasoning tests. Her speech recovery has been quite
remarkable. This morning, we conversed fairly
easily.
What is strange is that although Ms Gummer has
what I would call "general memory", the closer these
memories zero in on who she really is and her actual
past, the blanker her mind becomes. She is not lying;
I am convinced of that. It is almost as if her brain has
cauterised any dangerous memories to prevent post-
traumatic stress disorder.

Sometimes an extreme stress situation can trigger
psychoactive amnesia. The brain protecting itself in
the absence of structural brain damage, almost like a
crash helmet, so to speak.

It is important to be clear about this.

Right now, Ms Gummer is merely a witness to a
crime whom police would like to speak to—she has
not been arrested, let alone charged, and is simply
one of many witnesses, albeit the key one.

On top of any questioning by police, there would
also be press intrusion. Yes, we are isolated here and
could reject any interview requests. But seeing
herself reported on television and any recap of the
events of December 19, 2015, would be traumatic.

I am simply not prepared to put my patient at risk.
Please, can we hold off alerting the authorities until
I have had a chance to explain to Ms Gummer,
calmly and reasonably, how she came to be under
our care?
If the authorities do ask why we took so long to alert
them, I will simply tell them what I have told you:
that my patient's retrograde amnesia made her unfit
to be interviewed.

All I am asking for is more time.

Something I forgot to say during our phone call, and
I am speaking selfishly and somewhat hubristically
here, is that a case like Ms Gummer's comes along
once in a generation for a psychiatrist such as myself.
It is a case analysts dream of. As a psychiatric study,
she could be even more significant than Anna O was
for Sigmund Freud.

As you know, retrograde amnesia is thankfully rare,
and piecing together her memories is going to be like
mending the most fragile vase. It would be a tragedy
to trip and smash the vase to pieces. The Japanese
have a method of piecing back together broken
pottery called kintsugi. Often, the mended vase is
more beautiful than the original. That is what we are
attempting to do here.

With your permission, I would like to diarise our
therapy sessions with a view to later writing a book.
A memoir of her recovery, if you will.

The care given by the Hallam Group, without cost, to this poor young woman, hiding her away from the public to let her heal over so many years, would be heavily flagged throughout.

Think of the publicity if we could finally piece together what happened that night and answer the one question that has maddened the world, and especially ourselves, for so long.

Forgive my purple prose. I am not a natural writer, but I do think a diary of her recovery would be of immense interest.

I realise this is a big ask.

In exchange, I would be honoured if you would let me dedicate any such book to you.

I would appreciate your thoughts, particularly regarding the management of Ms Gummer's retrograde amnesia. Please let me know if you would like to review her file or discuss her case further.

Sincerely,
Doctor Max Quane

CHAPTER SEVEN

The woman who claims to be my mother sits red-eyed and gripping a scrunched-up tissue. We've been allowed in the day room with its strange Art Deco armchairs. In fact, this whole sanatorium has a nautical feel, like an ocean liner that's been stranded on the marsh.

Because it's just the two of us, she's the one who can answer my questions. I am painfully aware of the minutes ticking down. Any moment now, Nurse Bunny could reappear and tell us visiting time is over.

"Look, Mum—" I try the word out, but it sounds strange. "I-I-I don't really understand why I'm here." My voice buffers with a slight stammer. "I don't remember anything."

"You were knocked down by a car," she says.

Yes, I know all that, I want to tell her. *That's the one thing I do remember. Tell me something I don't know.*

"Oh Susan," Mum says, tearing up again, "I never thought I would see you again."

Don't start crying again, I think irritably. *I don't need your pity, I need answers.*

"Yes, but *why* was I knocked down by a car? What was I doing there?" She's moved by my pleading, I can tell. "All I can remember is... blood."

There, I've said it.

The woman's mouth tightens. "They told me not to say anything. They said it would upset you."

"Yes, but what? Please, I need your help, Mum. I have no idea who I am. Or what I'm doing here."

The woman looks around conspiratorially before leaning in to confide something. "I never believed them. They said that you—"

"Visiting time is over, Mrs Gummer," Nurse Bunny says loudly. "You'll have to hurry if you want to make the last boat."

We both sit back guiltily, as if we've been caught doing something we shouldn't have. The woman fusses about in her handbag, pulling out a gold pen and a diary.

"This is my number and my address, if you need anything," she says, tearing out a diary page.

"We have your details on file," Bunny interrupts smoothly. "There's no need for that."

Once I am well again, she makes me promise to come and live with her, so she can look after me. I am not sure that moving in with this frail, white-haired woman, who looks like she's been through enough already, is such a good idea.

That was one week ago.

Today, I have been allowed outside for the very first time. It feels good to have sun on my face. My skin hasn't felt the sun for ten years. Bunny parked me here after this morning's physio. It's a patch of garden to one side of the clinic, with a concrete patio and some wooden outdoor furniture. It's not much of a garden. One bed with roses heavily pruned for winter, a dead-looking rhododendron, and some perennials I can't name.

I scan the plants looking for a flower that's most like me. The one that speaks to me most is a weed that's choking one of the rose bushes. "Nobody wants me to be here," it seems to be saying, "but I'm tough and my roots have gone deep and you're not getting rid of me."

My physio is coming on well. I can walk on my own with the help of a couple of walking sticks, but I do get so tired. Even Bunny seems to have warmed to me, and jokes about my entering this year's London Marathon.

My memory, though, is still a complete blank. Doctor Max says this is completely normal. My brain had a massive shock when my head struck that tarmac. There was internal bleeding, despite the crash helmet of my skull. We just have to give my brain time to heal, that's all. Healing is a long, slow process. That's why it's called being a patient, he says.

A white van comes bouncing up the drive and I visor my eyes against the blue winter sky to get a better look. There's already one navy saloon parked outside the front entrance. This is unusual. We don't normally get many visitors here, just deliveries.

It's difficult to get cars onto the island, apparently. There's a ferry that's more like a rowing boat with an outboard for day visitors, and a landing craft for vehicles which dates to the Second World War. Most of Orford Ness —that's the name of this island—still belongs to the Ministry of Defence and is fenced off with Keep Out signs. So, I was right about it being something military. The rest of the island is a nature reserve, I'm told.

Our sanatorium is the anomaly, a relic from when they thought clean air and sunshine would be enough to get

tuberculosis patients well again. That explains the photograph I saw in the day room. And then they invented
penicillin.

The unmarked van pulls up beside the navy car and a
couple of workmen get out. They're dressed in painter's
whites. Only they're a strange-looking pair. The tall one
could be a spindly-legged, top-hatted figure, prancing about
in a frock coat and buckled shoes. The other one has a moon
face, greasy ringlets and a hook nose. They look like illustra-
tions out of a nightmarish Victorian children's book. They
don't look like plumbers or painters to me.

Both of them stand chatting before they spot me. The fat
one literally digs his friend in the ribs and points. I hope
they've come to fix the leaking roof. The drip-drip-drip of
rainwater into buckets outside my room at night is driving
me mad. Or even madder.

They amble over with their hands in their pockets.

"Alright, luv?" says hook nose. "Nice day, innit?"

It's hard for me to see them properly in this winter
sunshine, and I frown harder under my shielded eyes.

"Yes, the weather is lovely."

Compared to them, I sound like the Queen.

"You're Susan Gummer, aren't you?"

How do they even know my name? My throat narrows
and cold rolls down my spine. They shouldn't be here.
There's something off about them. They stand there, blankly
malevolent. Then the tall one pulls out a phone and snaps a
photo of me. They shouldn't be doing that. I didn't give them
permission.

"Hey, just a minute—"

"Thanks, darlin'." He smirks, and they both turn and

sprint for their van, just as Bunny comes down the front steps. She watches them clamber into the front seats.

"Who was that?" she asks, watching the van hurriedly make a three-point turn. When I tell her they were workmen, she frowns and says the repairs department isn't due until tomorrow. She watches the van tear off down the drive and, turning, says Doctor Max wants to see me.

I don't tell her about them snapping my photo. Something bad is going to happen because of that.

There's a reception area outside Doctor Max's office. A couple of deep easy chairs and a coffee table piled with magazines and the local newspaper. I park my new walking canes that Bunny has given me, those lightweight ones which hikers use, and settle in.

First, I pick up the *East Anglian Daily Times*. A teenage girl, one eye closed with a swollen black eye and half her face a livid purplish birthmark, stares out of the front page. Apparently, she's the latest victim of a burglar and serial rapist they're calling the Suffolk Beast. There's an artist's impression of the man police are looking for, a square-jawed thug with close-cropped blond hair.

Not wanting to read any more, I turn the page.

Next, there's a headline about protests over a housing development in a nearby village and a story about sewage on beaches.

The magazines are ancient: car enthusiast titles and gardening glossies, gossip weeklies (I don't know who Taylor Swift is but she's everywhere. I suspect she might be the new president). Right at the bottom I tug out a dog-eared trade magazine, *Health Investor*, and take in the headline, "Eagle swoops on Hallam in $500m deal".

Underneath the headline is a photograph of a woman

wearing oversized Jackie O sunglasses and a beanie, bundled up in an overcoat. The photograph is grainy, as if it's been taken from a long distance with a telephoto lens.

Something passes through me, a feeling or a piece of knowledge, something I once knew or felt. A memory I can't quite reach. Only I don't know if this is a lost memory or, more worryingly, a premonition.

My brain pulses with shock. The waiting room throbs around me because I know this is important.

I know this woman.

CHAPTER EIGHT

The caption says: "Reclusive Hallam Group chief executive Amanda Mawdsley", and I can't read the accompanying story fast enough.

US pharma giant Eagle Pharmaceuticals has made a $500m offer to buy troubled Anglo-American private healthcare provider Hallam Group. Its reclusive chief executive Amanda Mawdsley declined to comment on the US takeover, which was first reported in The Wall Street Journal...

Hallam Group. They own this hospital. You see the H logo on the walls everywhere. "Struggling healthcare business"—that explains the buckets along the top-floor corridor collecting rainwater, the damp on the walls, the sagging feeling of everything collapsing, as if it's being pulled back into the marsh.

Doctor Max pops his head out round the door, calling me into his office. I stand up, still clutching the magazine, I'm so excited. This woman, she has something to do with me; I am sure of it.

It's like one of those photographer's trays they used to develop pictures in, details becoming clearer, images forming. My memory is coming back. I can feel it.

"Max, I've remembered something." I can't keep the excitement out of my voice as I hobble in with both sticks, still clutching the magazine. "This woman, *I know her—*" I announce, thrusting the magazine at him.

"Susan, not now," Max says irritably.

"Max, you don't understand. This woman, *I know her.* She's got something to do with why I'm here, I'm sure of it."

"Susan, please. There's somebody here to see you."

A stranger sitting opposite Max's desk stands up. "Ah, speak of the devil," he says, rising. He's a big, grave man with the solemn air of a funeral director or a disapproving bank manager. But the first word that comes to mind about him is *solid.* Whoever this is, he's solid like a wall, like there's no getting around him.

Ignoring this stranger, I shake the magazine at Max. "You're not listening. This woman in the magazine. *I recognise her.* I know who she is." I'm practically shaking the page in his face.

While I'm gabbling, this stranger looks at me like I'm some exotic caged animal, something dangerous to be kept at arm's length.

"Hello, Susan. It's been a long time," he says in a rich Yorkshire baritone. "Remember me?"

That brings me up short. Do we know each other? Because I've never seen him before in my life. For a moment, I wonder if this is my husband who's come to take me home. No, it can't be. He's too old. My dad, perhaps.

"I'm sorry, do I know you? I don't remember things. Perhaps Doctor Quane told you."

"Yes, Doctor Quane said that your physical recovery has been little short of... remarkable." The way he says this, rolling his tongue around his mouth, as if he's said something droll, is unsettling. Whoever he is, I don't like him very much. "My name is Detective Chief Inspector Horner from the Metropolitan Police. We know each other... from years ago."

"Susan, sit down," Max says testily. "The chief inspector has come up from London."

"First, congratulations on your recovery. None of us thought we'd ever see you again." This detective smiles but there's no humour in it. "Doctor Quane tells me you have total amnesia. That you don't remember what happened to you. Before waking up here, I mean."

"That's not quite true. I do remember things. From my childhood, I mean. It's just the closer I get to waking up here, the less I remember."

"How convenient," he mutters. Those same words Bunny used in physio.

"Yes, well—" says Max nervously.

"You don't believe me."

We're playing a game of snakes and ladders. If I ask the right question, I'll go up the ladder. Or I could land on a snake.

"It's not about what I believe or don't believe. I just follow the facts."

"And what are the facts? They won't tell me," I say pointedly, looking at Max.

I'm fed up with being treated like a child. I am a grown woman, and I need answers. If he's a police officer, then he *must* tell me the truth. If Max and the others won't say, then he will.

Max shoots him a look as if to say, "Don't go there."

"The facts are that you were knocked down by a car in central London on the night of December the nineteenth, 2015. You were covered in your employer's blood. You were seen crouched over his body before you bolted out into the street."

Shock drops right through me. The room sways, yet everything remains completely still. What does he mean, I was covered in my employer's blood? Who was my employer? The blood in my dream—I thought that was my blood, not somebody else's. My God, what sort of monster am I? So that's why Bunny and Nurse Linh are so afraid of me. Because they know what I've done.

That I'm a murderer.

"You really don't remember?"

"I remember running down a street. In a nightdress. A taxi coming straight at me. Then nothing."

"I've told you, Inspector. That is Susan's only memory. Everything else is still a blank."

"Nothing before that?" repeats the detective.

I can only shake my head. There's a cold ball of fear in my stomach now and suddenly, I'm not sure I want to know the truth, not if I'm this... this... monster.

The policeman turns to Max. "I'd like Miss Gummer to come down to Scotland Yard with me for questioning. The fact is," he says, turning back to me, "you're the key witness in a murder investigation, whatever your involvement."

"What do you mean, 'involvement'?"

I feel faint and need to sit down. This is all too much for me to absorb.

"It's far too early for any of this," Max interrupts. "I've told you that already." I have never seen Doctor Max rattled before.

"This is a murder investigation, and my duty is to the victim. Miss Gummer has to come down to London with me right now for questioning. I'm not asking you, Doctor Quane. I'm telling you."

"And my duty of care is to my patient," counters Max. "Susan's making good progress but right now her mind is fragile. I told you, it's far too early for her to be interviewed. As her consultant, I forbid it. You're going to need a court order, and I'll get it overruled by our lawyers. Or by the Royal College of Psychiatrists."

The detective stands there, getting angry. He's about to say something, then changes his mind. You can tell he's unused to not getting his own way.

"That's your final answer, is it?"

Max says nothing but sets his jaw. He may have won this particular game of chess, but there will be others.

"Don't worry, Doctor Quane. I will be back. Shielding a witness is not a good look, for either of you. I don't know what we can do about a psychiatrist who impedes an investigation, but I'll tell you this for nothing. You're going to find yourself in a lot of trouble. This time, I've asked you nicely. Next time, I'll have the full force of the CPS behind me."

He stands up, moving past my chair, something big and dangerous, a great white shark sliding into the murk with a dismissive flick of its tail. The detective almost slams the door behind him, and we both just sit there, in stunned silence. I'm not sure what has just happened.

Finally, I have to speak. "Max, what he said, that's not true, is it?"

I can't bring myself to say the word. The psychiatrist won't meet my eye, just sits there with his head in his hands, rubbing his temples.

"The police want to bring in their own psychiatrist. They don't believe you've got amnesia. They're pushing to move you to one of the big brain injury hospitals, take you out of my care."

"Wouldn't a specialist hospital be better?"

"You don't get it, do you?" He looks up sharply. "He doesn't just want to question you. He wants to arrest you for murder."

CHAPTER NINE

3:05

The digital clock on my bedside table tells me it's gone three in the morning. My throat is parched, and I desperately want a drink. I glug greedily from the plastic water beaker beside me. Better.

Max wouldn't tell me why the police want to arrest me for murder. He stayed tight-lipped, no matter how much I pressed him. "You witnessed a crime, that's all," he shrugged. He talked about recovered memory syndrome, when a therapist unwittingly influences how a patient recovers their memories or what they remember. He explained that he wanted my memory unpolluted.

My ears strain in the velvety silence. Everything's so quiet, marooned out here on this remote Suffolk islet. The answers I need are just forty feet away from this room, on that desktop computer behind Bunny's nursing station. Just a few clicks and I'll know the truth. *But can you handle the truth, Susan Gummer?* I mean, the police can't put me on trial for murder if I can't remember anything, can they?

Besides, I'm fully awake now. And so, I slide out of bed, a sly plan forming in my mind. If anybody asks why, I just needed to pee, that's all. Yes, I could have used the commode beside my bed, but that's so humiliating.

My tiptoes touch the cold floor and, by clinging onto the bed and then the visitor's chair, I negotiate the obstacle course to my bedroom door. I am getting stronger each day. I am going to do this using only one stick.

The corridor is empty.

Bunny is usually on duty at her nursing station overnight, although I suspect she sometimes takes a nap in one of the spare patient rooms.

Hanging onto the wall for support, I edge my way to the nursing station. That unattended computer on Bunny's desk will give me all the answers I need.

The corridor, this whole hospital, is fast asleep as I hobble over to the nursing station. Maybe Bunny really has gone for a nap. I sidle around her desk. Her PC is dark but wakes up with the shake of a mouse. Maddeningly, I am confronted by a password login.

Shit.

Maybe it's written down somewhere on a Post-it note. I fruitlessly scan above her desk. Nothing. Then I try each of her desk drawers. They're all locked apart from the top one, which slides out to reveal the usual Biros and staples and—

A spooled lanyard with an ID pass.

It's hopeless trying to guess a computer password, but this lanyard could give me access to the admin offices downstairs, the ones where they keep files. The answers I need must be somewhere in this building. Everyone creates a paper trail—invoices, prescriptions. And I have a good idea of where to start.

Hanging onto the corridor banister for support, I limp to the far end, towards what I call the airlock. That door opens onto the third-floor landing, and then the central staircase down to the ground floor. When I press the ID card against the reader, it turns green, and the door softly clicks open.

There's a central stairwell that leads three floors down. Wire netting has been strung across each floor of the stairwell, to stop the patients who used to be here throwing themselves down the shaft, I suppose.

Even with my cane, my progress down the stone steps is wincingly slow.

Stepping down onto the ground floor, the dining room is on my left, facing swing doors to the kitchen. To my right, the admin offices.

Every door stays stubbornly locked as I uselessly brush my ID against each card reader.

Peering in through one slit window, I see a bank of video monitors clicking between different views of the building: empty patient bedrooms and stairwells and then Bunny pounding along on the treadmill in physio. So that's where she is. She's always worrying about her weight.

There is one computer in the video room that does look switched on, but my ID doesn't work on this door either. I test the handle but it's no good.

I swear under my breath.

By the time I reach Doctor Max's office, I have all but given up hope. Swiping my pass against his reader, I'm about to haul myself back upstairs, hoping I'm not spotted, when it turns green.

Pushing the door gently open, I creep through the

waiting area into his office. The overhead lights automatically switch on. I clock the CCTV bulb high up in the far corner but it's too late now. There is CCTV everywhere in this place—ugly black bulbs high up in each corner, watching you all the time. In this place, there's nowhere to hide.

All of his filing cabinets are locked and so are his desk drawers. My patient file must be in there somewhere, tantalisingly out of reach. My fingers scrabble at the bottom desk drawer, the one where he keeps hanging folders, but it's useless. All I am doing is breaking my nails.

Looking up at the vapid posters on his walls ("Take a swim in a lake called you", "Mental health starts with Me") I feel hateful, resentful of my situation, of everything that's happened to me. I hate everything and everyone.

I have been asleep for the past ten years. While other women of my age have been getting on, forging careers, falling in love, having babies, I have nothing. That's all been snatched away from me. That policeman, he wants to arrest me for murder. The irony is, I'm as innocent as a newborn baby. Because I am a newborn. I don't have any memories of who I was before this.

There's another door behind his desk, some kind of anteroom, and I push that door open too. There's a toilet, a shower and a corner washbasin. An oxygen tank propped against one wall next to a bench piled with diving gear: a facemask, flippers and a weighted belt. Then I remember what Max said about his hobby being scuba diving. But it's what's above the bench that shocks me.

Dozens of photos of myself stare back.

Yellowed newspaper clippings pinned to a notice board. Printouts of web searches with sentences highlighted. A map. Date-stamped video grabs of what looks like a road traffic camera with a figure in a nightdress standing in the middle of a street.

Me.

All crisscrossed with drawing-pinned red string, connecting one to another. It looks like one of those murder walls in a detective movie. Or the paranoid obsessions of a serial killer.

I quail at what's in front of me but force myself to look closer. Fascinated yet repelled, I peer at one newspaper clipping showing a handsome man next to another snapshot of myself looking sullenly at the camera.

I know this man too.

I flash on him smiling at me, handing over a glass of champagne. This isn't really a memory, more of a moment. There's a hubbub going on around us. Were we at some kind of party?

I am peering so close now, I can even see the dots in the newspaper print. *Connect the dots, Susan. You have to connect the dots.*

'COMA KILLER NAMED AS PRIME SUSPECT' blares one headline.

'SHE WANTED TO KILL ME TOO, SAYS DRIVER.'

"Susan Gummer, 25, has been named by police as the key suspect in the murder of pharma tycoon—" The moment my finger dabs my name, it's like an electric shock. Once, as a child, I stuck my finger into an empty lamp socket. The shock threw me across the room. It's the same thing now.

The answers to my questions, literally all there in black and white.

This is who I really am.

A murderer.

They're calling me a modern-day Lizzie Borden, the daughter who took an axe to her entire family and never said why.

Ten years ago, I was knocked down by a taxi after fleeing the scene of the crime, covered in my employer's blood, just as the detective said. Apparently, I was the carer for my employer's paraplegic sister. We had a terrible row and I pushed him over a balcony. That's what his sister said, who saw everything from her wheelchair.

There are no other suspects.

Suddenly, I know I'm going to be sick. I grab the toilet bowl with both hands and vomit until there's nothing left. Wiping stringy phlegm away from my mouth, I stand up feeling giddy, hot and cold.

Hanging onto the corner basin, trying to get my breath under control, I then splash blessed cold water on my face. This has shaken me down to my core. I press my forehead against the mirror—real glass this time—and now there are two of us conjoined at the head like Siamese twins.

For a moment I stand there, as the full enormity of who I really am sinks in. Then, as I straighten up, I sense there's another person inside this reflection, someone watching me —the woman from that magazine photograph. She's there for a moment and then she's gone.

You're losing your grip, Susan Gummer. Seeing things that aren't really there. Shock does strange things to your mind. My heart is pounding and all the while, I'm thinking, thinking—

I am thinking so hard, I don't even hear him come into the room.

"Ah, you discovered my little secret," says Doctor Max behind me.

He's standing at the shower room entrance, and he doesn't look happy.

CHAPTER TEN

He's wearing a dressing gown and holding a mug of something. I am so angry. All these photographs, all this evidence... He thinks I'm guilty, just like that policeman. I thought Max's job was to protect me, to make me well, not to side with them, the police.

All along, he's been in the pocket of the authorities, helping them to build their case. I feel so betrayed.

"Susan, listen. I can explain..."

"Go on then," I say coldly, radiating with anger.

"Susan, you've got to understand how famous you are. Yours is one of the great unsolved mysteries. Susan Gummer, the servant who murdered her employer. Or did she? Everybody has a theory and, yes, you're right. I'm just as bad as the others."

"What do you mean, famous?"

"There's been a drama on Netflix, podcasts. You've gone viral. Everyone playing amateur detective, including me. Everybody has a theory. There's even a walking tour of your last night, the night you fled the scene of the crime."

He steps back into his office and places his coffee mug down on his desk, turning to face me. Instinctively, I take a step back away from this man, this betrayer, the person I thought of as my support.

"Look, I can understand how you must be feeling."

"How can you understand? You don't know anything about me," I spit. Then I cover my face with my hands, realising the truth. This has all been too much to take in. "I don't know anything about me."

Max comes forward, gently prises my hands away from my face and hands me a tissue.

"Susan, listen to me. You're the key witness *and* the prime suspect. Only you can tell the police what really happened that night. And once the world finds out that you can't remember anything, they'll only become more convinced you're hiding something."

"But *you* do believe me, don't you?" My voice trembles, because it's important that Doctor Max believes what I'm saying, that one single person knows I'm telling the truth.

"Do I believe that you've got amnesia? Yes, of course. As for the rest..." He shrugs. "I just don't know." At least he's being honest for once.

Despite myself, I still need to know the truth, no matter how bad it looks. It's like edging your toes towards the lip of a parapet. Once he tells me, there's no coming back. The hard ground rushing up to meet me as I fall and—

"You said everyone has a theory about what happened. Such as?"

Doctor Max looks at me dubiously, weighing up how much to tell me.

"That you killed your employer after he broke off your engagement. You were getting married, you see. That you poisoned their father because he objected to the marriage, and your fiancé found out what you'd done, so you had to get rid of him as well. I'm sorry, I could go on." He breaks off, embarrassed. "Having you lying there, asleep, it's been like having all the clues to a crossword puzzle right in front of you. I'm sorry, I owe you an apology."

"The Sleeping Beauty Killer, that's what they're calling me. You called me Sleeping Beauty. Is that how you think of me?"

"Look, I'll take this all down. It's not appropriate. Maybe the police are right. I have let my personal ambition cloud my judgment. I am ready to step aside as your psychiatrist. There are plenty of others better qualified than me."

Max is about to start tearing stuff off the wall, when I put my hand out to stop him. Deep down, I wonder if what they're saying about me is true. I know that I've done something bad. It's like a wound, deep inside, a wrong which I deserve to be punished for.

But not this. Whatever it was I did wrong, it wasn't this.

"Max, tell me. Do you think I did it? That I'm a killer?"

"What I think doesn't matter. I told you, my job is to get you well again."

"I don't want your disclaimer. You don't do all this—" I gesture to his horrid murder wall "—without some idea of whether I'm guilty or not."

Max contemplates me for a moment and then nods. Point taken. He looks at me ruefully.

"Listen, Susan. I want to write a book about you. A first-hand account of you recovering your memories. If I can help you remember, it would be one of the greatest breakthroughs in neuropsychiatry ever. The woman who woke up with a completely blank mind, at the centre of one of the most celebrated unsolved murders ever. And then there's the police. You need to give them a plausible explanation. An alternative version. Because I'll be honest with you, right now all the evidence points right at you."

"You still haven't told me. What you think."

"Personally, I don't think you murdered Jamie Mawdsley. Not for one moment."

Jamie Mawdsley.

I recognise that name too. I flash on Jamie's handsome face handing me that glass of champagne and the party going on around us. There are streamers and balloons. Were we at some New Year's Eve party?

A thought occurs to me, but I park it and turn back to the murder wall, tapping one brittle newspaper clipping. Max comes up alongside me and now we're both studying his morbid collage.

"It says here he fell down a flight of stairs. What makes people think it wasn't an accident?"

"Forensics said he was violently pushed. Your employer was six foot one and weighed one hundred and eighty pounds. That was one mighty shove. There were only two people in the house that night, you and the victim's sister, who says she *saw* you murder her brother."

"What about her, the sister? If there were just three of us in the house that night, couldn't she have done it?"

Max looks down at his feet and says quietly, "I don't think so."

"Why not?"

He looks me dead in the eye.

"Because she's been paraplegic since the age of eighteen. She's been paralysed in a wheelchair for the past seventeen years."

CHAPTER ELEVEN

I let that sink in.

"This sister, she was Amanda Mawdsley, wasn't she?"

The woman I saw captioned in yesterday's photograph, the one selling her business.

"Yes, you were taken on to be her carer, her companion."

"And then I had an affair with my employer, her brother," I say, running ahead. "You said we were engaged. Then why would I want to kill him?"

"Like I said, he broke off your engagement. Hell hath no fury— I'm sorry, I don't think you're allowed to say that anymore."

I am not sure I like this Susan Gummer very much. She sounds deceitful, conniving. On the make. Not who I am at all. Because when you don't know who you are, Max might as well be describing a total stranger.

It's gone four in the morning by now and we both stand there, me in my hospital gown and him in his pyjamas.

"What are you doing up so early?" I say, calming down.

"Couldn't sleep. My phone's been blowing up since midnight. Then there's this—"

He digs into his dressing gown pocket and pulls out what I think was called an iPhone, handing it across. Phones have changed. I dimly remember having something like this myself, except that it was just a simple handset with an LCD screen, a Nokia.

It's a photo of me shielding my eyes in the garden this afternoon taken by those builders. Except they weren't builders, they were paparazzi. And the *Daily Mail* headline shrieks, "SHE'S AWAKE – Sleeping Beauty killer wakes up after 10 years in coma".

"Someone tipped off the police. That's why DCI Horner came here. He *knew* you'd woken up. I've already spoken to the nurses and the hospital porter. They deny having anything to do with it."

"That was me."

"Sorry?"

Now it's my turn to feel ashamed about something I've done.

"I thought they were builders. It all happened so fast. I'd gone outside for the first time, and they sort of ambushed me."

"My phone hasn't stopped ringing. Reporters asking questions. The BBC wanting an interview. They're not going away. And it's only going to get worse. I can speak to our PR team, but I can't shield you forever."

Max looks at me frankly, treating me like an adult for the very first time. That's the funny thing about having been in a coma. I may be thirty-five years old technically, but inside I'm still twenty-five.

"I'll be honest with you, Susan. You could make a lot of

money out of this. Selling your story, I mean. Enough money for the rest of your life."

"Why don't we write my story together?"

"What do you mean?"

"You said the police are going to arrest me for murder. All the evidence points at me. I need your help. Can you help me to remember? I don't *feel* like a murderer, but I do feel guilt. Over something. What, I don't know. Maybe they're right—I did do all this." I gesture to the wall. "But I do need to know. Please, I want you to help me. I need you to help me. Will you help me?"

Max looks at me carefully and then reluctantly nods.

"All right, Susan. But I have to warn you. What we discover might not be what you want to know. The brain can protect people from themselves. It's like an involuntary detachment from reality. Sometimes, an extreme stress situation can trigger what's called psychogenic amnesia, which is the normal memory functioning in the absence of structural brain damage."

Max walks over to the bookshelf, searching for a book.

"I'm not saying whether you're guilty or not, but people can disassociate from their memories if they do something they can't reconcile themselves with. Or who they believe themselves to be."

He finds the book he's looking for and pulls it off the shelf.

"Here, this book can explain it better." He hands me a weighty tome. "Your memories from ten years ago are still there. They're just buried deep in your mind."

"What if I give you my only interview? Just me and you. You want to write a book. I need answers. The final chapter could be what I remember of that night, my final memory... that is, if I do remember."

I trail off because this all sounds so sketchy and insubstantial. But the police are going to charge me with murder unless I can come up with some other version of events. Some plausible explanation, that's what Max said. And that clock is ticking...

"What about now?" he suggests, yawning. "We're both up. Do you want some coffee?"

We walk down the corridor towards the side kitchen, where there is a hot water cylinder for staff to make drinks. Max finds some milk and stirs lumpy-looking instant coffee into mugs.

We settle back down in his beige office with its sofa and coffee table. There's an ominous-looking box of tissues. Max plumps the cushion at one end and drapes a dainty serviette over it as an antimacassar.

"Are you going to hypnotise me?" I ask nervously. It's a way of deflecting my anxiety.

Max smiles gently. "No, nothing like that."

Max takes the chair beside the couch and rests his notepad and his mobile on an armrest. I lie down, feeling self-conscious.

"I want to begin with some questions. You've told me the last thing you do remember, running down that street and being knocked down by the car. But what's the very first thing you remember?"

Suddenly, I'm not sure I do want to remember. What Max said about my brain protecting me from the truth, there's a reason it doesn't want me to know who I am. A murderer. A cold-blooded killer who pushed someone to their death because she couldn't get what she wanted. Hell hath no fury like a woman scorned, that's what Max started to say.

"Tell me a childhood memory, something inconsequential." Max's voice sounds high above me, somewhere far away.

I feel myself going, sinking deeper, and suddenly, I don't want to go there. I don't want to remember. The past is pulling me down and I'm falling into its black chasm and Max's face appears high above me, peering down, as if he's looking into an open grave and—

CHAPTER TWELVE

SESSION 1

"Okay Susan, I want to go back to what you were telling me. About working for the Mawdsleys. How did you get the job?"

I'm lying on Max's sofa with my head propped up on a pillow, my bare feet at the far end. Max is seated in his armchair wearing a dressing gown, a notepad on the armrest.

"I told you. Amy and I were at school together. She must have heard I was looking for work. I was a care home worker, you see. She knew that."

"Tell me about that care home. What do you remember about it? How long had you been working there? What sort of place was it?"

My childhood has come back clearly to me. I can see that in detail. The closer I get to working for the Mawdsleys, the more out of focus it gets. The nearer I get to what happened that night, it greys out. Eventually, all I can see is myself surrounded by blankness.

"It was pretty rubbish, to be honest. It was the only job I could get after leaving school. A friend of Mum's said she was leaving. Look, I was happy there, to begin with."

"So, you do have nursing experience."

"Not really, no. I was just a pair of hands. There were proper nurses though. I was more of a cleaner, like Mum."

"Describe a typical day to me. We're just warming up here, Susan. Flexing your memory muscles. Here, if you're uncomfortable, I can get you another pillow—"

THEN

— PILLOW.

Honestly, there are moments when I could pump this pillow between my hands, put it over her face and be done with it, she makes me so exasperated.

I've been searching for her non-existent brooch for twenty minutes now. My patient watches me balefully while I sort through her chest of drawers. Her claw-like hands grip the armrests of her easy chair as I turn over her underwear, raking through a mess of bras and big knickers.

Edith is one of our oldest residents in the nursing home, both in terms of how old she is and how long she's been here. She's always losing things. Worse, she accuses us of stealing from her. Still, that's what happens when you get dementia, I remind myself.

Often, I come into her room and find her distractedly looking for something. Or scraping imaginary insects off herself with her hands. All part of her dementia, and it's desperately sad.

"I'm telling you, it's not here," I repeat. "Are you sure your daughter didn't take it? Last time she came to visit?"

Edith sits in her armchair, watching me beadily.

"It must be somewhere in this room." I sigh.

And what a depressing little room this is, the kind you want to commit suicide in. A framed photograph of her unappealingly greasy-haired daughter as a schoolgirl. A divan bed with a nubby rose bedspread, a set of Formica white drawers, and a single overhead lampshade which I had to go into Clacton for and buy with my own money. Otherwise, the care home owner would have left her with a bare light bulb.

"Edith, I've looked everywhere. Are you certain Sheila didn't take it home with her?"

"You stole it," Edith says grimly.

"Don't be so silly. What would I want your old brooch for?" I say this in the brisk singsong voice I use whenever she's being difficult and I need her to do something.

"You stole it and I'm going to tell matron."

"Edith, we've been through this before. Your brooch will turn up, I'm sure of it. You've just put it somewhere."

Last week she accused our owner, Mrs Mkpeti, of leading her around by her nostrils. "Don't think I don't know what she's been up to," Edith said mysteriously. "When I go out of my room, she dresses up in my clothes."

This week it's me who's been stealing.

Her room has a sour, close smell and I am glad that it's nearly teatime. My swimming pool lane is booked for seven o'clock and I don't want to miss it.

I have always been good at swimming. It's the one sport I was any good at in school. For a large girl, I was even in the school swimming team. Okay, maybe not the first team but the *second. Because I'm weightless in water, I don't feel my size. Swimming is how I met her, Amy.*

Amanda Mawdsley.

No, Susan, don't think about her.

Don't think about Amy.

It's an effort to manoeuvre Edith into her wheelchair and then trundle her into the dining room.

They haven't changed the décor in this place since the nineties. Flamingo-pink curtains and walls. They keep the radiators on far too high to make residents sleepy. The place smells of dust and grease. Sweltering central heating is Mrs Mkpeti's one act of generosity since she took over as owner.

The truth is, most of us working here couldn't find another job working somewhere better. This ugly thirties detached house facing the North Sea is the last chance for most of us. Nobody asks about your old life, they're just grateful for another pair of hands.

Parking Edith at her regular table, I wait at the serving hatch for her tea. Shepherd's pie again with overcooked cabbage. At least, unlike some of my other patients, I don't have to spoon-feed her. Because Edith is a greedy old girl. Once I found her glugging an entire catering-size jug of cream.

Edith keeps her eyes fixed on her dinner, overwhelmed with greed as I adjust her wheelchair, making sure she's comfortable.

I once asked her what she'd learned during her ninety-four years of life. "Everything gets worse," she frowned. She's not wrong. Mrs Mkpeti hasn't spent a penny on upkeep since she took over Seaview Court, raking in as much money as she can from the local council.

Part of the deal was that she had to keep on existing staff, which she grumbled about. She would have much rather got rid of us all and replaced us with cheaper, hardworking teenagers from Eastern Europe.

The first time I met Mrs Mkpeti, I thought it was odd that she had the Boss logo on her trainers. Because that's what she is. A boss. She's a tyrant too, sending one of the younger girls home in tears this week. The only way to stay on in this place is to be invisible.

Which suits me just fine.

Quick glance at my watch. Half past five. Edith will take half an hour over her tea, as she always has a sweet, usually steamed pudding and custard. That gives me a golden half hour in the staff room before going back to collect her and then wheel Edith through to the TV lounge. Then three hours of television for her before bedtime.

What they laughingly call our staff lounge is basically a windowless store cupboard with a stained sofa, a kettle and a coffee table strewn with newspapers.

Nurse Tracy has already beaten me to it and has her feet up on the table, smoking a Superking. Unlike me, Nurse Tracy is a proper nurse, not a carer.

"I got the photographs back, Hermione," she says with a fag in her mouth. "There aren't any good ones of you though. You've always got your face covered."

They all call me Hermione after the Harry Potter character because I went to private school. I have worked in this care home ever since I left there, really. It gave me somewhere to hide, to forget about what happened. What they can't understand was why someone from what they think of as my posh background has hidden themselves away in this place.

Only I know that.

They're wrong about my being a posho too. What they

don't know is that Mum was a cleaner and Dad was a gardener. They have no idea of the hours spent cramming for the scholarship, the private tutors all paid for out of Mum working double shifts.

Then everything changed.

Unable to resist, I pick up the Snappy Snaps folder off the coffee table. We went to Wetherspoons after work last Saturday. Riffling through the photos, I see Nurse Tracy's right. While they're all grinning drunkenly at the camera, I've covered my face in every snapshot. Good.

Nurse Tracy is about to say something when Siobhan— another school leaver Mrs Mkpeti has taken on—sticks her head around the door.

"Tracy, you'd better come quick. Joan's got out of her room again. She's been found in a garden down the road."

"Oh my days," says Tracy, stubbing out her fag. "Wait a minute and I'll go and get my coat."

"IF YOU WERE HAPPY THERE, why did you leave?"

"It wasn't my decision. I— I—"

"What is it, Susan? What's the matter?"

"I didn't say I was happy. I was hiding. I'd done something bad... I don't know what. What difference does it make, anyway? I ended up working for the Mawdsleys, you know that."

I hid myself away in that place because I felt incredible guilt over something I did. But I still don't know what it was. It's welling up, how ashamed I feel.

"Susan, if this is uncomfortable, that means we're getting

somewhere. Tell me, Susan. Why did you leave the care home?"

"I don't know. Something I did. Please, can we stop? I don't know what this has got to do with Amanda Mawdsley."

My palms are getting sweaty and I wipe them down my hospital gown. Then it comes to me, the reason why they fired me—

THEN

IT TAKES ABOUT *twenty minutes for me to get the bus from Frinton-on-Sea to Clacton Leisure Centre.*

The changing rooms smell of chlorine and bleach. The tiles look dirty, and I carefully try to keep my bare feet off them. There's just one hour left before the swimming pool closes and, adjusting my swim cap, I pad out to the poolside.

This swimming pool isn't like the one where I first met Amanda Mawdsley—no, that was a cold and grey lido in the Midlands—and it's not like the one where we basked in the South of France either, Amy smoothing sun cream onto her legs. It's not like the basement one in their family home, the one where—

Ploughing up and down my roped-off lane, staring into the chlorine murk, I can't help but start thinking about Amanda Mawdsley again.

Sometimes, I am back in that basement swimming pool, playing out another version of what happened. Some way things could have been different. But it always ends badly, like an equation which will never work out.

Amy on that diving board, turning. The wicked thing she

said to me, the cruelty of it. Fear and hatred rushing up inside me. Looking at my hands. Why, I could just push her off that diving board and—

How I long to go back and throw my arms around the past to change things, but you never can, can you?

A siren sounds, telling us the evening swimming session is over. Having showered, I pad back to my locker to get dressed. Locking the rattly cubicle door behind me, the first thing I do is check my Nokia for messages. There's one message from Tracy:

You'd better come back quick. She's on the warpath.

It's gone nine o'clock by the time I knock on Mrs Mkpeti's door. Whatever this is about, it isn't going to be good. Being called into her office is never a good thing.

Mrs Mkpeti doesn't look up, pointedly keeping me waiting, as if her paperwork is more important.

Finally, she acknowledges me.

For a middle-aged Black woman, her skin is grey with fatigue. Grey dreadlocky hair pulled back and oversized red eighties-style spectacles.

"We've had a complaint."

"What about?" I ask her. Honestly, I can't think what I might have done. But then again, it's always some tiny detail that's your undoing. Something you missed, which you could never have anticipated.

"Edith says you've stolen her brooch."

"Oh, that," I say, relieved.

"The complaint didn't come from her but from her family. They're accusing you of theft."

"I searched through her room. Her daughter must have taken it home for safekeeping."

"That's not true and you know it."

"What do you mean?"

"Because we found the brooch in your bedroom."

"That's ridiculous," I say indignantly.

Mrs Mkpeti says nothing but dips into her desk drawer, scrabbling about for something. She opens her fist to reveal the missing gold brooch. Righteous anger wells up inside me.

"Now wait a minute—"

"I asked one of the girls to go through your things. She found it at the back of your wardrobe. I'm sorry, Susan, but I simply cannot allow stealing in my care home."

She sounds sympathetic but she's playing the more-in-sorrow-than-in-anger card. This has all been rehearsed. She's always had it in for me and now I am being framed.

"You had no right to do that. I didn't give you permission."

"Don't have a right?" she says acidly. "Don't have a right? I have every right. To protect my patients from a thief like you."

I am so angry, I want to swipe the things off her desk and bang my fist. I have never stolen anything in my life—no, that's not quite true, is it? I did steal something once. A paperweight.

"I'm sorry, Susan," Mrs Mkpeti continues, leaning forward on her elbows. She's coming over all conciliatory now. "I cannot have theft in my care home. Surely you can see that."

"I'm telling you, I never stole that brooch. I swear on my mother's life."

This is awful. It's all I can do to stop myself bursting into tears. Already, I can picture my mother's tight mouth when I walk in through our front door and tell her I've lost my job.

Somebody planted that brooch, Siobhan perhaps. She comes over as all smiley and nice-y and making heart shapes with her fingers but really, she's a bossy mare.

"You've always had it in for me, ever since you took over. I've worked here for five years and never had one complaint. Mrs Drinkwater said—"

Mrs Mkpeti waves me away.

"Mrs Drinkwater is in the past. I'm your employer now. Then there's your timekeeping, your rudeness... In all my years in care, I have never had a staff member as insolent as you."

"Are you firing me?" I ask, incredulously.

"You think you're better than us, don't you?"

So this is what it's about. In some weird way, she's jealous. And there's an inkling of truth in this. Mum might have been a cleaner but I did win a scholarship to private school. I did sit the Oxbridge entrance exam.

"I'm sorry, Mrs Mkpeti. I didn't steal that brooch, I swear. If you could just give me one more chance..."

She gives me a pained smile. "It's too late for that."

"Then you're just a bitch who's always had it in for me."

Slightly stunned by what's just come out of my mouth, we both stare at each other. I am young, I want to tell her. I've got my whole life ahead of me. I'm not frightened.

"Well, you can forget about a reference," Mrs Mkpeti huffs, getting on with her papers. "I have never been spoken to like that."

"Well, there's a first time for everything."

She flicks me away with her fingers, indicating our interview is over.

"Close the door on your way out," she says. "I want you gone by morning."

CHAPTER THIRTEEN

SESSION 1

"How did it make you feel, being told to leave like that?" Doctor Max asks.

"Angry. Resentful. That I hadn't been treated fairly. It still makes me angry thinking about it."

"So, you were in a bruised emotional state when you went to work for the Mawdsleys. Any slight or criticism, you would have taken it badly?"

I see where he's going with this and I don't like it. He's pushing me to say things I don't agree with. *Careful, Susan.* All of this is going in his report, one which will be sent to the police.

"I don't know. I honestly can't remember."

Can't remember, can't remember... I'm like a scratched CD that can't get past itself.

"Let's rewind a bit. Tell me what happened then, after you went home?"

THEN

THE FAMILIAR FIGURE *appears on the other side of the whorled glass. I stand outside, holdall at my feet. Mum opens the front door, and I step inside. Our narrow hall smells of rose air conditioner and, instantly, I'm back to being a child again.*

Home.

Why did I ever leave here when the world outside just wants to hurt me? Somewhere safe. Home-cooked meals and getting my laundry done. The same things, day in, day out. Countdown on the telly at two and Pointless while we have our tea. A place where nothing bad can ever happen. Where they can't get to you. I was mad to ever leave here. What was I even thinking of?

"You're late," *Mum says.* "You said you'd be here hours ago."

"Nice to see you too, Mum. The battery on my phone died. The coach was late."

"It's really not convenient you being here, not right now. I've got a lot on. I'm late for my Zumba class. I'm going with Auntie Jean."

She's wearing Spandex leggings and a fleece. Actually, Mum looks in great shape for somebody who's sixty-five. As I follow her down the hall, she's telling me how she also does a weekly step class.

"I've kept your room just how you liked it," *Mum says, ushering me in.*

Yes, my teenage bedroom is exactly how I left it. A time

capsule of 2008. My teddy bear with the scorched foot lies propped up against the pillows. Purple clothes I outgrew years ago folded and stacked on shelves. Teenage posters, a pouting Jonathan Rhys-Meyers—God, I had such a crush on him—Britney Spears and Avril Lavigne still Blu-tacked to my walls. Seven years since I left this room and now here I am, back again.

"I'll leave you to unpack. I'm making your favourite for tea, sausage and beans. I'll be back around five."

While she's talking, I touch a pair of teenage knickers, large white ones with a daisy on them. I really am back to being a child again.

"Thanks, Mum."

Hearing our front door close, I sit down heavily on my bed. Then I remember its hard, cheap mattress. Another dead end. There's a lucky Chinese cat on my bedside table and I give it a flick, watching it wave uselessly at me. Waving goodbye to my old life. There's a glass paperweight beside it, a scorpion trapped in glass with its tail raised. I was lying when I told Mrs Mkpeti I'd never stolen anything in my life. I stole this paperweight. The first time my entire world collapsed.

I lie down and gaze up at the ceiling. This bed's so uncomfortable, like lying on a mortuary slab. Mum had a leak in the roof last winter and water poured in through the attic. It's left a nasty scar running down one corner of the ceiling like a pan of milk that's boiled over. Then I flash on her, Amanda Mawdsley, self-consciously pulling down her jumper sleeve, covering the scar on her wrist. That must have been, what, the second time we met?

Children are playing outside in our cul-de-sac, beyond these curtains, closed against the penetrating afternoon sunshine. Old feelings are rising up again—being smothered by a pair of motherly breasts, and it's suffocating. The ties that bind. I've got to get out of here, but how? Apart from working in a care home, it's not as if I've got any other skills. And Mrs Mkpeti said I could forget about a reference.

Suppose I'd better plug my phone in. I fish my Nokia out of my jeans pocket and rummage through my holdall for its charger.

I could always work in Tesco, behind a till. Or retrain as a primary school teacher. I've always been good at maths and I like children and—

The waltz ringtone makes me jump. When I glance down, the screen says, "number withheld".

"Hello?" I answer cautiously.

"May I speak to Susan Gummer, please?" asks a cheerful man's voice, one I don't recognise.

"Susan speaking."

"Oh, hello, Susan. You don't know me. My name is Gary Vine and I'm calling from the Easy Living care agency. A job has come up that we think would be a perfect fit for you."

Blimey, word gets around fast. Then I remember that I did in fact register with several care agencies back when I was first looking for a job but I don't specifically recall this one.

"Go on," I say cautiously.

"It's working for a family with a disabled daughter. I'll be honest with you, Susan. We don't have many people on our books with your, um, background."

Having been to a posho school and yet ending up in a failing care home, that's what he means.

"When you say disabled, what do you mean? I don't have any nursing qualifications."

"Oh, she just needs a companion, that's all. Somebody to be with her. The father goes abroad on business a lot, you see. It would just be for over the summer."

My heart thumps against my chest.

No, it can't be her. That would be too ironic. Not after what I've just been thinking. Not after everything that happened.

"This family, can I ask where they live?"

"In central London. An area called Belgravia. Do you know it?"

"I know where that is."

Know it? I can retrace the walk from Victoria Station to that front door in every single step.

I ask what the name of the family is, knowing full well the answer. It's the Mawdsleys, I want to shout down the phone, it's the Mawdsleys.

"I can't tell you that at this stage. All I can tell you is that they are wealthy. Very wealthy."

The way he says this, it's like he's talking out of the side of his mouth. There's fat pickings here for both of us, that's what he means.

Of all the people he could have chosen, I'm the one person they don't want for this job. In fact, I'm the very last person they need.

"As I said, it would be a live-in position and just for over the summer."

"I'm sorry. I don't think I'm the person you want."

"Wait, I haven't told you the salary yet—" *I get the feeling that he's muffled the handset with his hand and is talking to someone.* "The position would be extremely well paid. And I mean, very. We're talking four hundred pounds a day."

I quickly do the sums in my head. That could be two thousand pounds a week or even eight grand a month. Eight thousand pounds. Enough to rent a place of my own for months. A fresh start. *And ironically, her family would be the ones paying for it.*

Take it, Susan. If it's just for over the summer. Well, what harm could it do?

And what about her, Amy? This could be a chance to make up for what happened, to repay the debt I owe her. I've spent years just wishing I could go back in time, that I could undo everything.

"How long are we talking about?"

"Between now and September. A three-month contract."

Pause.

"Are you still there?" he asks. "Do you want me to put you forward?"

"All right," I say reluctantly.

"That's wonderful news, Susan. They're really keen to meet you. Would you be free tomorrow afternoon at three? I can text you the address."

I know what the address is. There isn't a day that goes past when I don't think about it. I can picture the house, its vast atrium, the galleried bedrooms, the lift which takes you down to the swimming pool—

"This family. They do know who I am, right?"

"Oh yes, they specifically asked for you once they saw your CV."

I bet they did.

Knowing I'm doing the wrong thing, I can't seem to stop myself. I'm irresistibly drawn to this family, I don't know why.

"It's thirteen Chester Street, isn't it?"

I can hear him breathe on the other end of the phone.

"How do you know that?" He sounds genuinely surprised.

"*I know the family. I was at school with the daughter, the one you want me to look after. We were in the same year.*"

I cannot believe I am being given this second chance. Amanda Mawdsley, whom I have obsessed about for the past seven years, who still comes to me in dreams. And because she'll be in a wheelchair, this time she cannot hurt me. I will be the one in charge. This is my chance. Take it. No, it would be too weird. Dangerous. I mean, if she found out... It's only after Gary Vine rings off that I wonder how he knew I was even looking for a job.

CHAPTER FOURTEEN

SESSION 1

Doctor Max rubs his chin, thinking. "That sounds very paranoid, Susan. Do you really think they were watching you?"

"How else do you explain it? Nobody knew I'd lost my job. The only person I'd told was Mum."

"You hadn't updated your social media status, something like that?"

"I told you. I'd hidden myself away in that place. Deleted my Facebook account. There's no way they could have known unless they'd been spying on me."

Doctor Max picks up his notepad again. "You said that you first met Amanda Mawdsley at school. That's how she knew you'd become a care worker. Let's focus in on that. Often how you meet someone sets the tone for a relationship, how it will end. The clues are all there, you just don't know how to read them."

"Amy came to our school late, in the sixth form. There

were rumours about her. That she'd been expelled from her previous school. She seemed very exotic. You've got to understand, Doctor Max, it wasn't one of those big posho schools, it was a pretty dismal place. I don't think it even exists anymore. None of us could figure out what she was doing there."

"Yes, but describe to me the moment you met. What you thought of her. Your first impressions—"

THEN—2008

IT'S SO *cold this afternoon as we shiver beside the outdoor school pool. For some reason, this ugly thirties swimming pool is called "the Tosh". We stand huddled together like ponies in our lumpy one-piece swimsuits, towels draped over our shoulders.*

Mister Sibley is giving us a kayaking lesson. He's a burly man who wears silly tomato-red shorts. Today's lesson is learning how to roll a kayak. The idea is that you pitch your-self headfirst into the water, somersault and resurface smiling.

Myra Didcock floats in a kayak at the deep end with her paddle across her chest, waiting for his whistle, a plastic apron sealing her in. I just wish she would hurry up and get on with it. I've got gooseflesh.

The whistle blasts and Myra dunks herself into the pool, snapping off the plastic skirt, and swims free of the upturned kayak. She doggy paddles to the side.

"You forgot the kayak, Didcock," Mister Sibley bawls at her.

Myra nods and obediently doggy paddles back to the over-turned kayak, rights it, and drags it back with her.

"Right, Mawdsley, your turn."

The moment I see her, I think, I'm going to come into great conflict with her. I can't explain it. I don't believe in horoscopes or palm reading or any of that stuff—numbers, that's my thing—yet the moment I spot her, I think, I am going to come into great conflict with this person. It's a premonition.

Mad, bad and dangerous to know, that's what the other girls are saying about her. Amanda Mawdsley arrived here to do her A-levels. There are rumours that she's been in a psychiatric hospital, somewhere in America, which of course only fascinates me more. America is a long way from Leamington Spa. I've never even been outside of the Midlands.

Amy steps forward but she's nervous, not her usual confident, slightly disdainful self. Maybe I'm the only one who notices. Gingerly, Amy lowers herself into the waterlogged kayak and pushes away with the paddle until she floats above the deep end.

Mr Sibley blows his whistle and she dunks herself as ordered, while we wait for her to resurface.

Nothing happens.

The upside-down kayak just bobs there.

The other girls get restive and I turn to look for Mister Sibley, only he's too busy flirting with Fiona Younger, a Scottish girl with one hand on her sexily cocked hip.

The kayak still hasn't moved.

I call out, "Sir, there's something wrong."

Our teacher just stands there looking stupefied, gawping at the water. It dawns on me that he's not going to do anything. Without thinking, I dive into the water, which explodes around me as I right myself. It's absolutely freezing, almost painful.

Everything goes into slow motion as I kick up towards Amy. She hangs upside down through the chlorine murk, her hair floating around her like ectoplasm. Her eyes are wide open but there's nobody there, as if she's gone into a trance.

I grab her around the waist, my fingers almost curling lazily around her, and try pulling. No good. My lungs burn and I kick back up to the surface, take a huge gulp of air, ignoring the shouts, and dive straight down again.

This time I kick towards her, tackling Amy in a clumsy embrace as I force my mouth onto hers, breathing air into her.

This time she convulses, brought back to life.

There's a commotion to one side of me as Mister Sibley finally jumps in. The water's churning. Together, we manhandle Amy out of the overturned kayak. My lungs ache as my head breaks the surface. I want to laugh, cry and shout as the same time.

The two of us drag her dead weight to the poolside and then the other girls pull Amy out, water streaming off her. She coughs and spews water onto the flagstones, her lungs heaving with effort.

We gather around like concerned cows looking down at somebody lying in a field. When she rolls onto her back, still coughing, mine is the first face she sees.

"You saved my life," she says weakly. "Maybe you should teach me to swim."

Like I said, it was a premonition. The first time we met, I saved her life in a swimming pool. Isn't that what they say about life, that it repeats itself, first as a comedy, then as a tragedy?

Second time around, Amy wasn't so lucky.

CHAPTER FIFTEEN

SESSION 1

The morning lightens outside Doctor Max's window. It's daylight by now. We're still in his office, me stretched out on his sofa and him in his dressing gown sitting opposite. The effort of remembering the past, all those ghosts crowding me, jostling for attention, it's exhausting. I see now why Max calls it "doing the work". My brain feels so tired.

"You still had misgivings though, about working for this family. Despite the salary they were offering."

"Yes. I felt guilty about something. I don't know what. Maybe it was that paperweight. I stole it from them. I'd been fired for theft, remember?"

"Susan, nobody buries themselves away because they stole a glass bauble. There has to be more to it than that. Why were you so reluctant to see this family again? This is important, Susan. It could unlock everything."

"Max, I want to stop. These memories, they're too painful. Haven't we done enough for now?"

"One more question. How did you feel about seeing Amy again? Would you call it an infatuation? To be honest, the way you talk about her, you come across as obsessed."

THEN

I DON'T SLEEP *well that night.*

I toss and turn, unable to get comfortable, having lurid thoughts about Amy, imagining what it will be like to meet her again for the first time in seven years. Wondering if she's changed. Because to me, she's always exactly the same as that first day we met at the swimming pool.

Next morning, Mum smiles tightly when I tell her I'm going down to London for a job interview. Because if they don't take me on, I'm not quite sure what I am going to do. I have no references and it's not as if I have much money saved from my minimum wage job. It's not as if Mrs Mkpeti is going to recommend me, is it?

The more I think about it, that care agency phoning me up out of the blue was too weird. Were they watching me? Stop being so paranoid. You're overthinking this. They were looking for a carer for Amy and saw your name, that's all. Somebody they know. You were a name on a list put forward by the Easy Living care agency, whoever they are. Trouble is, I don't remember signing up with any Easy Living care agency.

From what I know of this family, money just magnifies your problems. When everybody wants something from you, whom can you even trust? That's why this family wants me, because they think they can trust me.

If only they knew.

And how would they know where I even was anyway? I haven't been in contact since it happened. Amy left a message about a year later, but I never returned it. I have not spoken to handsome—no, beautiful—Jamie either. It's their father I feel sorry for. How much bad luck can one family have? First, his wife, then his daughter. I shiver. Bad things come in threes, don't they?

A paid companion. It sounds so Victorian somehow. I picture the two of us, me pushing Amy in a bath chair around the boat pond in Kensington Gardens. But this isn't some genteel Victorian novel, this is my one offer of employment. A second chance.

That afternoon there's a little girl on the train down to London. Was I really that girl once, her mouth smeared with chocolate, jumping up to point excitedly out of the window? Rain trails hang over the city as our train gets nearer. By the time we arrive at Euston, it's raining hard. Cold sluicing rain.

I take the tube from Euston down to Victoria and it's sheeting outside the station with a huge queue for taxis. I grimace. I don't have an umbrella. For a moment, I debate whether to wait out this thunderstorm but there's nothing to do but make a run for it if I'm to make the interview on time.

Rain explodes on the pavement as I scurry past office workers also hurrying to get out of the wet. I am completely drenched. My tights are wet and my hair is plastered down. Barging past other pedestrians, I must look like a drowned rat.

I remember the very first time I came to Chester Street, the night of the party. It was a summer evening like this one, only it was humid. Poor, dumpy Susan, standing in the garden making awkward conversation with Amy's father, looking up at her bedroom window where her London friends gazed coolly down at us. Edgy Black music blasting from her room.

How I longed to be up there with her, hanging out with the cool London girls.

I turn into Chester Street, remembering that it's the first house on the left. As I climb those front doorstep, the voice in my head tells me this is my last chance to turn back. Forget it, Susan. Do you really think you're going to get away with this? Turn back, turn back, Dick Whittington; isn't that what the fairytale says?

The glossy black door stands as impenetrable as ever, guarding its secrets. I quail. Once I go through that door, things are never going to be the same again. I will be on the wrong side of my old life forever.

"THIS IS GOOD, SUSAN," says Max. "What's stopping you? Why can't you get through that door?"

"Shame. Guilt over something I've done. Please, Max, let's stop now. We've done enough for one session. I'm tired. I want to go back to my room."

"No, Susan. You've got to stay with it. Resistance is good. Now we're getting somewhere. You've got to push past this, Susan. Kick down that door, Susan. Tell me what's on the other side."

THEN

I CAN'T SEEM *to move my feet on those front steps. They won't do what I want them to. I am stiff with fear. Smokey dark tendrils appear at the edges of the glossy black door, over-*

lapping each other like tongues, spreading across the brick-work. "Come inside, Susan," those tongues whisper, "it's time for you to repay what you owe. You didn't really think you were going to get away with it, did you?"

The man who answers the door is a blond giant, well over six feet tall with the build of a soldier or a bodyguard. He looks at me uncomprehendingly.

"It's all right, Pavel," says an unseen voice high above us. "I'll come right down."

As if a silent dog whistle has been blown, this Pavel steps smartly aside to let me in.

Oh, I recognise that voice.

I look up to see Mr Mawdsley with his arms folded across the third-floor balcony before giving me a cheery salute. "I'll be right down," he says.

The interior of the house is just as I remember it. I still want to stand in the middle of this atrium and twirl around to drink it all in, it's so overwhelming.

It's an amazing building. From the outside, it looks like all the other white stucco houses in the street until you realise that it's two of them knocked through. You gaze up at three floors of arcades running around the atrium where the bedrooms were. Years ago, I came across a magazine where the architect said he had based his design on a Shakespearian theatre, although I'm not sure whether he meant it to be a comedy or a tragedy.

Is she here? In one of those bedrooms up there? Is this the moment I have obsessed about, meeting her again? Or is this a trap, a way for the family to confront me, to get me to tell the truth?

An open marble staircase flows down to the ground floor. I know that the marble was imported from Italy and that building work took over a year, and there's still another third of the house underground. Amy told me all this the last time I stood in this hall. Three floors below us include a gym, a cinema and a swimming pool.

Don't think about the swimming pool.

Amy clowning about on the diving board while all that hatred and resentment boils up inside me.

What she said to me.

The cruelty of it.

Don't think about any of that. Stay in the moment. You are here for a job interview, that's all. Stay focused.

Mr Mawdsley descends in a golden lift, the Sun King himself, the man nobody says no to. This lift wasn't there before but I can guess why they need it now. A deus ex machina, isn't that what they call it? God descending in a machine to put everything right. But if he is a god, then his power has faded, you can tell.

He's aged since we last met. The last time I saw him was outside this very front door, out in the street, his face lit up with strobing blue lights. His hair is still leonine, but it's gone quite grey and his belly hangs over his open-necked silk shirt. He's wearing a pair of suit trousers and, oddly, is barefoot.

"Susan, how lovely to see you," he says, extending his hand. His lion's paw completely covers mine and he double-grasps it with both hands. "Come, sit down. Goodness, you're completely soaked. Would you like a towel?"

"That would be great, thanks."

To my surprise, he barks what sounds like an Eastern European language at his major-domo. This Pavel exits smartly, almost clicking his heels. The kitchen, if I remember right, lies off to the left of the lobby. I remember the kitchen too with its marble work surfaces, the silent American refrigerator, the astonishing kitchen island.

Mr Mawdsley pads over to one of the thick, comfortable sofas and sprawls across it, waving airily for me to join him. His butler or manservant or whoever he is comes back from the kitchen, handing me a tea towel. Rubbing my hair, I sit down across the coffee table, on which Mr Mawdsley puts up his bare feet.

"You can't imagine my surprise when I saw your name on the CV. I thought, 'It can't be her,' yet here you are."

He's all charm now. You catch more flies with honey than vinegar, that's one of Mum's sayings, and I am the fly creeping deeper into his spider web.

"Yes, I decided to become a carer after leaving school. I never did go to university."

"And I always thought you would become an academic. Maths was your thing, wasn't it? You remember our holiday in the South of France? You always had your nose in a textbook. Never mind," he says, shaking his head.

I smile meaninglessly at him and, for a moment, we sit there in silence. Is this it? The moment he leans forward and says, "I know it was you, Susan."

Finally, I say, "I'm afraid I haven't been a very good friend to her. I feel bad about that."

"You're not alone. People find tragedy difficult to deal with. A few friends stuck by her at the beginning but they drifted away. Some of them came to visit in the early days and then stopped. That's how people are." He shrugs. "I say tragedy but nobody died, did they?"

No, nobody died but confined to a wheelchair for the rest of your life, dependent on the charity of others, that's not much of a life, is it?

"How's she been?"

"She's angry at what happened, of course. The worst of it is, she knows it was all her own fault. So she lashes out at people, whoever's nearest to her. Usually, that's her carer." He pauses and says ruefully, "We've had a succession of well-meaning ladies, earnest Christians from South Africa, but she reams them out. Tears a new hole in them, as the Americans say. So they leave. I can't blame them."

"So, who's looking after her now?"

"Poor Pavel has been trying but he doesn't speak much English and I need him with me in New York. You remember my son Jamie?"

Parting leaves between my fingers that sweltering summer, sweat stinging my eyes, as a beautiful teenager jack-knifes into the cold, clean water.

"I think so," I reply, my voice catching.

"He's been running the American arm of the business but it's overwhelming. He needs my support. It's a lot for a young man of your age to take on. I've got to go away for three months and I need someone to be with Amy."

I don't understand why Amy being in a wheelchair should stop her from working for her father—I mean, it's not as if her brain is impaired, is it?—but I don't say anything.

"She suffers from depression, black moods," he continues, answering my unasked question. "There's no reasoning with her when she's like that. She can't help herself. You can't have that in a corporate environment."

"What do the doctors say?"

"Well, as you can imagine, we've been to the best clinics in the world. Seen the top consultants. She spent a year at Shirley Ryan in Chicago. None of it did any good."

He swings his bare feet off the table and hunkers down,

getting down to business. I've seen him do this before. First the soft talk and then the hard negotiation.

"I'll be honest with you, Susan. I'm desperate. She needs someone with her on her own intellectual level. Somebody she can talk to. And I'll pay you well, double what we advertised."

Eight hundred pounds a day?

"And there are benefits. On top of your salary, you'd be living here rent-free. You wouldn't have to pay for anything. And I'd give you a credit card with unlimited expenses. But I do need you to decide quickly. I'm leaving for New York the day after tomorrow. Please, Susan, I'm begging you."

Really, Susan Gummer, you should be the one down on your knees begging him for forgiveness, not the other way round. At the same time, my other voice whispers to get out, get out, GET OUT.

"All right, I'll do it," I hear myself saying.

His shoulders actually slump with relief. "Oh, thank goodness. I have to warn you though, she can be difficult. When she gets into one of her rages—" He breaks off, suddenly. "Oh, hello, darling."

"Hello, Susan," Amy says behind me.

CHAPTER SIXTEEN

TO: █
FROM: Doctor Max Quane
Dear █

I have to tell you that Ms Gummer is now fully
aware of who she is and how she came to be in the
Hallam Clinic. Perhaps it was only a matter of time.
It is very difficult to keep anything secret in our
connected world and maybe it is best that Ms
Gummer understands the gravity of her situation.

Although it must have come as a great shock, she
now understands the facts and the need to protect
her privacy.

She has begun to show significant signs of memory
recovery. Remarkably, she has regained access to
childhood memories up to leaving school and getting
her first job at the age of 19.

The rest, however, is still a complete blank.

Happily, her recovery trajectory aligns with the latest peer group research that some individuals can recover consciousness and rebuild memory much quicker than previously thought.

Of course, helping Ms Gummer untangle which memories are true, and which are hallucinations the brain has created to protect her from the truth, is the job of the psychiatrist. To that end, I am co-authoring a book with Ms Gummer detailing this extraordinary recovery process. Our last chapter would be her final memory. Assuming, of course, we can retrieve what her brain has wiped.

It may be that we never recover what actually happened that night. The group's incredible generosity in paying for Ms Gummer's care will have been for nothing, and it will be up to the police to press charges.
Given the sensitive nature of this case and the potential impact of our findings, we need to conduct our research and treatment away from public scrutiny and media attention. This controlled environment is crucial to maximise Ms Gummer's chances of recovery and to maintain the integrity of our study.

To that end, I have made a complaint to the newspaper regulator about photographers ambushing a hospital patient. There is no public interest in photographing a young woman who may or may not be a witness to a crime. The police have yet to question her formally, let alone make an arrest.

In any case, there will be no more reporters trespassing onto the property. The gates are now locked at all times. Only deliveries and pre-screened visitors are admitted. Any interview requests will now be routed through the group's press team, so thank you for that.

There will be great interest in this book, as you can imagine, especially, as I am now coming to believe, because what happened was a tragic accident and not murder. I realise this may not be what you want to hear.

As agreed, I propose sending you the manuscript chapter by chapter. If Susan does remember in detail what happened that night, then it will be up to you to decide what next steps to take.

The police have not returned since their visit yesterday, although I suspect they are just regrouping with a court order. Of course, I apologise for any bad publicity, but I maintain that my first duty is to protect this vulnerable young woman.

Thank you again for your patience and understanding. The most valuable commodity is time but as Ms Gummer herself said last night, that clock is now ticking...

I would greatly appreciate your discretion regarding the contents of this email.

Max

CHAPTER SEVENTEEN

A child's voice brings me back. I'm in the day room, thinking about that moment when I saw Amy Mawdsley again for the first time in nearly a decade. A little girl stands at the entrance to the day room, too afraid to come in fully.

"Are you the very ill lady?" she asks shyly.

She must be about four or five, chubby, with an unbecoming pudding bowl haircut. Maybe she's been told not to come into this room. Who is she and what's she doing in this place? As far as I know, there's just Doctor Max, myself and the two nurses, Bunny and Linh, here. There's a hospital porter but I haven't met him yet. Then, further off, I hear the grate of a vacuum cleaner.

"Come in. I won't bite," I say, sitting up in my chair. "What's your name?"

"Jade. Jay. Ay. Dee. Eee," she says, spelling it out.

The girl dawdles by the doorway, still unsure. "Mum says you've been asleep for a very long time," she says.

"That's right, I was, but I'm awake now."

"Like a princess in a fairy story. Is it true you can't remember anything?"

"No. I can remember some things, just not everything."

"What's it like not being able to remember?"

It's like watching a movie when the screen goes white, just the film end uselessly slapping around the projector.

"I don't know. I can't remember," I say, pulling a stupid face.

The girl chortles and steps further into the room, reassured.

"That's silly. Everybody can remember something. Can you remember when you were a baby? Can you remember what you had for lunch?"

What *did* I have for lunch? I suddenly panic, then remember chicken stew, tepid mash potato and overcooked green beans.

"Shouldn't you be in school today?"

"I'm still on school holiday. My nan's too ill to look after me. That's why Mum brought me with her."

Of course, it's still the Christmas holiday, out there, beyond these windows. That's ten Christmases I've missed.

"What's your favourite subject at school? Do you like maths, you know, counting?" I ask hopefully.

"Maths is boring," Jade says firmly. "I want to be an artist when I grow up." Pause. "Or an influencer."

I don't know what an influencer is, so I ask her if she'd like to do some drawing now, getting up to find a pen and paper. I can move around quite easily today, without Bunny's walking sticks, and I root about in old board games to find a pencil stub and the back of a scorecard.

We sit cross-legged on the floor together as I watch Jade draw. I have always got on with children. It's just a question of literally getting down to their level. Jade even lifts her arm and points the pencil straight up at me, like a proper artist would do, something she must have seen on TV. She takes this all very seriously.

"What is it that you're drawing?"

"It's you," she says.

She's drawn a stick woman standing beside a boxy house marked with a red cross. Out of the mouths of babes and innocents.

An image comes into my head, something from a black-and-white film—a little girl by a lake, holding out a flower to Frankenstein's monster, the two of them sitting together casting flowers onto the water until, having run out of flowers, the monster throws the child into the water.

Where on Earth has that come from? I don't even like horror films, do I? Am I that monster, sitting cross-legged on the floor with this little girl?

"Mum says that you're fibbing when you say you can't remember," says Jade, still drawing.

Does she, indeed?

"Finished."

I sense that we're both getting bored of this drawing game, and so I ask her what she would like to do next. Hide and seek, she says, and I tell her to run off and hide downstairs. "Don't go too far though; my legs aren't very good still." Jade clatters down the main staircase, shrieking with laughter, while I hobble towards the patient lift.

Once I get downstairs, it's easy to see where she's hidden. The double swing doors to the kitchen are still flapping to a close. I push my way in, exaggeratedly making a lot of noise, to hear her giggling from somewhere inside this stainless-steel professional kitchen. Then I spot her. She's pushed her way inside one of the pan cupboards with a sliding door underneath the work surface.

"Colder," she says from underneath the counter. "Warmer," she giggles, as I turn with my arms raised like the boogie-man or the big bad wolf, about to pounce.

"Jade. What the eff are you doing in that cupboard? Get your arse out here now!"

Her mum's voice cuts through, and I turn to face an indignant-looking woman struggling with a mop and bucket. Jade laughs though, still thinking this is part of hide-and-seek, shrinking deeper inside the pan cupboard.

"Really, she's no trouble. We were just playing a game—" I begin.

Her mum, though, isn't messing about, and lurches for the pan cupboard, dragging her daughter out. Jade's laughter turns to yelps and then to frightened wails as her mum violently pulls her by her arms. Jade's really sobbing now.

"Stop, you're hurting her," I protest, putting my hand on her mum's shoulder. "She's no trouble, really."

She whirls around, incandescent with anger. "Get your filthy hands off me," she snarls. "It's not you I'm worried about, it's her. I don't want her going near a... murderer."

A murderer.

That's what she called me.

Murder, murder, murder. That same word I screamed that night, running down the street in my bloody nightdress.

So, this is how the world sees me, is it? The servant who murdered her employer. That same word shrieked again and again in all those newspaper clippings.

MURDER.

CHAPTER EIGHTEEN

SESSION 2

We're back in Max's office for my second session of forensic psychotherapy, as he calls it. This time we're sitting in armchairs facing each other with that ominous box of tissues between us.

"Susan, I need to explain something. About the work we're doing. Being knocked down by that car, you had a terrible accident. When a plane goes down, it has a black box that records everything that happened. Divers go down to the seabed to retrieve that black box. That's what we're doing. Diving deep into your brain, retrieving your memories."

"What happens if we can't find the black box?"

"Oh, it's there... we just have to keep searching. Now, I want to pick up where we left off. Tell me about the first time you met James Mawdsley. What did you think of him? Where did you meet him?"

"I think we met on holiday." I frown. "Amy's family had a place in the South of France. I think I met him there. Yes, that's right."

Max raises his eyes at this. "You certainly got on well then. I mean, with Amanda. First, you save her life in a swimming pool. Next, she's invited you on holiday."

I shake my head as if I've got water trapped in my eardrum. "It wasn't as fast as that. I *thought* I was Amy's friend but really, she just needed a maths tutor. That's something you've got to understand about the Mawdsleys. Everything was a transaction to them. You give me this, I'll give you that. That's why they had so many people around them. Protection. Everyone wanted something from them."

"Tell me about that holiday. How did it come about?"

THEN—2008

I'VE ALWAYS FOUND *maths easy and am helping Myra Didcock with her homework. All you have to do is explain things slower and more clearly. Fractions, equations, algorithms, they're as simple as basic arithmetic once you explain them clearly.*

"Mister Sibley says I'm mathematically dyslexic."

"There's no such thing as being dyslexic at maths. He's just a crap teacher."

Mister Sibley is her maths teacher. He takes the bottom class of girls. He also teaches PE. Because he's the youngest master in our dismal boarding school, some of the girls have crushes on him. Not me though. He sits too close to you when he's correcting your work, his jean trouser leg jiggling with excitement.

Amanda Mawdsley leans insouciantly against the door-frame, watching us. She's one of those cool London girls whose skirt is shorter than everyone else's, showing off her legs. Her tight V-neck jumper shows off the exciting plunge of her breasts.

That's when I notice the ugly, thick cut across her left wrist, where the skin has healed. This isn't a dainty cut on her thigh with a razor blade, like some of the girls do, more like she's attacked herself with a bread knife. Noticing where I'm looking, she self-consciously pulls down her jumper sleeve.

There are rumours about her. That she was expelled from her last school because she had an affair with one of the teachers. And then there's that one about her spending time in a psychiatric hospital.

She only joined our school in the sixth form. Quite what she's doing at our third-rate Midlands public school, nobody can figure out. She's already gathered a coterie around her. Christina Walsh also stands in the doorway. Her parents run a chain of pawnbrokers in the northeast. She's a nasty piece of work with a sullen, mean face.

"You're the one from the swimming pool, aren't you?" Amanda remembers. "I didn't think they allowed tanners in here after the bell."

A tanner was what they call us day girls who live in town. Like everything else in England, even our second-rate school has snobberies and cliques.

"I'm helping Myra with her prep."

"Yes, I've heard you do that. You can help me with mine." It's a statement, not a request.

"I'd be happy to."

Already I feel as if I am betraying my ugly duckling friend, siding with the pack, which makes me uncomfortable. That's the thing about bullying—you find yourself being pulled into it, encouraged by the others.

I help Amanda ("Call me Amy") with her homework the next afternoon. Even her study bedroom is cool compared to Myra's squalor. We sit beside each other at her desk, uncomfortably aware of our knees brushing.

"I don't know what it is but I'm hopeless at maths," Amy says. "I've already got a place at St Andrews studying art history. But I've got to get this maths exam, otherwise they won't let me go there. Porca puttana."

"I didn't know you spoke Italian."

"I was expelled from my last school in Switzerland. They spoke four languages there."

"How many languages do you speak?"

"Italian, French... some German. Then there's the language that everybody knows."

Then she burst out laughing, breaking the moment.

"Maths is just another language," I say, blushing.

I stand up to stretch my legs.

A collage of photographs covers her study wall. Floppy-haired boys in black tie sprawled across gilt chairs. Pretty girls in spaghetti-strap black dresses. Amy caught by fizzy flash-bulbs at various parties. She watches me touch some of the society magazine photos. It's all quite unlike anything I'm used to. You're only the prettiest girl in the room once, I think sourly.

There's one black-and-white photograph of an older woman, her arms crossed at defensive angles across her bare breasts. Her head is turned to the side, inviting and defiant, and her lovely face is mostly covered by molten, dirty-

blonde hair. She looks as alien and golden as a Viking goddess.

I sense this is a special photograph.

"Oh, that's Mummy. She used to be a model in Sweden. She died in a skiing accident when I was thirteen," Amy says matter-of-factly.

I'm shocked and don't know what to say.

There's also a holiday photograph of a younger Amy grinning beside a handsome boy in a restaurant. Sunburnt and happy. "That's my brother Jamie," she tells me. The snapshot looks as if it was taken abroad and so I ask her where.

"We've got a place in the South of France." She shrugs. "I'm going there for the summer once we break up. You should come. You can be my maths tutor."

"I SPENT a month waitressing in our local restaurant so I could take Amy up on her offer. Two whole weeks in the South of France with occasional maths lessons, which her dad offered to pay for."

Max rubs his forefinger against his lower lip, looking thoughtful. "The way you talk about them, money was no object. They could have afforded the very best tutors. Why you, do you think?"

"Amy liked having me around. Teenage girls... they're very competitive. Me and my friend, you know? I wasn't any competition. My Little Pony, she used to call me."

"Harsh. That must have made you feel resentful, no?"

"Look, I see where you're going with this but that's not true. The truth is, I had something over her and she knew it."

THEN—2008

THE MAWDSLEYS' *villa is hidden in the hills inland and difficult to find.*

I barge through a wall of pampas grass and start up the rocky track towards what I guess must be the house. As I lug my suitcase, its unsuitable wheels twisting on the stones, I imagine the grass curtain sealing up behind me, almost as if the house doesn't want to be found.

Walking up this track, kicking stones with my sandals, the heat and stillness become overwhelming. The throbbing insistence of cicadas, what looks like a farmhouse flashes between olive trees and, as in a mirage, I can never quite seem to reach it.

I stumble downhill into a thicket with the heady smell of pine and lavender. The almost tactile absence of sound is broken by the splash of somebody diving into a swimming pool. I put my hand on a tree branch as dry as cracked crocodile skin to peer through its spiny leaves. Sweat stings my eyes.

A boy about my own age pounds through the swimming pool doing the butterfly and, when he reaches the far end, launches himself up onto the poolside. The powerful V of his back and shoulders are enthralling as he hauls himself out, still dripping.

I recognise him from the happy snapshot on Amy's study wall. This is her twin brother, Jamie.

He's stark naked.

I accidentally scuff the dirt and he pivots, hearing some-

thing, and looks straight at me. I shrink back into the under-growth as he covers himself with a towel.

How on Earth am I going to get to the house?

I watch him climb back up to the main house and wait for a few minutes until he's gone.

Amy is sitting on the veranda reading a magazine when I finally emerge up the stone steps. "Susan, you got here at last," she cries, getting out of her chair. She's wearing a bikini top with a sarong and a daffy straw hat. Dots of sunlight play over her beautiful face. She looks tanned and happy, and I have never seen her like this before.

"God, you must be exhausted. Do you want something to eat? Do you want to rest?"

She shows me around the villa, which is more like a hamlet than a farmhouse, with outbuildings converted into bedrooms.

We head into the kitchen and she asks if I want breakfast. Her brother Jamie went to the bakery first thing, she says, watching me eat a croissant that's so delicious I want to rub my face in it.

"It's just going to be the three of us until Daddy gets here in a week," she explains. "All the other girls have dropped out." I feel quiet satisfaction when she tells me this.

My bedroom is in an outbuilding halfway between the villa and the swimming pool and I'm so exhausted that I fall asleep in the clothes I have travelled in all the way from Leamington Spa.

Later, a scalding shower washes off the grime and I unpack my few clothes on the bed. For once, Mum isn't going to tell me what to wear. The tiles under my bare feet feel deli-ciously cool as I change into a hippy skirt and white cheese-cloth blouse.

The sun is fading when I climb the steps onto the terrace. I have slept most of the day. Amy's brother stands by the rail peering at his mobile phone. Jamie is meltingly handsome... No, more than that, he's beautiful like that poster of Jonathan Rhys-Meyers on my bedroom wall.

"Oh, hi," he drawls. "You must be Amy's friend, right?"

His accent is bored and sleepy, as if everything is a bit of a puzzle.

"That's right. My name is Amy," I say brightly, sticking out my hand, then flushing when I realise what I've just said.

"Funny." He nods.

"I mean, my name is Susan. I'm a friend of Amy's from school."

"Yeah." He nods slowly, absorbing this new piece of information, then goes back to his mobile phone.

"Anything wrong?" I ask, just making conversation.

"My girlfriend just broke up with me. Sent me a text. Says I don't love her." Beat. "Whatever love means."

He's holding what looks like a fat cigarette in his other hand and he gestures, asking if I want it. It has an acrid, unpleasant smell. I have never even smoked a cigarette in my life, let alone marijuana. Not wanting to appear uncool, I tentatively take a drag but nothing happens. Coughing, I hand the joint back and turn to look out over this beautiful landscape.

Japanese watercolour mountains stain the silence. It is so beautiful here. You can still feel the heat and the warmth of the day. I could stay in this place forever.

Jamie comes up beside me and now both of us are looking down into the valley. The air becomes dangerously still, almost liquid.

"Beautiful, isn't it?" he says.

Leaning over the railing, I want him to cup my bottom with his hand. Later, Jamie will tell me that he wanted to do the same thing but he was too nervous.

"What do you think love means?" he asks, still not looking at me.

"I think it means when you're both looking in the same direction," I reply, not having any idea where that came from.

I turn and realise that the pot has taken hold, after all. His cloudy face occupies the whole of my vision and he is so beautiful, I want to reach forward and kiss him. I want to kiss them both. Can you fall in love with two people, because that's how I feel. I love this place, I love this house, I love everything. It's as perfect as a circle.

"Christ, it's Stevie Nicks," Amy interrupts from behind us and we step apart, embarrassed. "What's going on here then? Come on, don't bogart the joint."

The three of us stand in a triangle as Amy and her brother pass what's left of the joint between them. I've had enough. Whatever it has done to me, I want it to stop.

"Amy says you're going to college in the States," I begin, not knowing what else to say.

"Not yet." Jamie coughs, shaking his head and passing the joint back to his sister. "I've still got my SATs to do. I go to this awful private school outside New York. I've been offered a place at USC."

"On a swimming scholarship," snorts Amy.

"Los Angeles. How amazing."

"University of spoilt children," teases his sister.

"At least it's better than going to the arse end of Scotland because you couldn't get into Oxbridge," he counters. "Amy says you're going to Cambridge, yeah?"

The two of them bicker good-naturedly while privately I

crow because I am the one who's been offered a place at Cambridge, not her. Okay, it depends on my exam results. And there was that awful moment in my final maths paper when my scratchy pen seemed to dry up and I just sat there, staring at equations I've done hundreds of times in mock papers, not knowing the answers. Don't think about that. I might not be as beautiful or wealthy as bloody Amanda Mawdsley but this is the one thing I do have over her. And right now, in this moment, my future is as infinite as pi.

"DON'T TAKE this the wrong way but I don't really remember much about that holiday. Not in detail. You never really remember being happy, do you?"

"I don't understand," says Max. "There you are, having this millionaire's holiday in the South of France, all set to go to Oxbridge, but then you end up working in a care home. What happened?"

"I got a phone call." I sigh. "That changed everything."

THEN—2008

IT'S ABOUT HALFWAY through my second week when everything changes. Already, I'm feeling a bit melancholy because the sand is running out of the hourglass. Soon it will be time to go home.

Jamie stands at the record player with Amy sprawled across an armchair, reading an art book. I glance over at what she's reading. She turns over pages showing strange, empty

Italian piazzas, odd Renaissance colonnades where the perspective is all wrong. There are no figures in these spooky paintings, just the shadow of a young girl running. Or fleeing.

She puts the coffee table book down and picks up a supermarket gossip magazine. Madonna is on the cover and the headline screams about her divorce.

"Oh, that's a shame," I say limply. "I thought they were happy."

"I'm amazed any of them stay married as long as they do," says Amy, flipping the page. "All that money, all that opportunity. Everybody betrays each other in the end."

Mr Mawdsley has gone out for the evening with his Italian girlfriend, Mrs Paolozzi, whose husband died suddenly of cancer, so we call her the Merry Widow.

"I'm going to have a party," Amy announces. "One last hurrah before we all go off to uni."

"When were you thinking?" asks Jamie, choosing another LP and putting it on the Bang & Olufsen record player. This time it's the plaintive, hesitant trumpet of Miles Davis echoing down the valley.

"You can invite some of your oiky friends," Amy says. "Susan, who shall we invite?"

Friends? I don't have any friends. Just you, Amy.

I am about to reply when the phone rings, the landline. It's such an unusual sound that it takes us a moment to even find where the handset is. Nobody ever rings this number— then I remember I gave it to Mum in case of emergency.

Feeling apprehensive, I'm the one who answers.

"Hello?"

"Susan, it's Mum. Your exam results have come through. Do you want me to open them?"

Her voice sounds distant and crackly like one of those old

78rpm records Jamie has found, as if it's costing her great effort to speak across such a long way or this is a message sent from the past.

"Sure."

The others are looking at me as if to say, "who's on the phone?" I reassure them with my eyes it's just Mum. I can hear her looking for something nearly a thousand miles away and I go a bit deaf with anxiety. So much is riding on this.

Eventually she says, "Susan, are you there? It says a B in maths and two Cs in physics and chemistry." Pause. "That's not very good, is it?"

My dream of going to Cambridge, those beautiful stone buildings and my wheeling my bicycle across those elegant bridges, evaporates right in that moment.

"No, it's not."

My throat is painful. It's difficult for me to swallow as my new reality sinks in. I can picture Mum's pained expression, the embarrassment of having to tell the neighbours how I've disappointed everyone.

Instead of saying something comforting, Mum says, "All that money I wasted. Those private lessons I paid for. You can forget about going to university. You'd better start looking for a job."

It's as if I've been punched in the face.

We ring off and my other voice says, this must be a mistake. They must have marked the papers wrong. Maybe I can write to the college tutor who interviewed me. All those times I was last to leave the school library, the hours I spent poring over old examination papers, the reams of notes I made, and for what?

They talk about the stages of grief, but everything hits me

right at that moment—denial, anger, bargaining, depression—they're all happening at once.

Jamie and Amy look at me with real concern.

And meanwhile, the two of them just sail through life. Amanda Mawdsley wasn't so much born with a silver spoon in her mouth as had an entire canteen shoved in her gob. It's like those card games we play at night, except when I look down at my hand, it's all ones and twos while they've been dealt aces and kings. They always have been.

Turning, I say, "I think I'd better go home."

CHAPTER NINETEEN

SESSION 3

"—and that's why I came back home."

I'm back on Doctor Max's couch with my head propped up on cushions and that dainty piece of tissue behind my head. So far, I've remembered everything from my early childhood right up to that holiday in the South of France. I flew back home the day after Mum telephoned with my exam results, and that's how I ended up working in Seaview Court.

But what happened after that?

Why do I have this crushing guilt about Amanda Mawdsley? What was it that I did to her that was so bad? It's something to do with the swimming pool at Amy's house, that I do know. But it's still a blank. I can see myself but everything else is blurred out.

Max doesn't reply.

Surprised, I sit up on my elbows and watch him impatiently click his Biro top.

"It's all coming back, Max. I thought you'd be pleased."

"All this la-di-da stuff. What we did on our holidays. It's not helping." He rubs his forehead. "I'm sorry, that was uncalled for. I'm under a lot of pressure. I've been ordered to release your medical records to the police. They don't believe you. They don't believe in the work we're doing."

He puts his notepad down and sits forward in the chair. Just like Mr Mawdsley in my job interview.

"We need to move faster," Max says. "I don't know how much longer I can fend them off."

"What happens if I just refuse to cooperate? They can't make me, can they? I mean, what if I just say no?"

"They can, actually. They can arrest you for obstructing an investigation. Please, Susan, we need to drill down into what your brain is shielding. Back in the Middle Ages, they used to make holes in people's skulls to let the devils out. That's what we're doing."

"I had a dream last night."

"Go on, I'm listening."

"I was sitting at a table with playing cards face down. The nearest card faced three cards like an upside-down triangle. I turned over the nearest card and it was a two of clubs. I thought, that can't be right, and when I turned it over again, it had transformed into the queen of hearts. Then I turned the next card over and it was a queen of diamonds. Only, you know how cards have mirror images? The bottom half was missing."

"Go on, Susan. This is good. Keep going."

"The next card was the king of diamonds. The final card was the jack of hearts, only there was something wrong about that too."

"In what way?"

"You know how playing cards are the same whichever way you turn them? Well, this card was also different. He was the jack of hearts on top but the king of spades at the bottom. And his face had this horrible manic leer. I reached onto the table and put the jack on the king, but the king had changed as well and upside down his face was rubbed out, as if somebody had really gone at it with a Biro. It sounds mad, I know."

"This dream, it obviously upset you."

"And then the jack became life-size... It grabbed my throat. He was strangling me. Even now, I can still picture him, his distorted face throbbing with fury, throttling me, bearing down and—"

I don't want to die.

It was only a dream, yet it felt so real.

"Pretty stupid, huh?" I say, embarrassed.

"What you can't remember, it's trying to tell you something. We need to give your brain a jolt. I want us to play to play a game of word association. I say a word and you say the first thing that comes into your head. No matter how silly, okay?"

I nod.

"Mother," he says.

"Lonely."

I flash on Mum sitting in the picture window of our bungalow, looking out at our cul-de-sac. I never realised right up until this moment quite how lonely she was.

"Father."

That one's a blank. Mum went on a destructive binge after Dad walked out, I remember that, destroying nearly every photograph of him. He left Mum for a barmaid in our local pub. I have only ever seen one snapshot of him, the three of us somewhere hot, me a pudgy four-year-old, looking uncomfortable in a wool jumper, shielding my eyes from the sun. Mum told me it was taken in Skegness.

"Missing."

"Birthday."

Standing up to thank the other children at a children's birthday party. I must have been seven years old. What felt like a hail of cocktail sausage sticks being thrown at me. Even then, I knew I was unpopular. The fat girl in the playground corner nobody wants to play with.

These memories are getting uncomfortable, and I want them to stop. Whatever Max is doing, it's working.

"Holiday."

"Embarrassed."

I remember shyly undressing in a caravan bedroom I was sharing with Mum and being ashamed of how fat I was. We were in a caravan park. "It's just puppy fat," she tried soothing me. "You'll lose it."

"Beach."

"Towel."

I flash on that holiday in the South of France, the three of us sprawled on beach towels. Amy sits up on her elbows to watch a plane crossing the blue sky with an advertising banner. Jamie says something, making me laugh. He's so meltingly handsome. That's when I realise, I'm falling in love with him and—

"Animal."

This one's easy. Even I chuckle at this one. Mum used to have a Scottie dog and a caged canary she used to keep on a table in our kitchen. The dog was jealous of this bird. It used to sit on its haunches watching it, biding its time. One afternoon, Mum and I went to the cinema but came home unexpectedly. I think the film was sold out. Anyway, we found the dog with one of the canary's legs sticking out of its mouth. Somehow it had bust into its cage and eaten the bird whole.

"The dog that ate the canary," I finish.

Even Max laughs, which makes me feel good. "Good, Susan. You're doing well. Let's try another one. Swimming—"

Something glitches in my memory.

THEN—2008

"YOU'LL BE SHARING *a twin room with Christina Walsh. Hope that's alright," says Amy.*

"Great," I say, trying to hide my disappointment.

"Let me show you where you're sleeping. Then I can show you around the rest of the house, if you like."

I stand there with my nylon holdall at my feet and twirl around to take it all in. There are squeals from the upper floors as the other girls explore their own bedrooms.

A barman in a white dinner jacket is setting up a champagne bar in the atrium. It all feels so incredibly grown-up and sophisticated.

Amy takes my sausage bag and we climb the dangerous-looking open staircase up to the first floor. I have never liked heights and try not to look down.

"Jamie's invited some friends from his old school. They're a bunch of pikey chavs, as far as I'm concerned," she says as we walk up.

"How is Jamie? It'll be nice to see him again. Did he get into USC?"

"Oh yeah. His grades weren't good enough but Daddy crossed some palms with silver. He always says his favourite weapon is an endowment."

We turn right along the first-floor corridor and I catch tantalising glimpses inside bedrooms where my school friends are already changing. Friends. Whom am I kidding?

Everything looks incredibly well made and tastefully done compared to our cul-de-sac bungalow. At the same time, it all feels a bit impersonal, like living in a luxury hotel.

"That woman, Daddy's girlfriend, Mrs Paolozzi, the one we met on holiday—she did the interior design. It's not all finished yet. They're still working on the swimming pool."

They have a swimming pool?

"Here you are," she says, opening the door into a delightful twin-bedded room decorated in soft pinks and golds. It looks both Art Deco and modern at the same time and it's all very clever.

Amy dumps my holdall on the bed and says she'll leave me to change. Her bedroom is just down the hall, so do come and say hi.

Christina Walsh hasn't arrived yet, thank goodness, and I wonder about having a shower in the en-suite bathroom. I unzip my bag and hold up my evening dress critically against myself in the full-length mirror. Mum bought it for her company Christmas party years ago. I suspect that it was out of fashion even then. Of course, she had to let it out for me. It's made of thick, uncomfortable material and has large flowers all over it, making me look like a walking chintz seat cover. Still, it's the best I have.

Amy is still changing when I knock on her door. She's

wearing the clinging black cocktail dress with the spaghetti straps I saw in that society magazine photograph. Her shoulders are still sun-kissed from our holiday.

The red chiffon scarf draped over her bedside table lamp gives her room a piratical, Boho feel and the photograph I saw on Amy's bedsit wall, that one of her mother with her arms crossed defensively across her bare chest, is now framed on her bedside table. A collection of glass paperweights sits beside the photograph. They're fascinating. Exploding flowers, insects and reptiles all trapped in perfect glass spheres. I pick one up and weigh it in my hand. It's heavier than I expected.

"Beautiful, aren't they? Mummy collected them. They're not even very good ones. The best ones can go for thousands. Which one do you like best?"

The one I like best isn't the biggest but the smallest—a flawless crystal ball with what looks like a scorpion trapped inside it.

"I was given that one as a christening present. I'm a Scorpio, you see. Burying secrets with my tail." She raises her eyebrows, mocking herself.

"They're fascinating. Like bubbles of memory." I have no idea why I say this. It makes me sound so pretentious.

Amy hovers and I sense there's something else she wants to say to me.

"Listen, I'm sorry about what happened with your exams. Or that you left so soon. I get it, sure, but have you decided what you're going to do next?"

I've gone back to waitressing in our local steakhouse but I'm not even very good at that. In fact, I am possibly the world's worst waitress. Last week, I was on duty and took a customer's order but instead of handing it in to the kitchen, I just stuffed it in my trousers. When the couple called me over *to complain that they hadn't had anything to eat after an hour, I reached into my pocket and felt their paper chit. "I'm so sorry," I told the furious customer. "It was my mistake. Missed steak, geddit?" He looked as if he wanted to throttle me. I was demoted to dishwasher after that.*

"I thought I'd go into nursing."

"What, like become a doctor?"

No, like work in a nursing home cleaning shitty bedpans and giving bed baths and wiping old ladies' bottoms. Honestly, Amy, her family, they live in a completely different world to the rest of us. They never have to think about money. They just imagine something and it's theirs. For the rest of us, life is as difficult as algebra.

"No, more like a care home," I admit. "Become a carer. There's good money in it," I continue, seeing the look on Amy's face. "Mum's got a friend who works for one."

She wrinkles her nose at that. "All those old people, smelling of wee. I don't think so." Then adds hastily, "Not that you shouldn't, I mean, if you want to."

You patronising cow, I think, but instead I say, "What about you? When do you start uni?"

"I'm driving up to Scotland next week. It's where Prince William went, you know. A corner of Fife that is forever Sloane Square. Lots of American girls looking for husbands. The cream of East Coast society."

Yes, rich and thick.

Already, she's leaving me behind, a forgotten children's toy left in the back of a wardrobe. A plaything to be discarded once you've outgrown it.

Amy turns her back to the full-length mirror and hoiks up her cocktail dress. She's wearing black panties and a suspender belt. It's the boldness of her move that astonishes me, her effrontery, like she just doesn't care what people think of her.

"Not bad. You'll get to meet Teddy tonight."

Teddy or Edward du Cann is her new boyfriend, one of Jamie's friends. His father's a judge. Mum excitedly showed me a story about them in the Daily Express *gossip column.*

I'm so shocked, I hear my childhood stutter come back. "I-I-I—" I stammer.

Amy mimics me cruelly and then laughs. For the first time, I'm not sure I even like Amanda Mawdsley very much.

One of the other girls calls out and Amy goes to investigate, leaving me alone in her room.

I don't know why but all the resentment I feel at her boils up. Why should Amy have everything when I have nothing? Right at that moment, I close my fist around that perfect tiny crystal weight and steal it. It was hers and now it's mine. I'm going to have a piece of her—isn't that what they say?—payback for all those barbs and putdowns I've had to put up with, all those sniggers behind my back.

I wander downstairs and back out into the garden to stand chatting with Mr Mawdsley, looking up enviously at Amy's bedroom window while her new London friends gaze coolly down at us.

Then I spot Jamie standing with a group of his own friends and my throat narrows. He looks so handsome in his dinner jacket. The boys around him are all boarding-school good-looking too, like those male models who preen in Abercrombie & Fitch.

They're laughing oafishly—Amy was right when she described them as oiks—and, as I approach, I get the distinct impression they've just been talking about me. Stop being so paranoid, Susan Gummer. Nobody cares about you.

I raise my champagne flute and congratulate him on getting into USC.

"Yeah, thanks," Jamie acknowledges sheepishly. "I fucked up my SATs but they're still letting me in. They really want me on the swim team. Dad's rented me a place in Venice."

I have a vision of him ploughing up and down the Grand Canal.

"Italy? I thought you were going to California."

"It's a place in Los Angeles. On the beach. You must come and visit."

I flush and his friends look at me as if I'm some ugly, flat-footed creature who's embarrassed herself. Los Angeles? He might as well have said come and visit me on the dark side of the moon.

Jamie tells me how sorry he was that I didn't get into Cambridge, and I tell him about my decision to go into what I grandly call nursing. We stand there chitchatting and my grin gets so fixed my jaw hurts.

As I drift away, there's a guffaw of laughter behind me.

Back inside the house, a disco has started in an unseen room. Music booms through the atrium, the song which everybody has played all summer, "I Kissed a Girl".

I have no desire to be a wallflower all night, waiting for some boy just as desperate as me to pull me onto the dance-floor trying to cop a snog. No, thank you.

Instead, I wander back upstairs to find out where Amy has got to. She's not in her now-empty bedroom, so I head back to mine.

Christina Walsh and a couple of other girls are crouched over the far side of her bed.

"What are you doing?" *I ask, intrigued.*

"Being naughty," *says Christina.*

The three of them are bent over an upturned wall mirror, spreading what looks like baking powder with a credit card. Sophie Hare bends down, holding a straw to her nose, and inhales deeply. She gasps as she lifts her head.

"What's that?" I ask, slightly shocked. I have never seen cocaine before in my life and it frightens me.

"Hey, there's a CD player over there. Let's put some music on," says Christina. "There are some glasses in the bathroom."

Downstairs I can hear the thumping bass of the Pink song, "Get the Party Started".

"Yeah. I stole a bottle of Stoli from the bar."

Great. I can't even hide in my own bedroom. They're probably going to be in here for hours.

So, I head back downstairs again, avoiding the disco (by now it's the thudding robotic beats of Kanye West) and decide to explore what Amy calls the iceberg.

There are another three floors that have been dug out beneath the ground floor and the building work has cost hundreds of thousands of pounds, Amy told me.

There's a gym with a treadmill, a rowing machine and a rack of free weights, a temperature-controlled wine cellar, and a plush home cinema.

The absolute basement is where they are still building the swimming pool.

Amy was right about not everything being finished yet— about a third of the empty pool has yet to be tiled. Unlike our holiday, there are no pulsing spangles of sunlight at the bottom of this swimming pool, just an unfinished jigsaw of tiles.

It's more like a spa really, with a sauna and a steam bath and even a hot tub. Just like in a luxury hotel, there are a pile of fluffy white towels and a rack of towelling dressing gowns. I touch their thick, fleecy softness, appreciating their quality— what I wouldn't give for a life like this—when I hear some- body outside.

Amy stands on the end of the diving board with her back to me and a bottle of champagne in her hand. The way she's behaving, she's almost comically drunk.

"I used to be a ballerina, you know," she says, swaying. "Only I wasn't tall enough. I still do my barre exercises though." She tiptoes on one leg and leans forward, stretching her other leg behind her. The classic dancer's pose.

The board wobbles. I swallow hard, cold, cold dread in my guts. One slip and she could break her neck.

"Amy, come down. It's dangerous. You've had too much to drink."

"Mummy said there are three types of women: birds, cats and cows. Birds flit from tree to tree, unable to settle. Mummy called me her cat, watchful and sly, but watch out." She turns and mimes slashing with her fingers. The board wobbles again, deeper this time. "You, though, you're a cow. You're so trusting, so... bovine."

It's just the drink making her say this, it has to be. She looks over her shoulder with something like contempt.

"You could never have been a ballerina though, could you? Look at you, a pig in knickers. That's what Jamie calls you."

It's the moment when the scalpel presses down, turning your skin white, cutting through with a sudden rush of hot pain.

What a wicked thing to say.

Her cruelty shocks me.

"That's not true. I don't believe it. He wouldn't say that," I say, getting hot.

"You were a bet. I bet Jamie he could take your virginity. You know, like that film, the one with Buffy the Vampire Slayer. He said he would do it only if you had a paper bag over your head."

It hurts to swallow and my throat feels painful. I'm about to burst into tears.

"You lost your bet then." I gulp.

All the fear and hatred I have for Amanda Mawdsley boils up inside me. All this time, I've just been a joke to her. Why, I could just rush at her and push her off that diving board. Break her neck.

What happens next goes into slow motion.

Amanda bounces on the board, testing it, loses her footing. She looks like a comically bandy-legged drunk. Or Charlie Chaplin doing his silly walk. She does a spectacular belly flop onto the board. Our eyes meet and the look on her face says, not now.

Then she disappears.

I must have gone deaf with fright because this all plays out silently. I don't hear her head smack those tiles.

It's like putting your foot down, expecting a step which isn't there. Something bad has happened and I don't know what to do now.

"Amy, are you okay?" I call out, knowing full well the answer.

I edge along the board, not daring to look. Cold fear crawls up my body. I ask her if she's all right, my voice echoing around the half-tiled pool.

Amy lies at the bottom of the unfinished deep end with

her legs and arms at funny angles, like a puppet which has had its strings cut.

Already I have a sense I am performing, going through the motions. Really, I'm not going to do anything. I know I should run for help but something stops me. Instead, I just stand there, staring down at her.

The most shameful thing is that part of me gloats. The golden girl, the one whose life was mapped out for her—the wealthy husband, the happy family—and now this. All those times I hung back and said nothing when she bullied the others.

Well, look what's happened to you now, Amanda Mawdsley.

Then another thought hits me.

She'll say I did this. She won't remember that she was drunk. They'll blame me for the accident. Because that's what this is, an accident. I didn't push her. Already I'm rehearsing what I'm going to say to people.

But what if they don't believe me? Then it would be your word against hers. Whom do you think they're going to believe? You or her?

Say you weren't here.

So, instead of calling for help, in a moment of panic which I will regret for the rest of my life, I just bolt. Run. In fact, I can't get out of that basement swimming pool fast enough.

CHAPTER TWENTY

SESSION 3

So, there it is.

I left her in that swimming pool when maybe the paramedics could have saved her. Perhaps I didn't cause Amanda Mawdsley's accident, but I was the one who left her for dead. If I'd gone for help, she might have walked again.

As to why I bolted, that's something I have tormented myself over for years, the shame of it. Mr Mawdsley was right. I didn't call. I just wanted to forget about Amanda Mawdsley and pretend none of it had ever happened.

It was a wicked, wicked thing to do. Something I can never forgive myself for.

Even Doctor Max looks shocked as I sit up on my elbows. The reason why I felt so guilty is clear to me now.

"You were teenagers, children really," Max says, trying to make me feel better. "Who knows how any of us would behave if confronted by the same situation?"

I don't think so, Doctor Max. You're a good person.

There's something rotten inside me, and if I could leave Amy there, knowing she'd broken her back, why, what else am I capable of? What's to say I didn't push her brother off that staircase, just as they said I did? Max thinks the same thing, I can tell.

It's morning outside. Max says he's used to getting by on not much sleep and will power through on coffee, but I feel spaced out and my eyes are gritty with tiredness.

After lunch, I take a nap and it's so deep that, for a moment, when I wake up, I don't even know where I am. There's somebody at the door. The knocking gets more insistent and Max's face appears in the porthole. I swing my legs off the bed. *Sure, come in.*

He's not dressed in his lab coat this time but more for going outside, with a thick zip-up fleece, windbreaker and walking boots.

"I got the results of your bloods back," Max says. "Your Vitamin D level is way down. That's hardly surprising. You need some sunshine. Get some Vitamin D into your system. As your doctor, I recommend you come outside with me for a walk, seriously."

Outside my window, the weather is still very bright. It's cold, sure, but this is the kind of sunny January afternoon that you do want to put a coat and scarf on and go walking in. I point out that I don't have any outdoor clothes—what clothes I do have were transported up from London and they hang off me.

"Don't worry about that. We've got loads of coats and welly boots you can borrow."

Until now, I have only ventured onto the patio at the side of the hospital, where those photographers ambushed me.

"What makes you think there won't be any more of those photographers?"

"We've tightened up security since then. Nobody gets onto the island without our knowing."

This is the first time I have been allowed through the security gate and up onto the metal bridge that connects the hospital to the rest of the island.

Orford Ness turns out to be weirdly desolate. The first thing that strikes you is the utter silence and flatness of the marshland. Walking along this long, straight road, Max striding ahead, we could be the last people on Earth.

Max explains that Orford Ness is where Britain tested the atomic bomb. The site was shut down in the seventies and its scientists mostly went to work further up the coast at a nuclear power station.

"The hospital was originally built in the twenties as a hotel," Max continues, "before it was converted into a tuberculosis sanatorium before the war. After they'd invented penicillin, there was no need for it."

He tells me all this as we stride along. What I told him this morning, the revelation of the kind of person I really am, hangs over us, unspoken, a crow circling overhead.

We walk past strange stagnant ponds and the only sound is the hiss of long grass. The horizon is littered with strange bunker-like mounds, some topped with barbed wire, others Japanese-style pagodas. We cross a mysterious concrete ring with a red-and-white lighthouse in the distance. There's an ebony-black building on our left like a windmill without arms.

"What's that place?" I ask him.

"They invented radar in it. In the thirties, before the

war," he says. His words are swallowed by the wind. "All this land still belongs to the Ministry of Defence."

The landscape is changing now and, on our left, a moonscape of shingle leads down to the sea.

"Stay on this path," Max warns. "There's still unexploded ordnance on the beach, they say. Also, they don't want you disturbing the wildlife."

We're getting closer to those strange bunkers, like Anglo-Saxon burial mounds with shingle poured over them. The distant pagodas are the strangest buildings of all.

"There's a path this way that's safe," Max says. He's enjoying playing tour guide. We turn off the track and crunch over the shingle moonscape.

It's wonderfully bracing.

Wind scours my face and the sunlight and ozone smell energise me. Max strides on ahead and, for a moment, I glimpse the little boy in him, the one who built forts or raced twigs downstream.

It's the kind of weather that reminds me of when we used to go to Skegness at Easter. Dogs bounding along the beach, people flying kites, families behind windbreaks having picnics. Except this place is empty. It's just the two of us.

Max strides on, enjoying himself. In another life, maybe I would have slipped my arm through his and leant against him, the happy couple.

Finally, I have to say something, and I brush his arm with my fingers. Max turns.

"Do you think I'm a bad person? What I told you."

"Do I think you're a bad person? Well, I think you made a bad choice. Listen, when I was eighteen, I did something stupid too. I borrowed my parents' car and went for a drive. I didn't have insurance or even a driving licence. I clipped a car and it all went to court. I was fined, banned. Does that make me a bad person? No, it makes me a bloody fool. But there's a big difference between not calling for help and murder."

I feel warmth in my heart. He's the one person in the whole world who doesn't believe I'm guilty, that I'm a murderer. Nurse Bunny, the cleaning lady, those photographers, they all think I did it. I imagine them all stamping their feet, shouting in unison, "Murderer. *Murderer*. MURDERER."

"Can I ask you a personal question?" I ask.

"Sure, go ahead."

"What made you become a psychiatrist?"

He ponders for a moment, then decides to tell me.

"I had a bad divorce. We married too young. I was still doing my post-grad in psychology when it happened. There was no warning. One moment I had a wife and young baby and was planning my career as a brilliant psychiatrist, then everything collapsed. The Chinese have a saying for it. Once everything in the garden is perfect, a strong wind will come along to knock everything down. I ended up in therapy myself. Physician, heal thyself, right? Being in therapy made me realise that analysis could be as powerful as the atomic bomb. Although you might not like what you hear."

So he's divorced.

We plough through shingle down to the North Sea and a sailing boat glides serenely past. A fisherman's hut stands in the middle of the beach. A rowing boat lies beside it at an angle, its once-white fibreglass covered in greenish algae.

Max stomps through the pebbles and I hurry to keep up.

The door to the fisherman's hut is ajar and we push our

way in. Inside smells musty and damp. I touch the wood
where it has rotted, brushing weird butterfly growth from my
fingers. Looks like nobody has been in here for years.

The floor is dirty with old tins of lager, scrunched-up
newspaper pages and rusty paint cans. There's a single shelf
with a wood trug of useless tools: forgotten old pliers and
strange metal protractors and a blunt plane. I guess they're
for mending boats. I pick up one ancient metal spike that
must have been used for tethering a boat.

"Careful, you'll get tetanus," Max warns, and I place it
carefully back down.

There's even less to discover on the abandoned boat.
Nobody has sailed in her for years. It smells of old fish. The
one thing of interest is a still-padlocked box on deck marked
"Emergency".

"What's in there, do you think?"

"Life jackets," shrugs Max. "Or gin."

"Let's hope it's gin. I haven't had a drink for ten years."

"Susan, what you told me early this morning. About
running away from the accident. Okay, that wasn't good, but
any of us might have done the same thing. Fight or flight
kicked in, that's all. You were just children, remember?"

"You're saying this to make me feel better."

"That's my job."

Pause.

"Did the family know what you did? When they hired
you to look after their daughter?"

"Of course not."

"What about Amanda? Did she know?"

"No, Amy just accepted it was all her own fault. She was
so drunk when she went into the swimming pool, she
blacked out. She couldn't remember anything."

"And you never spoke up."

Cold shame runs through me, like a wind shadow rippling through long grass.

"We talked about it once. I was terrified she would remember. But she never did. Ironic, don't you think? First her, then me."

How things will end is there, right at the moment of the first meeting. The clues are all there, it's just that you just don't know how to read them.

A swimming pool.

The dead space in both our memories.

Her, the moment she toppled off that diving board; me, what happened that night, when I found myself screaming in the middle of a London street, drenched in blood.

What I did to her was a kind of murder too.

Neither Max nor I say anything, but we silently agree to trudge back up the beach towards the Ministry of Defence site, the labs where they tested those weapons.

"Susan, you've got to start forgiving yourself. Haven't you been punished enough already?"

"That's easy for you to say. Maybe some things are unforgivable."

"Such as?"

"Murder."

"You've got to stop this. You don't know that you've murdered anyone. That's the point of the work."

A diamond-link fence run between concrete prison-camp posts stops us from getting any further. Ministry of Defence signs warn us to keep out. There are holes in the fence though.

"They closed this place down fifty years ago. Teenagers sometimes break in as a dare."

"How do they get onto the island?"

"It's not that difficult. All you need is a rowing boat."

"There isn't still radiation in there?"

Max laughs and shakes his head. "They didn't set off any atomic bombs here. They tested the explosives. Heat. Cold. Back then, Britain's atomic bomb was going to be dropped by plane. Vulcan bombers. They wanted to see if it could withstand the flight."

The more he talks, the more excited he gets, and again I can see the little boy in him, the one who glued together model aircraft in his bedroom.

We stand closer and I put my fingers through the diamond-link fencing to peer through. It looks like a vast necropolis where they buried the dead after a human catastrophe. It gives me the creeps.

"Max, could we get out of here? I really don't like this place."

I flash on one of those paintings Amy showed me in her art book, the one she was reading on holiday. It reminds me of this place: still colonnades and the horizon dotted with brick towers, the silhouette of a young girl running between them.

Fleeing for her life.

CHAPTER TWENTY-ONE

SESSION 4

Max says, "So, you accepted the job, despite knowing the risk you were taking. About being discovered. You were taking one hell of a chance."

"I told you. I felt bad about what I'd done. It was my way of saying sorry. Most people are never given a second chance, but I had been given one. I had to take it."

"Let's be candid. You took the job because you felt guilty. Did you think you ought to suffer?"

"I suppose so, yes. I deserved to be punished."

"Most people would have stayed away, Susan. But you didn't. Despite the risk you were taking. I would say that you have a deep sense of right or wrong. That's something to feel good about, Susan."

"Is it? I don't think so. It was just my way of saying sorry—"

THEN

"—SORRY," *says Amy.*

It's my first day in my new job as her carer. We're going up in the lift all the way to the top floor. Amy sits in her wheelchair beside me. Like in a first-class hotel, Pavel will bring my suitcase upstairs.

"We've put you in the attic, I'm afraid."

The lift door slides open to reveal what looks like a sumptuously decorated flat. Attic? This is more like a luxury hotel suite spanning the length of both houses.

Amy wheels herself into the sitting room while I inspect each of my new rooms. There's a master bedroom with a huge black staring television opposite the super-king-sized bed, a dressing room, and a single spare bedroom. The enormous wet room has a walk-in power shower and one of those rolltop baths for luxuriating in. I even have my own steam bath.

It's incredible. Forget three months, I want to stay here forever.

Amy waits for me while I gawp at everything. It seems so wrong. I did that to her and yet I'm rewarded with all this. It's pathetic to see her compared to how she once was. Trapped in a wheelchair for the rest of her life.

One that you put her in.

Now it's my turn to ask Amy the question, one which I have been dreading. I've been rehearsing it in my head ever since they offered me the job. I've even practised the conversation in a mirror. I can't not ask her.

"Amy," *I say lightly.* "What do you remember... I mean, about that night?"

My scalp tightens as I say this, expecting her accusing finger to point straight at me.

"You mean the night of the party? Not much. I remember doing some coke with Christina, then going for a boogie on the dancefloor. I even remember the song, 'Faster, Better, Stronger', that one by Kanye West." She slaps her armrest. "Funny, no?"

Which means she was in the disco as I was coming downstairs, heading into the basement.

"I remember taking a whole bottle of champagne from the bar and swigging it, going down in the lift. I felt so good, everything ahead of me."

I know how she felt. It was the same thing when we were on holiday in the South of France. Until Mum telephoned. Then everything changed. God laughs at our plans; isn't that what they say?

Amy is getting tearful. Please don't cry. I couldn't bear it if you cried.

"What about the actual accident?"

The moment tightens. Everything hinges on what she's about to say next. Even the walls seem to hold their breath.

"Nothing. I remember stepping onto that diving board. And that's it. The doctors said I landed badly when I fell. Like, duh. They said it was like I'd twisted the nerves in my spinal cord with both hands, giving them a real wrench."

She mimes wringing out a wet towel.

"So, they're not severed? It's just like they're dead?" I frown, trying to understand. "What I mean is, there's nothing that could stop you walking... in theory?"

"Daddy paid for me to be seen by the best spinal injury clinics in America. I spent months in California. The way they explained it was that the wiring has blown. They all said the same thing. My brain can't get through to my legs. And I was the one who did this to myself."

Self-pity isn't going to help, I want to tell her. That's when I decide. I am going to get Amy walking again. It's the least I can do.

"In time, they will be able to run new wires, fibreoptic ones, better ones, up through my spine. I'll be able to control them, that's what they say. Daddy's funding the research. They want to put an implant in my brain but the technology's not there yet."

"Amy, in the care home, we had a lot of stroke victims. People who couldn't walk. I got them moving again—" *That's not really true. I just helped them shuffle along on their walking frames.* "—and I could do the same for you... if you let me."

"That's very sweet of you, darling," —*a flash of the old condescension*— "but I'm never getting out of this chair. The best doctors in the world told me that."

"Yes, but if you could let me try."

"Regular miracle worker, aren't you? Heal the lame. Do you do laying on of hands as well?" *She waggles her fingers like an evangelical preacher.* "Praise the Lord." *Now she's being sarcastic.* "I've just got to live with it. Look, I can still think, I can still read, I can make decisions. My life isn't over yet."

"Amy, I'm serious. I want to help you, but you have to meet me halfway. Deal?"

I stick out my hand, wanting her to grasp it. Amy considers for a moment—what has she got to lose?—and then we gravely shake hands. She's so desperate, so trusting. What she said to me that night in the swimming pool, now it's the other way around. But we all need a bit of hope in our lives, don't we?

Right at that moment, I make a silent vow. I swear on Mum's life I am going to get this girl literally back up on her feet, so help me God.

CHAPTER TWENTY-TWO

SESSION 4

THEN

Amy and I are mostly left alone in the big London house over the summer. Mr Mawdsley has gone out to New York to be with Jamie, just as he said. Maybe he needs a break from his daughter too.

One of the first things I do is explore this amazing house from top to bottom.

I discover a stash of their old children's toys at the back of an airing cupboard—a teddy bear, dirt-smudged Barbies and obsolete Gameboys—along with a beautiful handmade theatre, its puppets hopelessly tangled up together with their strings.

I enter Mr Mawdsley's very masculine bedroom with its super-king-size bateau-lit bed and his double-quartz sink bathroom, his badger shaving brush and his military hair-brush. Even though he's not here, you can feel his presence.

His bathroom cabinet is shockingly crammed with every type of painkiller, from pharmaceutical-strength ibuprofen through to brown plastic bottles stamped with warnings. It's strong stuff. Working in a care home, you get to know about pain relief. Most of those pills I recognise, others are new to me, and I examine the tiny writing on each blister pack the way a collector might inspect a rare stamp.

Jamie's bedroom, which has been mostly empty since he went away to college, still has touches of him as a teenager. A Radiohead poster on his wall. Swimming rosettes. I riffle through his underwear drawer and lift a pile of his ironed boxer shorts to my nose, just to see if I can smell his musky sourness, but there's nothing, just fabric conditioner.

Sometimes I do feel like Cinderella living in the castle with an absent Prince Charming and Baron Hard-up—even Pavel could pass for Buttons at a pinch. And just like in a fairy tale, the one room I am told is out of bounds is Mr Mawdsley's study.

One thing I didn't realise until now is the extent of the Mawdsleys' philanthropy after Amy's accident. Amy personally gives generously to charities supporting the paraplegic and the quadriplegic. Research labs. Spinal repair clinics. Holidays for wheelchair-bound children. We're talking hundreds of thousands of pounds.

Part of my job as Amy's carer is to be a kind of secretary, keeping track of all those donations and thank-you letters. One spinal trauma unit wants to name its new wing after her. There's a heartbreaking letter from a mum thanking Amy for the gift of a converted minivan so they can get around—a hit-and-run driver has left her thirteen-year-old paralysed from the neck down.

It must have been my third or fourth weekend in the

Mawdsley house when I discover the real reason for their generosity.

Turns out, I'm not the only one who's guilty.

It's early on a Sunday morning and I'm boiling the kettle to take Amy her morning cup of tea. Only when I open the fridge, we've run out of milk. Never mind, there's a newsagent outside Victoria Station which opens early.

I'm buying a litre of milk when I glance down at the piles of Sunday newspapers on the floor. "PAIN AND GAIN" shouts The Observer *headline. "How one of Britain's richest families makes millions out of US misery." With a photograph of Mr Mawdsley right beside it.*

Thumping the newspaper down beside the till, I pay for it and, clutching the milk, go and sit in the communal garden. One of the perks of this job is that I've been given a key to this private garden, which is out of bounds to the public. Amy and I sometimes sit here in the evenings, she in her wheelchair, I on a rug. It's going to be a hot one today; you can feel it. Sitting on a park bench, I open the newspaper feature.

Yes, the family owns a chain of rehabilitation units and private psychiatric hospitals across America. But the real money comes from a powerful painkiller they've developed, one used for treating cancer patients. Only they're running out of hospitals to sell it to, so now they're targeting family doctors. Offering cash bonuses. Prescribing what the newspaper calls "synthetic heroin" for any kind of pain.

"One physician, who asked to remain anonymous, said: 'We're creating a generation of addicts. The sickest thing is that once these people are addicted, they're often referred to a rehab centre run by Hallam Group. It's a racket.'"

So, that's why something feels so off about the house. For a moment, I'm back in Sunday school, listening to the parable about the house that's built on sand.

Only this house isn't built on sand, it's built on poison.

CHAPTER TWENTY-THREE

SESSION 4

Now it's Max's turn to look uncomfortable. Because he's the one who's taken the Mawdsley shilling, just as I did. They own this psychiatric hospital, which is being kept open for just one patient. Me. What is it about me that's so special? Why do they want me kept away from prying eyes?

Because I know something, that's why. Only I have no idea what it could be. And they don't know that.

"But you carried on working for them, despite knowing where the family fortune came from?"

I say nothing but carry on looking at him, until he shifts in his armchair.

"I know what you're thinking," says Max. "But the Hallam Group got out of the opioid business over a decade ago. Months before your accident."

"We're both their servants, aren't we? You may have the fancy degree and the doctor's coat, but we're both on the payroll."

Max recrosses his legs and consults his notes. The tongue touches where the tooth hurts.

"Let's go back to what you were saying, those early days when you first moved in. Apart from that newspaper, was there anything else that struck you as off about the family?"

THEN

I'M *ashamed to say I go along with it, despite what I now know about them. I fall in love with the amazing house and the Mawdsleys' incredible lifestyle. I could get used to this. It's as if I've won the lottery.*

Amy treats the restaurants around Mayfair like her canteen; I wheel her into Le Caprice or The Wolseley the way other people pop out for a sandwich.

On good days, Amy has a voracious appetite for culture— every first night, we are there. If you've been to the cinema or the theatre, we'll have seen it before you. Pavel drives us in the minivan to the latest art exhibition or ballet or theatre show. There's nothing you can do or see in London that we haven't done first.

The one thing I don't share, though, is the family's taste for opera. The company has a box at Covent Garden and the first time Amy takes me I fall asleep, only to jerk awake when a character in a big hat jumps up through a trap door. Amy thinks this is highly amusing.

Of course, we don't go out every night. Sometimes we sit up in bed together, side by side, eating frozen yoghurt and watching those old horror movies that Amy enjoys, the creaky black and white ones with Frankenstein and Dracula.

Japanese horror movies are the ones she likes best, vengeful ghosts and dripping water.

One afternoon I wheel Amy through Tate Britain, the art gallery. She wants to see the Turner Prize exhibition. What I love most is the Victorian solidity of the foursquare building, the reverent hush as people mill around looking at paintings.

We roll to a stop in front of a small Elizabethan oil painting, artist unknown, showing identical twins. They are seated upright and side by side in bed, each holding a baby in a christening gown.

"Two Ladies of the Cholmondeley Family, Who were born the same day, Married the same day, And brought to Bed the same day," I read aloud, studying the inscription in gold lettering.

There's something about them, their imperiousness, their starchy whiteness, how they look at you almost with contempt. And the coffin-like babies they cradle in their blood-red christening robes, are they even alive or stillborn?

"That could be us, don't you think?" Amy says. She's thinking about those nights when we sit up in bed together, watching TV.

"They're identical twins," I disagree.

"No, they're not. Look closer."

She's right. The more you go inside the picture, the more differences you notice between the two women—one is timid, looking out of the frame apprehensively, the other almost malevolent, looking at you with disdain.

"One of them is weaker and the other's stronger. Which one of them is you and which one is me, do you think?"

"Can't they both be the same?"

"No, there's always a strong one and a weaker one. It's a

law of nature." Pause. "Come on, let's go and eat. I'm starving."

The Rex Whistler Restaurant is in the gallery basement.

"There's something I need to say to you," Amy says over her chopped salad. "I'm sorry I was such a bitch. I treated you badly. I'm sorry about a lot of things. You get a lot of time to think when you're in this thing." She slaps the side of her wheelchair.

I have never seen this side of her before, this humility; the cold, superior Amy seems to have disappeared.

Yes, when she taunted me about her brother, that still hurts. It's like a deep wound that you think has healed; I can still feel its hot otherness from where she stuck the knife in. But haven't I repaid her a hundredfold? Because whatever she said to me, I did a thousand times worse to her. Really, I should be the one getting down on my knees right here in this restaurant, begging her forgiveness, not the other way round.

But she can never know that.

"You've got nothing to apologise for."

"Really, why's that?"

Careful, Susan. She mustn't know the truth.

"It was all such a long time ago," she continues when I don't say anything. "We all thought we were so grown up but really, we were kids. Children say a lot of cruel things, especially girls."

"I should be the one saying sorry. After the accident, your dad said nobody came to see you. I was just as bad."

"Christina Walsh was the first to drop me. Then Sophie Hare. Remember my boyfriend, Teddy du Cann? He sent me a bunch of flowers and that was it. Charming."

Amy breaks off, noticing something across the room. I turn my head to follow where she's looking.

The person we've just been talking about stands at the restaurant entrance, waiting to be shown to a table. Talk about a coincidence.

"My God, it's her," I gasp, stating the obvious. "What are the chances?"

I don't remember what we talked about during the rest of our lunch. All the while I was conscious of Christina Walsh staring at us from across the room. "Don't look at her," says Amy.

The waiter clears our plates and stands over us as I greedily scan the dessert menu, choosing a chocolate ganache with extra chocolate soil for a sweet.

"With two spoons?" the waiter asks.

"One spoon," says Amy.

The reason she stays so slim in her wheelchair is because she doesn't eat very much.

Out of the corner of my eye, I notice Christina get up and leave her table, and I debate whether to follow her into the ladies. For once, I am not going to be cowed into not saying anything. I am going to tell Christina Walsh just how I feel, about how badly I think she has behaved, having nothing to do with Amy after her accident.

Christina is washing her hands as I walk in.

"So now you've become her servant, have you?" she says, flicking water off her fingers before reaching for a napkin.

Through my trainers, I grip the washroom floor with my toes, determined to have it out with her.

"At least I've tried to be her friend. I think it was wicked what you did, abandoning her like that. You were meant to be her friend."

Christina studies me for a moment and then says, "Is that what she told you?"

"She needs my help and I'm going to get her better."

Christina humphs and shakes her head.

"She really hasn't told you, has she? I was doing your job when she first had the accident. I was her first carer."

That brings me up short. Amy never said anything about this.

"She didn't tell you, did she?"

"No, she just said you never called her."

"Susan, let me give you some advice." Christina steps forward and takes my wrist—it's a warning or a way to stop me from leaving. "Listen to me, you need to be careful. The Mawdsleys, they're not good people."

"I don't know what you're talking about."

"They're dangerous, the lot of them. The father, the brother, they're all the same. They're utterly selfish. All they ever think about is themselves. I don't want you to get hurt."

"You're being ridiculous."

"Am I? Really?"

She lets go of me and shows me her hand, turning it over. It's red and crinkly and crisscrossed with scars, the hand of an old woman. It makes me wince.

"She did this to me. Once, she got so angry, she poured a boiling kettle over my hand. I had to have a skin graft. That's why I left."

I'm so shocked, I don't know what to say.

The swing door bangs open and I glimpse restaurant hubbub as another woman pushes past us, breaking the moment.

Christina tries to take my hand again, but I step backwards.

"I don't believe you," I say. "You're making this up."

I am still absorbing what she's just told me as I weave my

way back to our table. Amy said nothing about Christina being her first carer, she'd just given me a sob story. The whole family has.

"How was Christina?" *Amy asks as I sit back down.*

"I don't know. I didn't see her."

"She's a liar and a thief, you know. She stole one of my glass paperweights on the night of the party. I thought she was my friend. You never know about people, do you?"

And that's when it comes to me. All this rich food, the French cuisine smothered in butter, the premier-cru Burgundies, they're the gloop which runs along this spider's web, trapping me in it, binding me ever closer to the Mawdsley family.

Because luxury corrupts and absolute luxury corrupts absolutely.

CHAPTER TWENTY-FOUR

SESSION 4

"But you chose to ignore this woman's warning."

"I had made a vow to get Amy better and that's what I was going to do. I spoke to physiotherapist friends about the equipment we were going to need. Inversion frames, Swiss balls, stuff like that. I even bought a massage table, as if I was going to knead Amy back to health."

"Did your efforts work?"

"Yes, they did... There was one time. But that came later, maybe after a couple of months."

"Tell me about those early days of looking after Amanda. How did she behave towards you? She was bitter, I would imagine."

"There were many Amys. On good days, she was interested and funny. Then there were the bad days, when she went to what I called 'the dark place', when she couldn't even get out of bed because she was so depressed. I used to dread those days. Yet part of me accepted them, even welcomed them."

"Because you deserved to be punished."

THEN

"JAMIE'S COMING BACK TO LONDON," *Amy announces. "In the middle of September."*

She's lying face down on the new massage table. My heart gives a little leap and then I remember his betrayal, what he'd said about me, Amy's cruel words that night in the swimming pool.

"You know, I was the one being groomed to take over from Dad, not him," Amy muses, turning her head. "As the eldest child, I should be the one who becomes CEO, not him. That won't happen now."

"Why not?" I say, working one of her dead calves. Then I remember the conversation I had with Mr Mawdsley, about Amy not having anything to do with running the company. I feel indignant on her behalf. "There's nothing wrong with your brain. Plenty of businesses are run by people with a disability."

"The heir and the spare." She sighs.

"I thought you were twins."

"We are but we were born twenty minutes apart. I'm the oldest. Now I'm just the crippled spare."

"Amy, you've got your whole life ahead of you. Your life isn't over."

That afternoon, I ease Amy into the swimming pool in her wheelchair—they've rebuilt it with a ramp. I read some-

where that they mend horses whose backs have been broken in swimming pools. Ironic, no? Here we are, getting her better in the very place where she had her accident.

"It's cold," Amy says, water rising over her useless legs.

That's when I spot it.

The black bulb of a video camera, high up in the ceiling above the diving board. Watching us.

"That camera, that wasn't there before, was it? You know, on the night of the accident?" I ask, trying to sound as casual as possible.

"Oh yes," Amy replies, floating free of the wheelchair now. She wallows in the pool, doing a lazy breaststroke to keep afloat. "It was all caught on camera. The police asked for the CCTV footage."

My brain thumps. It's the moment when you think you've lost something, then realise it's still on you.

If the police had seen you, they'd have questioned you by now. You'd have been called in and everyone would know the truth.

Amy turns away, preparing to do her nervous breast-stroke, her dead legs trailing behind her.

"Dad kept the footage if you want to see it. It's all there in black and white," she calls out, her voice echoing.

I have to find that CCTV footage and destroy it.

Part of me knows I'm being ridiculous, that you can copy anything hundreds of times, so what good would it do? Yet I have to watch it, see for myself if I'm caught on camera, some shadow which gives me away.

And I know exactly where to find it.

Mr Mawdsley's study is on the first subterranean level, the one room I am forbidden to go in.

It's a windowless room designed to look as if it belongs to

a South American dictator: fake louvred shutters and a wooden ceiling fan. A large desk devoid of any paperwork, with a vast curved monitor and a wireless keyboard. There's a gallery of Mr Mawdsley snapped with famous people: a grinning holiday photograph standing next to an amused David Bowie, doing the thumbs-up beside a bouffant Donald Trump, another with his arms around Barack and Michelle Obama. Politicians, movie stars and athletes all pay court to Brian Mawdsley, who gives generously to both Democrats and Republicans.

Remembering to lock the door behind me, first I go to his bookshelves and sort through racked DVDs, mostly old war films and classic westerns. Nothing. Then I turn to his desk and impatiently rummage through the central pull-out drawer: dried-up Biros, Post-it notes and boxes of paper clips. Not what I'm looking for. It's in the second drawer down that I find it, buried underneath a tangle of old computer leads.

A DVD in a paper sleeve stickered "Metropolitan Police" and inside, a silver disc Sharpie-d with Mr Mawdsley's scrawl, "Amy accident. 15/09/2008".

There's a TV in the corner with a dusty-looking DVD player beneath it. I slide the disc in, and the television jumps into life. There, in ghostly black and white, is Amy clowning around on the diving board, just as I remember her. It's silent. She turns, clearly talking to somebody off-camera.

A hand reaches in to squeeze my heart. The corners of the room close in on me.

If I can see this, why haven't the police?

Somewhere further off, lift machinery starts up but I am too engrossed, watching this accident about to happen. Then the awful moment when Amy topples off the board, disappearing from view.

I freeze the image, listening hard.

Somebody is coming down in the lift, Pavel maybe. Quick, put the DVD back, just where you found it. No, steal it, destroy it. Torn, I stand there with the incriminating evidence in my hand. This DVD has lain there, undisturbed for years. If you steal it now, Mr Mawdsley might notice and questions will be asked. That's just what you don't want.

I bury the DVD sleeve back under the tangle of leads and, sliding the drawer firmly shut, that's when I notice the drawer underneath is also unlocked, stuffed with hanging files. Susan, what are you doing? You could get into real trouble. If anybody asks, part of my duties as Amy's carer is to run a Dyson around the place. I'll just say I'm cleaning.

I run my fingers along the plastic tabs, boringly filed under cars, insurance, medical and the like—all apart from one tab labelled "Amy medical". I'll say I was looking for doctors' assessments to help me with her recovery, that's all.

I stop, my ears straining. All clear. Whoever was descending in the lift must have gone on down to the swimming pool.

Spreading the manila folder out on the desk, I find it's crammed with bills and medical correspondence, letters from spinal injury clinics. Quickly, I drink in the paragraphs, scanning page after page, words such as "traumatic fall", "complete spinal cord injury" and "total loss of motor function... permanent and irreversible".

There's one older piece of paper though, already yellowed and brittle, dating back to 2006—two years before I had even met Amy at school.

I recognise the name on the letterhead—it's from Silver Pines, one of the Hallam Group's most luxurious private hospitals outside of New York.

PRIVATE & CONFIDENTIAL
Silver Pines Psychiatric Hospital
208 Forge Road
Millbrook, NY 12545
February 8, 2006

Dear Mr. Mawdsley,

Re: Amanda Mawdsley (DOB: 30/10/1990)
Admission date: February 6, 2006

I am writing to inform you about your daughter
Amanda's admission to Silver Pines Psychiatric
Hospital following an acute psychiatric episode. As
her attending psychiatrist, I want to provide you with
a comprehensive update on her current status and
treatment plan.
Amanda has been admitted under Section 2 of the US
Mental Health Act, allowing for an initial assessment
period of 28 days.
Initial medical assessment revealed multiple
instances of non-suicidal self-injury (NSSI),
primarily manifesting as superficial lacerations to the
forearms.
Amanda also presents with severe anorexia nervosa
(AN), with a current BMI of 16.2. During intake
interviews, she disclosed regular engagement with
pro-anorexia online communities, which have demon-
strably contributed to the maintenance and deteriora-
tion of her eating disorder behaviors.
Amanda exhibited acute agitation during admission,

resulting in an incident of physical aggression toward nursing staff. While this required brief physical restraint and PRN administration of lorazepam 1mg, she has since stabilized and shown remorse for her actions.

We have initiated the following medication regimen:
- Sertraline 50mg daily (SSRI antidepressant)
- Olanzapine 5mg at bedtime (atypical antipsychotic, primarily for thought disorder and appetite stimulation)
- Lorazepam 1mg PRN for acute anxiety/agitation (maximum twice daily)

The lift starts up again. I hear it through the wall. Probably Pavel coming back upstairs from cleaning the pool. I know I should stop reading, stuff the folder back, but I can't help myself.

Through our initial psychological assessment, we've identified that Amanda experiences significant survivor's guilt related to her mother's death six years ago in a skiing accident.

Through our psychiatric interviews, we have uncovered that your daughter's self-harming behaviors stem from profound guilt associated with her mother's passing. She has developed a fixed false belief that she was responsible for your late wife's tragic skiing accident, specifically fantasizing that she caused her mother's death—

There's a knock on the door.

I stand there, senses palpitating, urging them to go away. If I don't make a sound, they'll lose interest. The knocking starts up again, more like banging this time. They know that I'm in here. Face it, you've been caught red-handed.

I cross the room to open the door. Amy sits outside in her wheelchair. She's white with anger. In fact, I've never seen her so angry before.

"What are you doing in Daddy's study? You've been told never to come in here."

CHAPTER TWENTY-FIVE

TO: Doctor Max Quane
FROM: DCI Graham Horner

Dear Doctor Quane,

This email is to formally request the release of your patient, Ms Susan Gummer, from the high-security wing of the Hallam Clinic.

As you know, the Metropolitan Police are currently re-investigating the murder of Mr James Mawdsley, which occurred ten years ago.

During the initial investigation, Ms Gummer was identified as a person of interest. We are cognisant that Ms Gummer has been in a coma for the past ten years and only recently regained consciousness. However, based on assessments conducted by our own psychiatric professionals, we have reason to believe that Ms Gummer's claim of total amnesia regarding the events surrounding Mr Mawdsley's death on December 19, 2015 is not entirely accurate.

Therefore, we require Ms Gummer to attend Ipswich Police Station for questioning tomorrow at 3 p.m. We expect you to facilitate her safe transfer to the station at this time.

Please be aware that failure to comply with this request will be considered an obstruction of a police investigation.

If you do not cooperate, we will be compelled to seek an arrest warrant for Ms Gummer on suspicion of obstructing an ongoing murder inquiry.

We appreciate your cooperation in this serious matter. Please confirm receipt of this email and your intended course of action at your earliest convenience.

Sincerely,

DCI Graham Horner
Metropolitan Police

CHAPTER TWENTY-SIX

SESSION 4

THEN

"Why did you lock the door?" Amy asks coldly. *Calmly, I remove my iPod headphones, yellow duster in hand.*

Out of the corner of my eye, I can see the hanging file drawer hasn't closed properly. Files still peek out from the gap. I stuffed the psychiatrist's letter back in too hastily.

"Sorry, couldn't hear you. Listening to music."

"You know Daddy doesn't like people in here," she says accusingly. *"What were you doing?"*

She's like a dog with a bone. She won't let go.

"Cleaning," I say, waving the duster. *"Just trying to be helpful."*

"It would be more of a help if you came upstairs. Fortnum rang and said their delivery is on its way. It needs unpacking."

Even as she says this, the front door entry buzzer sounds.

Thank God, saved by the bell. "Come on, I'll wheel you upstairs," I say in that singsong voice I used with the old ladies when I wanted to cajole them.

All the while, my mind races.

Did Amy really push her mother off a mountain top? Or was she saying that to shock her doctors, the way she used to provoke me?

What Christina Walsh said in the restaurant bathroom, about Amy being so angry she once poured a kettle of boiling water over her hand. Was that true? Had she lost her temper once before, pushing her mother off that mountain?

Did Amy really murder her mother?

The lift door slides open and I park Amy in the atrium as the buzzer sounds again. "Coming, coming," I say out loud. Honestly, these delivery people give you less and less time to get to the door.

But the man standing on our front doorstep isn't a delivery driver at all.

He's a police detective.

"Miss Mawdsley?" he asks, holding up his warrant card.

"How can I help?" I say, flustered. "I'm her carer."

"My name is Detective Inspector Horner," he says, taking in the vast atrium behind me.

A detective? I keep one hand on the door, not wanting to let him in. I told Mr Mawdsley the truth when I said I left Seaview Court voluntarily. Surely, Edith's family hadn't pressed charges. I mean, I didn't steal anything. I am completely innocent—of that at least.

"That's me," Amy says, wheeling up behind us. "You'd better come in."

How ironic it would be if I lost this job because of a crime

I didn't commit, when my real crime—leaving Amy crippled for life—lies undiscovered.

Standing in the hall, the detective looks around, admiring the galleries and the glass lantern roof, just as I once had. It's easy to be overawed. That's the point.

Amy asks the policeman if he'd like something to drink, a cup of tea perhaps.

"That would be lovely, thanks. It's very muggy out there today," he says.

Amy tells me to serve tea in the drawing room and, refraining from doing an ironic little curtsy, I walk into the kitchen and switch on the kettle. Waiting for it to boil, I ransack the cupboard for biscuits, wanting to stuff them all in my face.

What does this detective want? Why has he come here? The police don't send a detective to investigate a lost brooch in Clacton, that's for sure.

They're onto me. They've seen what's on the tape. They've figured it out. They know I was the one Amy talked to that night in the swimming pool.

Stop being so ridiculous. They don't know anything. What happened took place seven years ago. This is about something else.

I look out the kitchen window, part of me wondering about scaling that garden wall and running away. Getting the hell out of here. Only I would look even more guilty.

When I enter the drawing room with the tea tray, DI Horner is admiring the paintings; the hip-hop squonk of the Jean-Michel Basquiat above the fireplace, the cursive hand-writing of a Cy Twombly which dominates another wall. His ox-like brow is furrowed, as if he doesn't quite understand what he's looking at.

"*I always like to take my watercolour brushes on holiday,*" he's saying. "*Views of the Turkish coastline mostly.*"

He turns back to Amy, who's parked her wheelchair beside the fireplace.

"*We always like to buy a painting on holiday too,*" he adds, as I set the rattly tea tray down. "*It's a way to support local artists.*"

"*How can we help you, Detective Inspector?*" Amy asks.

We're all being so polite, like actors in an episode of *Midsomer Murders* when the detective visits the house and asks questions. It feels almost surreal, acting out a scene I've watched hundreds of times on TV, yet this is happening to me, right now, in real time. And there's so much at stake. Everything I've worked so hard for, getting Amy better, it's all about to come crashing down.

"*Would anyone like a biscuit?*" I interrupt.

"*It's about the night of your accident,*" he begins.

I was right—this is it. The moment when we're all gathered in the drawing room and the detective reveals the real killer.

"*A witness has come forward. Well, not exactly a witness... more of a bystander.*"

I look down, appalled. My hand is shaking like a spider that's been injected with adrenalin. I just can't stop it.

"*Careful, you'll drop those biscuits,*" the policeman breaks off, taking the plate of biscuits from me. His large hairy paw covers the shortbread fingers. "*Really, I shouldn't. Mrs Horner has put me on a strict diet.*"

His hand drops down, greedily taking two at the same time.

"*You said an eyewitness has come forward,*" Amy presses him.

"Somebody who was in the pool area at the time of the accident. A Mr Edward du Cann."

"Teddy?" says Amy, blinking.

Amy hiking up the back of her skirt in the full-length mirror, telling me I'm going to meet her boyfriend.

"You were there too the night of the accident, weren't you —" he consults his black notebook "—Miss Gummer?"

A frill of fear runs through me. Nobody could have seen me. That CCTV was trained on the diving board. I was out of sight the whole time. There were just two of us in the swimming pool that night, no one else. I remember inspecting the sauna and the steam room. Both empty.

My mouth is full of cotton wool. I can't get the words out.

"Did you see anybody coming out of the swimming pool?" the detective asks me.

"What's this got to do with Teddy?" Amy says, puzzled.

"Because Mr du Cann has given a statement saying he overheard you talking to someone in the pool area right before your accident. As you know, he was the one who found you. Who called for help."

My stomach falls away.

"Bit late now, isn't it?" says Amy. "Why didn't he say something at the time?"

"Apparently—" DI Horner shifts in his armchair, which is something I've only ever seen people do on TV. "—Mr du Cann was being intimate in the sauna with another guest. After what happened, he was too embarrassed to speak out. He didn't want to cause you any more pain."

Already, in my mind's eye, I am picturing another version of events. I'm peering in through the sauna window and clocking it as empty, only Teddy and whoever he's with are in there, sitting out of sight, ashamed of being caught.

"Who was this other person with Mr du Cann?"

This detective probably doesn't know that Teddy was Amy's boyfriend seven years ago.

"A Miss Sophie Hare," the detective enunciates as if he's having trouble reading his own handwriting.

So that's why Sophie never visited Amy either. She was too petrified. She and Teddy Du Cann fooling around behind Amy's back. I feel sorry for my friend. Another betrayal. Amy was right; everybody does betray each other in the end.

"Does he know who I was arguing with?" Amy asks.

DI Horner can only shake his head.

"At least, was it a man or a woman?"

As she says this, Amy turns to me. I want the ground to open up and swallow me whole. No, she can't know. I've been so careful.

"He says it was a woman. Someone your own age, another of your guests."

Amy looks straight at me. She has to know. It has to have been me. Who else could it have been?

She knows, Susan. That you were the one who left her for dead.

CHAPTER TWENTY-SEVEN

This is all so familiar from television, it takes a moment for me to realise that I have never actually been inside a police interview room before.

The interview room is dingier than I expected. Cramped and stuffy. Grey baffled walls like bulletin boards. Around them runs a waist-high panic alarm.

Hard institutional echoes outside.

My chair won't budge—to stop people throwing them around, I suppose. There's also an ominous-looking black voice recorder on the scarred table between us.

A mirror along one wall distorts us, like something you'd pull faces at in a fairground. I guess DCI Horner's colleagues are behind that mirror, watching us, listening for one wrong word.

Ten years later and this same policeman, DCI Horner, sits opposite me once again. It's like we're having the same conversation, interrupted by the inconvenience of my having been in a coma.

Most of all, I feel frightened and tearful.

"You're not under arrest," says DCI Horner, getting comfortable. "You do have an entitlement to legal representation."

"I haven't done anything wrong."

There's a stack of plastic files in front of him—really, have I generated so much paperwork already?

DCI Horner nods and then presses record.

"It is Thursday the seventeenth of January. The time is four p.m. This interview is being conducted in interview room three at Suffolk Police Headquarters.

"In attendance are myself, Graham Horner, a detective with the Metropolitan Police, collar number five-oh-seven, and Detective Sergeant Kavi Shah of the same unit. Subject of the interview is Susan Gummer, born ninth of October 1990. Susan—do you mind if I call you Susan?—Susan, you are being interviewed under caution. As such, I will remind you that you do not have to say anything, but it may harm your defence if you do not mention when questioned something which you later rely on in court. Anything you do say may be given in evidence. Do you understand?"

I'm having trouble hearing him. Fear has made me go deaf. I nod.

"Yes, I understand," I say quietly.

"Susan, do you know why you're here today?"

"Yes. About Jamie. Jamie Mawdsley's death."

"Right. I want to go back to the beginning. You were at school with Amanda Mawdsley; is that correct?"

"Yes, we were school friends."

My voice sounds weirdly high-pitched because I'm so nervous. Although it's my voice, I sound like somebody else.

"So much so that you went on holiday together. To France; is that correct?" he asks mildly.

"Correct."

He actually licks his thumb before turning to the next page.

"Was that the time you first met Mr James Mawdsley?"

"Yes. He was on holiday before starting college in California. On a swimming scholarship, I think."

"Mmm, that's right. Seventeen years ago. Nothing wrong with your memory, is there?"

"I told you. I can remember things from a long time ago. Things from my childhood. It's when I get closer to now, that's when I can't remember."

"Can't remember or don't want to remember?"

I say nothing.

Max told me this morning the police were taking me in for questioning. There was nothing he could do about it. He could accompany me as far as Ipswich Police Station, but he couldn't stop them. He's sitting outside right now, waiting for me.

"Did James Mawdsley become your boyfriend on that holiday?"

"I don't remember us ever being boyfriend and girlfriend, sorry."

"How exactly did you become Amanda Mawdsley's carer? What was it about this wealthy family that made you want to go and live with them?"

He glances sideways at DS Shah and rolls his cheek as if he's said something droll.

I try to sound as dignified as possible.

"I am a qualified care worker. I have worked in care homes since leaving school. Helping my friend to literally get back on her feet was the least I could do."

"Ah yes, you were there that night, weren't you? The night of her accident."

"You know I was."

I cross my arms tightly, whether to hold something in or to keep something out, I'm not sure.

"The one witness, Mr du Cann, said he was sure Amanda was talking to a woman before her accident. That was you, wasn't it?"

My queasy feeling only grows stronger as I sit there. Dreadful, animal unease.

"No, no, it wasn't," I lie.

Don't let him in. He can't read your mind. He mustn't know the truth.

"You were spotted leaving the pool complex by another guest."

"I was exploring the house. The swimming pool was empty when I was in there."

I will myself to believe what I'm saying.

An empty swimming pool with tiles missing, your voice echoing around an empty basement, nobody in the sauna. Think about the bottom of the pool. Just an empty unfinished swimming pool, that's all. You never had that encounter with Amy.

Don't let him in.

"How did you end up working for the Mawdsleys seven years later?"

"They found me through an agency."

"When did you first become romantically involved with Mr James Mawdsley?"

"Were we? I told you, I don't remember any of this."

Stymied for a moment, DCI Horner turns to another plastic folder.

"Yes, I can see why it was an attractive position. Eight hundred pounds a week. Free board and lodging. Looking through the receipts, you certainly didn't stint yourselves, did you? The best of everything."

"Amanda was a wealthy young woman. Why shouldn't she have enjoyed things? Hadn't she been through enough?"

"Living well is the best revenge, eh?"

For one awful moment, I think he's about to wink at me. My fear and resentment of DCI Horner climb higher, like the eczema creeping up my neck.

"I don't understand."

"The point I'm getting at, Susan, is that you got used to this lifestyle. You weren't going to let go of it. Once Jamie Mawdsley made it clear that he no longer wanted to be involved with you—or for you to look after his sister—you reacted badly. A woman scorned, eh?"

"I don't know what you mean."

"I'm sorry, let me rephrase that." The detective gives a pained, winsome smile. "The point I'm making is that having got used to this way of life and seeing yourself as Mrs James Mawdsley, you weren't happy to be sacked."

"I told you, I don't remember."

I don't remember. I don't remember.

It's like one of those true crime TV police shows where the suspect keeps saying "no comment".

"Right then, Susan. I'd like to ask you a few questions about the night of December the nineteenth, 2015. Can you walk me through your movements that evening?"

"I don't know. I suppose I was at the Mawdsley house, if you say I was." My voice trembles. "But everything that night is... just a blank."

"Well, let's review what we do know, shall we? At

approximately 0400 hours, the victim, Mr James Mawdsley, was found deceased at the foot of the stairs in his home. Cause of death, blunt force trauma to the head. Consistent with a fall downstairs after being pushed with considerable force. We have CCTV footage showing you leaving the premises at 03:37, visibly distressed."

"I keep telling you, Inspector. I don't know anything about that night. Why won't you believe me?"

"Susan, our forensics team found your fingerprints on the banister and your DNA under the victim's fingernails. Care to explain that?"

"I don't know. I used those stairs all the time. I had to— Amy, I mean Amanda's bedroom was on the second floor. I might have scratched James accidentally while helping Amanda. That doesn't mean I killed him."

"Specifically, we have a witness statement from his sister, Amanda Mawdsley. She distinctly heard you shout, 'You can't do this to me!' Does that jog your memory?"

My throat is painful. It's difficult to speak. My eyes prick with tears, and I let out a great convulsive sob.

"Please, you must believe me," I say, shaking my head. "Why are you doing this to me? It's cruel. I don't remember any of this."

"Let's cut to the chase, shall we? We know Mr Mawdsley recently broke off your relationship. Motive, means, opportunity—it's all there. This alleged amnesia won't hold up in court."

"There must be some reason why," I say, wiping my eye with the back of my hand, "but I really can't remember."

I'm like an animal that's got itself caught in a hunter's trap. The only way out is to gnaw your own leg off. The way he's badgering me, he's relentless. I'm going to be sick. I press my hands to my temples.

"Everybody keeps telling me what happened that night, but I just can't... It's like there's just this... this hole. All I remember is running down that street, covered in blood."

DCI Horner leans forward, almost in my face. There's a silver-grey flash of that old danger, those shark's eyes turning white with ecstasy as it bites down.

"Are you aware that sudden amnesia following a traumatic event can be a psychological response to guilt?"

I can only shake my head, sobbing harder now. Knowing when to ease off, DCI Horner sits back.

"Susan, we also found a diary in which you wrote, and I quote: 'He can't just throw me away like this. After everything I've done for his family.' Would you care to explain that entry?"

"I don't know... But I would never... I couldn't."

That's when I spot it. Up there, high up in one corner: a cobweb with a dead fly caught up in it. The fly is dusty and forgotten. The spider just sits there, waiting.

I was that fly.

All along, I'd walked into their trap. They set me up. They must have done. Just as Christina Walsh warned me, the Mawdsleys were the spider.

CHAPTER TWENTY-EIGHT

SESSION 5

It's the morning after my police interview. The detective's badgering, his insistence that I pushed Jamie Mawdsley to his death, has left me unnerved and shaken. He was pushing through the wall I'd erected around the truth, brickwork bulging under the weight of his questions, mortar and dirt raining down, as he pushed through to reveal my deepest secret—

That I was the one who left Amy for dead in that swimming pool, crippled for life. It was easy to see where he was going. That her brother found out, and that's why I pushed him down those stairs.

Max sits in his Art Deco armchair, his ankle crossed over his knee. I'm not in the mood today. All these men, asking me questions. Prodding me, poking me. Like I'm some laboratory experiment. Trying to get to the truth. And what is the truth? There's what I remember and what Amy remembers.

If I go on trial for murder, then it will be my word against hers. It always will be.

"Okay, I want to try something different for this session. Have you heard of something called EMDR?"

I can only shake my head.

"It's a form of therapy that's been proven to work really well with people suffering from PTSD." Max clocks my blank look. "People who've been through trauma, like you. It's a way to look at memories, but from a distance. Make them safe."

"Sounds scary. Does it involve electric shocks?"

Max uncrosses his leg and hunkers down, levelling with me. "Nothing like that. I just want to wave my fingers in front of your face and for you to follow them, okay?"

"What difference does that make?"

"It's a way of telling your brain there's nothing to be afraid of. They're just memories, alright? I want to go back to something you said in our last session. About getting Amy better. You implied that it did work. Tell me about that."

Max reaches forward and starts making what looks like the sign of the cross, waving his peace fingers across my eyeline.

THEN

AMY'S KNUCKLES *are white on the parallel bars, she's gripping them so tightly.*

"I can't do it. It's too much," she grunts.

She's on the verge of giving up and collapsing.

"Come on, Amy. Just one step."

Amy's forehead pops with a sheen of sweat. Her legs are stuck, even though she's willing them forward. Just one movement, that's all I need. Come on, Amy, you can do this.

"It's like my brain is telling my legs what to do, but they won't listen."

Suddenly, her dead plimsoll twitches for a moment. It's literally one tiny step forward.

She's walked.

I want to cry and laugh at the same time. Finally, after all the hours we've spent on these parallel bars, the procession of acupuncturists she's had to put up with, all that time I've spent massaging her useless legs, the aqua therapy, it's all paid off. I can't believe it. I want to fling my arms around her neck and hug her, I'm so proud.

Amy will defy the doctors.

Amy's so astonished, she stumbles and nearly lets go of the bars, as strong arms grab hold of her and I find myself staring into Jamie's eyes. Gratefully, she grabs back hold of the rails.

He must have landed back from America this morning.

"You did it, sis. Amazing. You're walking again," Jamie says, helping her back up. "It's a miracle."

"Step by step," she says bashfully and, careful not to fall this time, flings one arm, then the other, around her brother.

"When did you get back?" Amy asks, hugging him tightly.

"My plane landed at half nine. Pavel met me at the airport," he says, muffled, because his sister's hanging onto him so hard.

"You're the one who did this," she says to me over his shoulder, shaken and tearful. "All those California consultants, all those specialists, you've proved them wrong."

I think both of us are on the verge of crying and I'm about to say something about it being the only way I could repay her —careful, Susan—when Amy asks her brother if he'd like anything to eat. He must be exhausted after his flight.

"I think I'll have lunch in my room," Amy says, getting comfortable in her wheelchair as I strap her in. "I'm tired. Jamie, will you take me upstairs? There're things we need to talk about."

The three of us squeeze into the lift and, as he stands behind his sister, I get a better look at Jamie. He's changed in the seven years since I last saw him. He's not a boy anymore. His face has lost that puppyish quality and his hair is cut short and business-like. He's still ridiculously handsome though.

I'm making soup for lunch, spinach and chestnut, when Jamie walks into the kitchen. "Smells delicious," he says, crossing over to the range cooker. "Remember that Shepherd's pie you made, in the South of France?" We stand together over the saucepan, watching it blip and blop. I could barely boil an egg when I got here. I sit up in bed at night watching YouTube videos and have become so confident, I even invent my own recipes. Like this one.

Something has happened upstairs though. The joyous bouncy energy of Jamie's homecoming has gone, and he looks a bit shaken, to be honest.

"Everything all right?" I ask, moving to the American fridge and taking out a wedge of greaseproof paper-wrapped pate.

"Amy tore a new hole into me upstairs," he admits. "She's bored at being stuck here all day with you. No offence," he adds, realising what he's just said. "She wants to come out to New York and be part of running the company."

"Well, she's got a point," I say, remembering our conversation on the massage table. "She's got a supple mind."

Jamie, though, shakes his head, frowning. "She wouldn't be right. She's too much like Dad—impulsive. Only wants her own way. With a board, you have to get consensus. I have a hard enough time managing Dad." He looks up. "Not the easiest, is she?"

He grins and we both become conspirators.

"After what she's been through, wouldn't you be angry? I think she just lashes out at me sometimes because I'm the closest to hand. Your dad did warn me. I don't take it personally."

This is a white lie. Sometimes the things she says can be incredibly hurtful. It's all part of my penance, I remind myself.

"Yeah, well, don't let her bully you. I've seen her do that with her previous carers. By the way," he says, changing the subject. "I love your hair."

"It was Amy's idea," I reply, touching my newly dyed hair, flattered. "She thought it would be fun for us to be twins."

"It's uncanny. And a bit creepy, to be honest."

Our eyes hold for a moment longer than they should, and there's an exchange of energy between us, all questions asked and then answered. The energy shifts again, warmth dropping from my heart. I'm getting hot down there. Don't even think about it, Susan Gummer. Sleeping with your employer's son will get you fired.

"What's New York like?" I say, flustered.

I reach for the baguette I bought this morning and saw through it with the bread knife.

"It's a wonderful city. Especially in the fall. The light is magical. It's bloody cold now though. Your clothes feel like you're not even wearing them, the wind cuts through so much. Sometimes I even wear long johns."

"What, those things that grandads wear?"

He nods ruefully and we both laugh.

"How long will you be staying for?"

"At least up until Christmas. We've got an AGM coming up soon and Dad wants me to prepare for that." Then, seeing my incomprehension. "Annual general meeting. It's when all the shareholders come up to London and grill Dad over the share price."

"It's good that you're here," I say shyly, looking down at the work surface. That's the first time I ever think about becoming Mrs Jamie Mawdsley. It's ridiculous, a faint thought, more like a feeling, right at the back of my mind.

Why, if I married Jamie, then the three of us could carry on living together in this amazing house, or in New York maybe, and I could keep on helping Amy to walk again and—

Going upstairs in the lift with Amy's lunch tray, I daydream about what life might be like in New York. To think that, before I met this family, I had never really been outside of Leamington Spa. Of course, I have only ever seen it on TV —the huge avenues, the constant stream of traffic, the hotdog stands on each corner. The Statue of Liberty and the Empire State Building. The city that never sleeps.

Setting the tray down beside her bedroom door, I knock gently in case she's having a nap after this morning.

"Come in," she says.

Outside, summer is over and it's grey and wet with fallen leaves on Chester Street. Children going back to school for the autumn always feels like the real start of the new year. With a pang, I realise that my three-month contract is nearly over.

"Here, let me help you sit up," I say, setting her lunch tray down. I move the cursed hoist standing over her bed to one side. Grabbing Amy under her armpits, I drag her up onto her pillows.

Funny how we've changed places. Amy is never going to have children or a proper family life. The golden girl who once had everything now has to rely on me to even go to the toilet. Now I'm the one who runs this household—the servant who's become the master.

Amy carefully skims the top of the soup bowl and smells what's on her spoon before swallowing it. *"Delicious,"* she decides, before spreading a chunk of bread thickly with pate.

"He's got a fiancée out in New York, you know," she continues, digging in with gusto. *"So don't think about making big eyes at him."*

"I don't know what you're talking about."

"Don't play all innocent. You know exactly what I mean. Here, pass me my iPhone."

She dabs at her mobile before handing it across.

Jamie's fiancée has that winsome California blonde all-American look. She could be a swimwear model in her stars-and-stripes one-piece.

"Pretty, isn't she?" says Amy drily.

No, she's more than pretty, she's beautiful and Amy full-well knows it. This is another of her little cruelties, her jabs, to keep me in my place.

"Her name is Claudia Patitz and her family owns a lot of real estate out on the West Coast, including the only privately owned chunk of the California coastline, can you imagine?"

I can imagine only too well and my inner swan shrivels back into an ugly duckling.

Marrying Jamie Mawdsley—what on Earth was I even

thinking? The rich only marry each other. Heirs to family fortunes like Jamie Mawdsley don't go marrying poor girls from Leamington Spa, Susan Gummer, so just you remember that.

"Dad's very keen on the marriage," Amy continues, *twisting the knife a little deeper.* "Her dad's a big investor. Makes a lot of noise on the board. Dad thinks a wedding will shut him up."

"Is there a date yet?" *I say briskly, pumping her pillows.*

"No, not yet. Perhaps you could be a bridesmaid," *she says, scraping her plate clean.*

Point taken.

That was spiteful.

CHAPTER TWENTY-NINE

SESSION 5

"Yes, that was spiteful. What made her say that, do you think?"

"I dunno. Maybe she wanted to keep me in my place. Remind me who was the master and who was the servant. You'll have to ask her."

"You kept on going with the rehabilitation though. That was admirable."

"No. Our moment in the physiotherapy room turned out to be just that, a moment. If anything, she went backwards."

"How do you mean?"

"Sometimes she was so out of it, I suspect she raided her dad's medicine cabinet. Once I caught her wheeling herself out of her father's bathroom. I didn't blame her. She was in constant pain."

"But your relationship with James Mawdsley did change, though, didn't it?"

"Yes."

"Can you remember when your relationship changed? Did something happen that changed things?"

"Jamie and his father had a row. Over dinner one night. The research scientists at Hallam Group had developed a new super-painkiller. Only it was incredibly addictive. Mr Mawdsley wanted to release it onto the market, but Jamie objected. He said it was so addictive, it would create a generation of addicts. Even stocking it would put pharmacists in danger."

"What was his sister's view?"

"She agreed with her father. She was always Daddy's girl. Mr Mawdsley was unbearable that night, bullying. He was also pretty drunk. He stomped off to bed and Jamie was so embarrassed, he asked me to be his date to a film premiere."

"But you knew he was engaged."

"Yes, I knew he had a fiancée. I wasn't a homewrecker. He just needed a companion for the evening, a plus-one, that's what he called it. And I wanted to be a part of that world, just for one night. Cinderella going to the ball."

THEN

JAMIE IS WAITING *downstairs as I descend in the lift. He's changed into what looks like an almost black double-breasted velvet jacket with sharp lapels. Open white shirt. Skinny trousers that show off his snake hips.*

He looks absolutely gorgeous.

Jamie smiles when he clocks me, a smile which promises

excitement and adventure, a smile that I will remember for the rest of my life.

"So, the shoe does fit," he says, noticing my elegant Louboutins. "Wow, you look amazing."

"It's all your sister's. She let me borrow it," I lie.

There's a little sting because we both knew what that meant. Amanda Mawdsley won't be needing this little black dress again. Jamie gives a tiny shake of the head as if he doesn't want to think about that tonight.

Silent Pavel drives us in the black corporate Mercedes past Buckingham Palace and down the Mall into Trafalgar Square. Looking up at those magisterial grey buildings, I can't quite believe this is happening.

Things get even better when we get to Leicester Square.

There's a red carpet outside the Odeon with photographers and camera flashes. They go crazy when they spot Jamie, dishy heir to the Hallam Group empire. My knees shake as we walk up the red carpet. I have gooseflesh, acutely aware of just how exposed I am in Amy's backless dress. "Slow down, enjoy yourself," Jamie whispers, squeezing my hand.

One of the photographers shouts at me to stop and look at him. I even manage that over the shoulder shot you see all the actresses do at premieres. I'm just being campy really, having a laugh. In time, this will be the photo they use on tabloid front covers.

The one with MURDERER written beneath it.

It's all so incredibly glamourous, quite unlike anything I'm used to. Until now, growing up in a dreary Midlands town, it's as if my life has been in black and white and now the picture has switched to colour.

I don't really follow the film. What I am most conscious

of is Jamie's knee pressed against mine, his just being beside me, not daring to look at him, not daring to breathe.

The afterparty is in an art gallery in Chelsea. Jamie stares out of the car window as we drive back through Belgravia, preoccupied. I don't know what he's thinking about. Maybe the row he had with his father. I can barely see him in the dark, given the luxurious coat he's wearing. He takes my hand. The moment he touches me, my heart swells.

"Listen, I've been thinking. I want to kiss you now, before the party. That way we can break the tension and just enjoy ourselves, all right?"

"Okay," I hear myself saying.

He slides across and our kiss is deeper and more prolonged than I expected. My heart is pounding so loud, I'm surprised they both can't hear it. His thick lips are soft and the tips of our tongues explore each other.

Breaking off, I see Pavel in the rear-view mirror. Our eyes meet. He's watching us.

"Miss Amy. She's not happy when she finds you go out," he says. "Very bad mood. Angry."

That's just what I don't want to hear. I dread having to deal with Amy when she's in one of her implacable moods. Not tonight of all nights. If that's what's ahead of me, I might as well go home now.

"Don't worry," Pavel winks. "I take care of her. I give her big pill."

If Jamie heard, he pretends not to notice.

When we get inside, the party is raucous. The din of the partygoers sounds like greed. Here and there I spot famous actors and pop stars. You never think these people exist in real life, or at least I don't, but they do. There's a buffet at the far end, and a TV presenter walks past with a plate groaning with seafood. Honestly, you'd have thought these people were never going to eat again. By the time I glimpse the table, all the food is nearly gone.

"Wanna drink?" Jamie shouts over the noise.

Eventually, he comes back with two beaded flutes of icy champagne.

"Look, I'm sorry about earlier," he apologises again.

"You've got nothing to apologise for."

We touch glasses and the champagne tastes like dry honey. I could get used to all this.

"You'll never guess who I bumped into the other day."

"No, who?"

"Amy's old boyfriend, Teddy du Cann. He's working for one of the big brokerages on Wall Street. We met for a drink."

My throat tightens. I thought all that had gone away. We never heard back from the police inspector. He never followed up on whatever Teddy thought he'd heard. No, what he actually did hear. Amy taunting me from that diving board.

My other voice says, not here, not now.

"When I told him you were looking after Amy, he said the strangest thing. He said the more he thought about that night, the more he's convinced that it was you Amy was arguing with."

The room shrinks to a pinprick behind him. He's moving his lips but all I can hear is blood singing in my head.

"What did you say to that?"

"I told him you'd come to save my sister, not the other way round. Anyway, he was a bastard for what he did to big sis. Shagging Sophie Hare behind her back. He's a bad boy. I wouldn't believe a word he says."

The sound of the room roars back.

"Listen, can you keep a secret? I've called a board meeting

for tomorrow. That's why Dad's so pissed off. To talk about this new super-drug. He's going to be voted in as chairman emeritus."

"That sounds like a promotion," I reply, not understanding.

Jamie shakes his head.

"No, it's bad. He's being managed out of the company. There are others on the board who feel the same way I do. This opioid business has got out of hand. It's not good. Before the federal government shuts us down."

"What does your dad say?"

"He doesn't know about it yet. It's an ambush."

Or an assassination.

"What will he do when he finds out?"

"Well, he's not going to be happy, let me put it that way."

We do a tour of the party and I hang back as Jamie chitchats with people. He seems to know everyone. Eventually, he does drift back to me. Only I've got no idea what the time is. Nearly midnight, says Jamie, looking at his Rolex. Midnight already? It only feels like we've been here half an hour.

"I've got to get back. I can't leave your sister," I panic.

"Come on, Cinders. Your coach awaits."

Pavel drops us off at Chester Street and my heart is in my mouth as we climb those front steps. I know what I want to happen tonight but I could lose my job over this.

Sure enough, Jamie leans in the moment the front door closes. We're kissing deeply. I want him to push his hand up my skirt, slip his fingers under my thong.

He's the one who breaks off.

"Are you sure you want this?" he asks, breathing hard. "It will change everything."

I can only nod, I'm so wet.

"Come on, let's take this upstairs," he says thickly.

We ascend in the little gilt lift and we're both too hungry to wait, and my heart is pounding, pounding. He paws at my dress and I want him to take it off right then and there, not even caring if Pavel sees us from below. In fact, I want him to see us, I think tipsily, because I am going to be the new mistress of this house.

"Wait," I gasp as the lift jolts to a stop.

I trot down the bedroom passage with my shoes in one hand, Jamie waiting behind me. I need to check on Amy. Carefully, I ease her door open. Her snore is so loud, she could summon sea monsters from the deep. Whatever Pavel gave her, she's out for the count.

We don't make it as far as my upstairs bed.

"Slow down," I pant, thinking how ridiculous we must look. Jamie with his trousers around his ankles, me with my dress ruched up to my waist.

I want to take things slowly, get my breathing under control. Understanding, Jamie pulls off his shoes and shucks off his trousers.

"Wait," I tell him. "You'll have to unzip me." I turn my back to him and feel him unzipping me. My dress whispers to the ground. I can feel the heat of him.

"Pretty underwear," he says huskily as I take his hand, leading him into the bedroom. I scrabble backward onto the mattress and Jamie pounces after me, half joking, kissing me, working down to my bra. I can't believe this is happening and yet I so want it to happen. Now we're both impatiently taking off our underwear. Then we're back on the bed, and this time he does slow down and then does all the things I want him to. I want him to go even slower, but I can feel it rising and then

there's that whited-out moment when you don't think about anything.

Nothing.

Later, as the room comes back, I rest my head on Jamie's chest, playing with his chest hair, enjoying the afterglow, the quiet.

"You all right?" he asks, passing me a tissue. "Sorry, I got a bit overexcited."

I sit up on both elbows to watch him walk into the kitchenette, admiring his racehorse buttocks. He comes back with two glasses of water.

"You won your bet," I say, having drained my glass. I can't help myself, I have to say something.

"What are you talking about?"

"Amy told me about the bet you made. When we were on holiday as teenagers. About taking my virginity."

I become more embarrassed with each word, wishing I'd never even started this. I was just trying to be witty, that's all. Instead, Jamie frowns and shakes his head, not understanding.

"She's just winding you up. We never made any bet."

Suddenly, I feel quite nauseous. If Amy hadn't lied, if she hadn't said what she said, then I wouldn't have felt so betrayed. I would have called for an ambulance. It's all because of this, one catty remark, that she's paralysed for life.

And it's all her own fault.

There's something else I need to ask him.

"Amy also tells me you're engaged. Congratulations."

I wince as I say this, because it's painful. Again, Jamie frowns.

"No, that's not true either. Is that what she told you? It's Dad who wants me to get engaged. Her family does too. It's more like an arranged marriage, yeah? She's nice enough but

it doesn't have that—" he snaps his fingers a couple of times
"—you know?"

So, she's lied to me twice.

Seeing how hurt I look, Jamie clambers over the duvet
and kisses me again, gently this time.

"Look, I'm sorry about my family. My dad's a cantankerous old bastard and my sister's a vinegary bitch. I'm sorry,
but she is. She's always been that way. Even before the
accident."

"I've never had much family. I don't know who to
compare them to."

"You're worth the whole lot of them put together," he says,
stroking my hair.

Next morning, my bedside clock radio goes off at half past
six as usual. Opening my eyes, I know today is going to be a
struggle. All that champagne has left me with a hangover.
Still, it was worth it. Jamie was right. Cinderella did go to the
ball last night, in the golden coach with Prince Charming. So
what if you've got to deal with Baron Hard-up and the Ugly
Sister today?

Wrapping my dressing gown around me, I take the gilt lift
downstairs to make Mr Mawdsley his morning cup of tea.
Strong Earl Grey, that's how he likes it.

So, Amy fibbed about them having a bet whether Jamie
would get me into bed, and she'd lied about Jamie's engagement too. Then there was the business about Christina Walsh
being her original carer. And if she's lied about all this, what
else isn't she telling the truth about?

I take his cup of tea back upstairs, but there's no sound
from Mr Mawdsley when I knock softly on his door. Probably
still asleep. So I gently lever the handle and glide across his
darkened bedroom to set down his teacup.

The room is thick with sleep, as I pull back the heavy curtains. Bleary London morning outside. The pavement is greasy with leaves. Autumn has definitely arrived. Turning, I move towards the bedside table, which I notice is scattered with pills.

"Do you want me to turn the radio on?"

No response.

Something's very wrong.

"Mr Mawdsley?"

Now I can see him, staring up at the ceiling with his mouth open, as if he's witnessed something terrible. Still no movement. He looks like a waxwork, and I half expect to see him sit bolt upright any moment.

There's an overpowering smell of lilies and I know this smell from the care home. I've smelled it many times before. It's not lilies, it's the smell of death.

Mr Mawdsley is dead.

CHAPTER THIRTY

SESSION 5

Seeing Mr Mawdsley like that, staring up at the ceiling, his mouth open in horror... That sickly smell of death. And there was something crouched up in one corner—death. A gargoyle with the balls of its feet on the cornicing, looking down, taunting us. Or his soul. I don't know what it was, but it was definitely a presence.

I'm sobbing so hard, my fingers shredding wadded tissue, my whole body shaking.

"It's only a memory, Susan. Keep telling yourself it's only a memory."

I nod, coming back under control. My face is streaked with tears. These memories, they're too painful.

"Susan, on a scale of one to ten, how much pain are you in?"

"Eight, nine... I dunno."

"Listen to me. It's important that we stay with this. I

want you to cross your arms and slap yourself. Try and remember what happened next. Can you do that for me?"

"What good will that do?" I wail. "He was dead and it was my fault. I could have stopped him. There were pills everywhere, all over his bedside table."

Max crosses his arms and slaps each shoulder, showing me what to do. Sniffing hard, I copy him.

"What are you seeing, Susan? Describe it to me."

———

THEN

THE THREE OF *us sit in the hospital corridor on hard plastic seats, unable to comprehend what's just happened. It's like the three of us are children, sitting halfway up the stairs while the grown-ups downstairs make decisions.*

Mr Mawdsley, the patriarch, is dead and I don't think any of us knows what to do next.

Jamie stares pop-eyed at nothing and I want to put my arms around him and tell him that everything's going to be okay. It's just too much for him to take in. The news has flashed around the world and already courtiers are assembling to decide the fate of the company. Uneasy is the head that wears the crown.

But Amy is the one who's taken it most badly. She lay face down spreadeagled in her bed when I told her and just sobbed uncontrollably. She was the one who'd always been closest to her father, even if he'd cruelly cast her aside after the accident. Always Daddy's little girl. The way she's talking now doesn't make much sense, but then grief does strange things to your mind. She's sitting beside us, rocking backwards and forward in her wheelchair. "Daddy, Daddy," she keeps repeating. She's gone insane with grief.

"Oh for God's sake, stop it," Jamie snaps. "You're like some kind of pity monster, sucking up all the compassion in the room. Don't you think that I might be grieving too? That I miss him as much as you do?"

"Mr Mawdsley?" a nurse interrupts. It takes a beat for Jamie to realise that she's speaking to him. "They're ready for you."

The three of us are shown into a briskly municipal office where a hospital official already has paperwork spread out on her desk. Amy's rubber tyres squeak on the floor. While Jamie's signing paperwork, I gaze at the sepia photograph behind the official that shows a road cutting through a forest symbolising—what? The endless road? The final journey?

All around us life is going on, the daily hubbub of the hospital, busy nurses and porters navigating wheelchairs, frail patients being helped with walking frames. Someone left sobbing on a gurney. Yet for the three of us nothing will ever be the same again.

Then back down the hospital corridor, past those bucket seats where we were seated. To my surprise, we've unknowingly been sitting right outside the mortuary entrance.

The young woman who answers the mortuary door could be an angel. Her hair is dyed punk-ish red and above her paper mask, she has the most beautiful eyes. An angel who stands between life and death.

It's colder on this side with the hum of powerful air conditioning. The mortuary assistant shows us into a blancmange-pink waiting room with an ominous-looking box of tissues on a side table. Dainty pink satin curtains are drawn across an eye-level window, like a Punch and Judy booth. The assistant pulls back the curtains on squeaky castors to reveal a body covered by a sheet. A stainless-steel counter runs along the wall behind with blue hoses coiled on top. Another masked orderly stands behind the body, dressed in a plastic bib as if he's about to eat a messy seafood dinner.

I'm not sure I can go through with this, suddenly feeling nauseous as the mortuary attendant lifts the sheet. I flash on Mr Mawdsley looking belligerently at me last night over dinner. In a moment, everything can change. That's how life is. He was here and now he's gone.

Mr Mawdsley's profile has turned the colour of plasticine, muddy and bloated. His hair is scraped back and he looks so undignified with his head and double chins propped up on a block. Jamie nods; yes, this is their father.

"Susan, could you leave us for a moment, please?" he asks quietly.

Only too glad to be getting out of there, I sit back down in the hospital corridor, islanded by notices. There's going to be so much to organise—the funeral and then some kind of reception afterwards, a memorial service, all those letters of condolence to help Amy write. Maybe the living resent the dead for the amount of paperwork involved.

Any question over my not staying on once my contract has expired is obviously out of the question. They haven't said anything but it's clear. Amy will need me more than ever and whatever happens, with the coronation of Jamie taking over the Hallam Group, I will be by his side. Every king needs a consort. There's no question of my going home to live with Mum in Leamington Spa now this has happened.

"I'm sorry for your loss, Miss Gummer."

A voice interrupts my vainglorious daydream. It's the same detective from before, the one who told us about Amy's *boyfriend overhearing us in the swimming pool. What's his name? Hammer or Hadley, something like that. What's he doing here?*

"Oh, hello, Detective—"

"Horner. Detective Inspector Horner," he reminds me.

Whatever this detective wants, it's not going to be good. Careful, Susan. Stay on your guard. Whenever the police knock on your door, it's always bad news.

"Do you mind if I ask you a few questions?" he asks, sitting down anyway.

Somewhere further off, a mournful alarm sounds.

"What sort of mood was your employer in when he went to bed last night?"

"I don't understand."

"We just want to make sure there aren't any odd circumstances. It's just routine, nothing to worry about."

"He wasn't in a good mood," I have to admit. "He'd had an argument with his son. It was quite a bad one, apparently."

Yes, that's probably what happened. Mr Mawdsley stomped off to bed, guilty about how he'd behaved, took one of his horse tranquiliser-sized sleeping pills and then, forgetting that he'd already had one, took another and then another.

"What was the argument about?"

"Business stuff. I don't know really. You'll have to ask Jamie."

"What do you think happened last night?"

"I think Mr Mawdsley felt bad about arguing with his son. He was upset. He was drunk when he went to bed. I'm guessing that he accidentally took an overdose of pills. It was an accident."

"You didn't hear anything?"

"Jamie and I were out last night. Everyone was asleep by the time we got home."

Pushing Jamie up against the wardrobe because I'm so hungry for him. Wanting him to kiss my neck, feel my breasts, dropping my hand to his groin.

And all the while, directly below us, his father was dying. I should have done something, checked in on him, asked if he needed anything, but how was I to know?

Sure enough, DI Horner approaches Jamie when he and his sister finally emerge. The two of them stand conferring while I wait with Amy. Voices are raised. Jamie marches back to where we're waiting. I feel bad because I get the feeling that this is somehow my fault, that I should have asked for a lawyer to be present or something. I've implicated Jamie when it wasn't like that at all.

"Susan, would you take my sister back home?" Jamie asks coldly. "I've got to go to the police station to make a statement."

If looks could kill. I start to say something, but he cuts me off with his hand.

"What did that detective want?" Amy questions me as I wheel her back out to the car park.

"I told him Jamie and your father had an argument," I reply, pushing her through the revolving door. Pavel stands outside, waiting beside the blacked-out Range Rover.

"I don't think you should have said that," Amy says grimly.

Jamie doesn't come home from the police station until late that evening. Amy and I are having something to eat in the kitchen, not that either of us is hungry. We're just picking at leftovers. I feel exhausted, we both are. I can barely put one thought in front of another, and the prospect of getting Amy into bed and the rigmarole of dealing with the hoist isn't help-ing. What I really want to do is neck that bottle of wine on the table in front of us.

Jamie looks as shattered as we both feel when he comes in. He's dishevelled and has been caught in the rain. His Burberry raincoat is soaked and I stand up to take it from him. My first instinct is to mother him.

"Jamie, do you want something to eat? Let me get you a drink."

"Thanks to you, the police think I had something to do with Dad's death. That he went upstairs because he was so upset and topped himself."

"Jamie, I never—"

"Well, you did. If you hadn't stuck your nose in, instead of carrying on like a histrionic chambermaid..."

He runs out of words, exasperated.

I have no answer to that.

"Christ, what was I even thinking?" he continues, running his hand through his wet hair. I can't tell if he's talking to me or to himself. "You're just a—a servant."

That's a slap in the face.

I turn to Amy for support, but she says nothing, just sits there with a quiet look of satisfaction in her eyes, as if to say, "Told you so."

"I'm catching an early flight to New York. There's a lot to do out there. We're convening a board meeting. Miss Krige, Dad's assistant, will be making funeral arrangements on this end. You can liaise with her."

"Jamie, I'm so sorry... Anything I can do to help?"

"Help? We've had quite enough of your help already, thanks."

And with that, he turns on his heels and walks out. I have

never seen him angry like this before. He's stalked halfway across the atrium by the time I catch up with him.

"Jamie, stop."

He turns, ready to listen to my excuse. All I want from him is one soft word.

"Jamie, I love you."

There, I've said it to his face.

I touch his sodden shoulder, but he shrugs me off. There's always one who kisses and one who turns their cheek, that's what Mum says.

"I can pack my bags if you want," I blurt out, not that I mean it—it's like creeping your bare feet to a roof edge, feeling your toes over the parapet... getting ready to jump. I want him to save me. Don't make me do this. Besides, where else have I got to go?

"There's no need for that." He hesitates. "My sister still needs you. But it's over between us, whatever 'it' was..."

Shock spreads across my face and it's almost physical pain. Please don't say that. You can't say that. Then I feel myself shrivel to nothing, this hall receding into immense distance.

"I'll be back for the funeral," he says brusquely.

"Jamie, please—" I begin, but really there's nothing left to say.

CHAPTER THIRTY-ONE

SESSION 5

"Amy was the one who took her father's death the hardest. I was very worried about her. If she could have covered all the paintings and mirrors, she would have done. She wouldn't leave her room. She sat there, playing endless games of patience. The way she talked about him, it was as if a saint had walked among us."

"You didn't feel the same way?"

"I respected him, admired him. But not after the way he behaved. He was a cantankerous old bully who played his children off each other."

"How about you? The way Jamie treated you must have been hurtful."

"I felt embarrassed. Used. The young prince screwing the hired help. A servant, that's all he thought of me. Worst of all, I fell for it. Building up all those silly schoolgirl dreams in my head. I decided to hand my notice in after the funeral. Phone up the care agency and tell them I was available."

"Ah yes, the funeral. I read about it in the paper. You were still there then. What do you remember of that day?"

I run my tongue over my lower lip, thinking. "Amy said the strangest thing."

THEN

WITH JAMIE GONE, *the house descends into a kind of Victorian mourning. If Amy could have covered all the paintings and mirrors, she would have done. Most days she sits in her bedroom watching the October rain. The way she talks about her father now, it's as if a saint has walked among us and not an imperious, cantankerous old bully who played his children against each other.*

Pavel enjoys himself, with his old master dead and his new employer away for the next fortnight.

One evening he sits with his feet up on the kitchen table picking his teeth, having finished supper. It feels improper somehow.

"What would Miss Amy say if she knew you were sleeping with brother? Not happy, I bet."

"It's none of your business. Besides, whatever it was, it's over now."

That's true. I have gone to nearby St Peter's church when it was empty and knelt in a pew and prayed for God to help me. Let me forget about Jamie, it had all been a dreadful mistake. A servant, that's all he really thinks of me. I have been so stupid. Worst of all, I had fallen for it, building up all these silly schoolgirl dreams in my head. Now that I can see things as they really are, I won't be fooled again. I will hand in my notice the day after the funeral. Phone up that care agency, tell them I'm available.

"You know, if you lost few pounds, you're a good-looking girl," Pavel smirks.

I reach to take his plate, aware of the constant drip from the faucet which needs mending, like the tap tap tap of a child's toy drum.

"When the cat's away, the mice will play, yes?" he says, touching my bottom.

There's a knife block on the counter in front of me and I swear to God, I think about grabbing one of those knives and holding it against his neck, pressing down until its tip turns his skin white.

"If you touch me again, I swear I will kill you," I hiss, my eyes boring into him.

"Only joking," he laughs, throwing both hands up in mock surrender.

For some reason, the family decides to hold Mr Mawdsley's funeral in a ghastly crematorium on the outskirts of Reading. It's near the Mawdsleys' country house, which I have never been to.

The Scots have a word for this kind of weather, I recall, as I park our minivan in the crematorium car park that afternoon. Dreich. It's as if the weather knows it's a funeral, fine persistent rain which gets into everything, cold which reaches into your bones.

I trundle Amy in her chair up the path towards the grim mausoleum. There are photographers here too, snapping the two of us as I push Amy towards the crematorium. Amy covers her face with her hand. Can't they leave this family alone, after everything they've been through?

The crematorium is packed. People I have never seen before give grim nods of sympathy as I wheel Amy down the aisle. The coffin rests in front of the altar, and all I can think is how small it is. It's awful, like being in a mournful doctor's waiting room.

"Who are all these people?" I whisper to Amy, who's parked in the aisle.

The service starts. I close my eyes, trying to think about Mr Mawdsley, his face strobed with blue lights as they lifted his daughter on a stretcher into an ambulance, placing his hand over mine that afternoon during my interview, his baleful stare that final night over dinner, but my thoughts jump about, they won't stay still.

All their eyes are on me as I wheel Amy up to the microphone for her to give the first Bible reading.

When it's his turn to give the second reading, Jamie can barely speak, he's so upset. He stands behind the lectern looking so pale. His hands are shaking. Oh, and his fiancée is there too. I lean forward to catch Miss California dab her eyes with a tissue at precisely the right moment. How dare you upstage poor Jamie at his own father's funeral?

I don't recognise the man they describe in the eulogy. Loving husband, tragically widowed. Doting father. Philanthropist. The man they're describing sounds like a cross between Saint Francis and a genial family doctor, not the head of a corporation attacked in the press for flooding America with dangerous synthetic heroin. Well, all that's going to stop now Jamie is in charge.

Finally, a reedy harmonium pipes up at the back of the room, signalling the funeral is over.

We mingle outside under a canopy. People queue to offer

their condolences, give embarrassed smiles, pat Amy's hand. Jamie and his fiancée greet mourners as if it's a perverse wedding reception. The irony is that I have never seen Jamie more handsome than on the day of his father's funeral. And that Instagram post didn't do Claudia Patitz justice either. She's much more attractive in real life, full of California sunshine.

"Ah, you're the help," she says coolly when it's my turn in the queue.

Once I've done the receiving line, Amy gestures for me to bend closer and whispers, "I did you a favour. I told you he would break your heart. I warned you but you wouldn't listen."

"I'm fine, really," I reply stiffly.

I'm not going to give her the satisfaction. Only she can't resist twisting the knife a little deeper.

"You know what's the one thing the happiest marriages have in common?"

"Shared hobbies?"

"The size of their parents' bank balances."

She's right, of course. How can I compete with someone whose family own a chunk of California coastline? All I have is a bungalow in a Leamington Spa cul-de-sac.

My humiliation is complete.

Amy cannot face the reception the ever-efficient Miss Krige has organised and asks to be taken back to the minivan. It's raining even harder now. One of the funeral directors stands over us with a golf umbrella as I wheel Amy back to the car park.

Once inside the van, I lock Amy into place, making sure her wheelchair is secure. Swags of rain course down the windscreen, making it difficult to see through the glass. There's *something I want to say to her, about how sorry I am about her first losing her mother, then her father. Amy, though, just blindly stares ahead, quite dazed with grief. I don't think she can see or hear me.*

Then she says, "I'm glad he's dead."

CHAPTER THIRTY-TWO

SESSION 6

Max sits behind his desk holding what looks like a pile of large cards with their backs to me.

I take the wing chair opposite.

"Are you going to read my fortune?"

"In a way. Do you know anything about the Rorschach test?"

"Never heard of it."

"It was invented in the early twentieth century by a Swiss psychiatrist, Hermann Rorschach. It's a series of images shown in order. They're very helpful in telling me the kind of person you are. It's a personality test."

"What, like I'm an introvert or an extrovert?"

"More subtle than that. For example, one card makes men think about hunting while women often talk about parenting. Or vice-versa. There's no trickery, I promise. There's nothing up my sleeves."

He snaps his shirt cuffs back and smiles.

"Okay," I agree nervously.

"I'm going to show you these inkblots. Tell me what they look like. Tell me everything you see."

He places the first card down in front of me. This first one's easy. It's the black silhouette of a bat with spread wings.

"Well, this might be a bat. A strange kind of bat. Is that the right answer?"

"That's fine. There are no right or wrong answers. Can you see anything else? Take your time."

Looking deeper, I do see something else. A headless woman in a tightly clinched nurse's uniform with her arms raised in horror. Something unsettling shivers through me.

"I'm not sure. This might be a nurse. Or a prison warden. Is that enough?"

"The number of answers isn't important. Let's try the next one, shall we?"

The second card makes me smile. It looks like two elves in red pointy hats playing patty-cake. Or two Scottie dogs with their snouts banged up against each other, fighting. Their paws are bloody, which also unnerves me.

"It's two old men in red wearing pointed hats high fiving each other. But their legs are bloody stumps."

"Interesting," says Max, turning the card down.

The third card makes me smile too. This one shows hyper-polite waiters carrying what could be a tureen between them. They're bowing to each other and wearing women's high-heeled shoes. There's a red butterfly floating between the two of them. Or it could be a bow tie.

"I don't know what these bits mean though," I say, pointing to some ink splashes above their heads. "Am I supposed to look at parts or just all of it?"

"Anywhere at all. Just tell me everything you see."

Card four shows a horrible bear monster with powerful hind legs and disturbing furry claws. Its tiny head looks like a praying mantis's and it's poised to attack.

"It's a horrible monster that's going to attack me. Its tail is weird too, it's got eyes in it."

"Hmm," says Max, taking the card back. "That's supposed to be the father card. It tells me your attitude to male authority figures."

He turns over the next card and this one brings me up short. All I see is a man's head with his eyes staring straight at me. "What have you done to me?" he's asking.

"Susan, what's the matter?"

An unseen hand grabs me by the throat.

Can't speak.

Cannot get the words out.

Yes, I remember it all now. Blood pooling around his head, spreading across the floor tiles, in between the grouting, edging towards me. So much blood. There's just so much of it. They were all right, every one of them. Every single thing they said about me is true.

Because this is Jamie's blood.

I am the one who killed him.

It was me.

I taste blood in my mouth because I've bitten down on my inner lip too hard.

Blood.

THEN

IT'S OVER *blares the* Daily Mail *headline. There's a grainy telephoto picture of Claudia Patitz leaving the Manhattan apartment she shares with Jamie. And an inset close-up of her left hand without an engagement ring.*

Another long-distance photo pictures the two of them walking together in Central Park, bundled up against the cold. More than ever, Claudia looks like Jackie Kennedy in her oversized sunglasses. Jamie, gesticulating, seems to be angry about something.

Amy shows me all this on her iPhone while I massage her dead legs.

"You needn't look so pleased," she says archly.

"I'm not looking like anything."

"I told you he would get bored of her just like he got bored of all the others. You probably dodged a bullet, to be honest. I can't tell you the number of ex-girlfriends I've had crying on my shoulder. I told you, he'd only break your heart."

Sure enough, Pavel is summoned that afternoon to fetch Jamie from Northolt, where he's landed in the Mawdsley private jet. I don't want to be around when he walks in, deal with the awkwardness of it, not after what's happened. Rejecting me like that, treating me like the hired help. Whom am I kidding? That's exactly how he thinks of me.

My letter of resignation stands propped up on my sitting room mantlepiece, waiting to be handed in. I've already contacted some care agencies, enquired about my successor. I do want there to be a smooth handover. You got off lightly, Susan Gummer, remember that. You made your act of penance; you tried to get her walking again. Yes, you wanted things to turn out differently, but they didn't. Christina Walsh was right. Everything with the Mawdsleys is about their wants, their needs. Nothing ever penetrates their self-

ishness. Maybe there's a lesson to be learnt from all this, but
I can't think what it might be. The rich are callous,
that's all.

Cathedrals of the lonely, that's how I think about cinemas.
I'm in such a hurry to get out of the house, I don't even know
what's on. I take the bus into the West End and get off at
Piccadilly. It's a short walk through to Leicester Square.

"What are you showing?" I ask the woman at the ticket
counter.

"Fifty Shades of Grey," she says behind her plexiglass.

"What's that about?"

She reaches for a flyer and reads out boredly, "A naive
young woman finds herself having a passionate affair with a
hunky billionaire tycoon. Starring Jamie—"

No, thank you.

"Anything else?"

She peers at her monitor. "Star Wars: The Force Awak-
ens, starring Daisy Ridley and John Boyega. But it's already
started."

"Doesn't matter."

I slide my credit card into her bank teller trough, the
credit card which is going to be cut in two tomorrow.

Star Wars turns out to be boring and stupid, a film made
for children.

There's one moment, though, when the actor playing the
villain, who's darkly handsome and wears his hair long,
reminds me of him. Of Jamie. Something in the way he turns.
It's there for a moment and then it's gone. I want to stop the
projector, freeze this moment, run my finger down his on-
screen features with the movie projected onto the back of my
hand. Oh, Jamie, we could have been so good together. Then I
twinge with embarrassment at all the things I did, all those

absurdly in-love ways I behaved. I've carried on like a lovesick schoolgirl, not a twenty-five-year-old woman.

It's pouring again once the movie is over, and I can't face queuing for a bus. By now, we've gone from autumn to winter. Impulsively, I step out from the shivering, sodden queue and hail a taxi. It's extravagant, I know, but this is the last time I get to use this credit card. And it's not as if I'm getting any redundancy money — from tomorrow, I'm back on benefits.

Once inside the warmth and dry of Chester Street, the house is quiet. Everybody must have gone to bed already, which is a relief. Pavel has left a note: Amy eat good, sleep. I go around as I usually do, tidying up and switching off lights, shutting down the house for the night.

The drawing room is dark when I go in to check for any dirty glasses or anything else that needs carrying through.

"Hello, Susan," says Jamie, switching on a standard lamp.

He's been sitting here in the dark, brooding. He switches the lamp off again. On and off. On and off. It's disconcerting.

"I thought you'd be in bed."

"Too tired from the jetlag. But it's too early for me to go to sleep."

On the coffee table there's an empty whisky tumbler. I reach for it and he takes my hand. There's something needy about him, something he wants to get off his chest.

"Listen, Susan, I owe you an apology. Another one. Of course the police were going to hold an inquest. Why wouldn't they? I lashed out at you because you were the nearest person to hand. I'm sorry, I didn't mean what I said."

"That's all right." I smile tightly. "You'd just lost your father. Everything is on your shoulders. Heavy is the head that wears the crown, you know?"

Why am I always apologising to this family? They're the ones who are rude to me, who are always putting me down, yet I'm the one who has to pump up their fragile egos. My letter giving notice sits upstairs in a sealed envelope. I can't go on like this, this emotional rollercoaster. It's too painful.

"I guess you saw on the socials about my engagement. Another thing I've fucked up. I didn't really love her. It was just something we were being pushed into."

Pause.

"There's something else. The truth is I missed you. I've missed the sound of your voice, the way you move, your lovely face. I dream about you. Can you give me another chance? God knows I don't deserve one."

This whole family, their emotions are as complex as an equation. I don't know what to say. He's so earnest, so desperate, a little boy who needs his mother's approval, a side of him which I haven't seen before.

"Why don't we go out tomorrow night? I've got tickets for the opera."

My heart sinks at the thought of another interminable opera but I know how much Jamie loves classical music. He looks so unhappy. Even though my mind is made up to quit tomorrow, I find myself saying yes.

So, the very next evening, we are back in their private box with my letter of resignation still sat on my mantlepiece. This time, though, it's different. I can't really follow the plot, something about Jewish slaves in the Bible, but there's a moment when I finally get it. The music begins quietly with ominous strings and flutes and then there's a tremulous flute solo before an overwhelming orchestral blast. I've never heard anything like it. It's so dramatic.

Jamie can't see me. Side-on, his beautiful face looks trans-

fixed, like a Roman god who's been blinded by this music. He places his hand over mine on the balcony velvet. Admit it, Susan. You're in love with him. Like Jamie said, he's the one you still dream of.

I'm standing in the bar at the interval while Jamie goes and gets drinks. The room is packed as the audience stands around chatting. There's a long queue at the bar. They've already announced the performance will be starting again in ten minutes, when I turn to scan the room.

That's when I spot her.

Sophie Hare.

The girl who was in the sauna with Amy's boyfriend that night, who heard me arguing with her the night of the accident. She's framed by men. She turns, noticing me. She's put on a lot of weight since I last saw her, seven years ago. It's only when she comes forward that I see she's heavily pregnant. She's glowing.

"Hello, Susan."

"Congratulations. How many months?"

Ignoring me, Sophie takes a sip of cola. "I'm still in touch with Christina Walsh. She told me you're working for them, the Mawdsleys."

"I'm trying to help Amy."

"I'm still in touch with Teddy du Cann too. He told me not to say anything, said it would only make things worse. But I know what I heard. You've got a bloody nerve."

"I don't know what you're talking about."

"Yes, you do. I don't know what sort of sick shit is going on in your mind, and I don't want to."

Jamie's coming towards us, clutching a couple of glasses of white wine. I want to get away from her, but my legs feel unsteady, as if they belong to someone else.

"It was you I heard that night. Arguing with Amy. You were the one who pushed her off that diving board."

With that, she throws her drink in my face.

"WHAT IS IT, Susan? What's the matter?"

My hand trembles. I'm rigid with terror.

"I can't do this. Please don't make me."

These last words come out more like a whimper. I blink away a tear. The Rorschach test card stares back at me accusingly. More than ever, it looks like Jamie's battered head.

"I want to stop now."

Fight or flight kicking in.

Can't breathe.

Darkness closing in from all four corners of the room.

I stand up, needing to get out of this place.

"Susan, don't go. This is important. What is it that you've seen? What does it remind you of?"

I shake my head, revolted.

"Blood. A man's head. The man I killed."

"Stay with it, Susan. Tell me what you're seeing. This is it, the moment we've been waiting for. It can't hurt you, Susan. It's only a memory."

Sticks and stones may break my bones but words will never hurt me.

"Please, Max. Stop."

"Tell me, Susan. Describe it."

"Jamie staring up at me. Blood everywhere. His eyes... so accusing. Please, Max, I want to stop."

Gently, Max takes the card from my stiff fingers and shuffles it back into the pack. I've had enough. My shoulders actually slump with relief. If I hadn't experienced what has just happened myself, I would never have believed it.

"Susan, you've got to lean into this. If it's uncomfortable, that means we're getting somewhere. Don't give up now. You're so close."

My adrenalin fades and my breathing comes back under control. Suddenly, I feel immensely tired. Max looks at me earnestly. All he says is can't. Empty words, words, words. Why did I ever believe he could help me? The truth is, I *did* kill Jamie, and there's nothing Max can say that can undo that.

I'm as guilty as sin.

Everything they say is true.

CHAPTER THIRTY-THREE

SESSION 7

I'm sitting in an armchair wearing a cap, the kind of thing astronauts wear before they put on their helmets, with a data hose running off the back of it. The cap is dotted with sensors. And the lead snakes across the floor to the laptop on Max's desk.

The wall-mounted TV screen shows me what's meant to be a calming scene, sitting on a stone bench surrounded by cooling pine trees, dabbling my bare feet in water. Glimpsed through the trees, islanded on a promontory, sits a Greek temple. You can almost feel the heat and the grating cicadas.

This is my first session of what Max calls neurofeedback. The idea is that whenever I remember something with shuddering horror, such as seeing blood pooled around Jamie's head, I bring that memory under control. Almost direct it. Knowing that it's a memory, I can dial it down. Examine things in more detail. Then we can go deeper.

"You're not going to show me anything violent, are you, Max?"

What I saw this morning in those cards has left me shaken.

"No, nothing like that. This is about remembering something good. It's about establishing a baseline. Then seeing how your brain reacts under stress. Give me a happy memory."

THEN

IT'S *difficult to remember happiness, I don't know why. You only ever really remember unhappiness. What I do remember is lying in an enormous bath facing Jamie with hot water thundering out of the taps, then the two of us lying naked in front of the fire, me feeling very wanton wrapped up in a fur throw, eating smoked salmon sandwiches and drinking very cold Chablis.*

"I'll say this for Dad, he kept a very good cellar." Jamie grins, wiping his fingers.

"I barely knew the difference between red and white wine before I met your family. Now look at me. You've corrupted me, Jamie Mawdsley."

"I do hope so."

He reaches forward to stroke my face.

"Listen, there's something I want to talk to you about. What would you say to coming to live with me in New York? It's where the future of the business lies. Of course, we'd come back to London every month or so, and we can always stay here, but I want you to be with me in America."

America? New York? Canyons of skyscrapers, yellow taxis, whooshing steam. The constant sirens and horns. They call it the capital of the world, the city which never sleeps. Is he saying what I think he's saying? Trying to keep the excitement out of my voice, I reply, "What about your sister? I can't leave her, Jamie. I made her a promise. I said I would get her better."

What Amy said, about everybody betraying each other in the end, comes back to me. No, I wouldn't do that to her. I won't just throw her away for Jamie. I made a vow. And a promise is a promise.

"That's impossible, and she knows it. Dad paid for the best consultants. They all said the same thing."

I can only nod reluctantly.

"We can always find another carer." He kisses me again. "There's only one of you, though."

We make love but this time it's gentle, yearning, questioning, with none of the impatience of that first night, going up in the lift.

By now, it's cold outside. You can feel it through the thick curtains. I go upstairs to get changed and, when I come back down, Jamie is nowhere to be found. Amy is asleep in her bedroom. I don't want to call out and disturb her. He's not in the kitchen or the sitting room either. So I take the lift all the way down to the basement swimming pool and work my way up.

Eventually, I find him on his mobile phone in his father's study. He's left the door ajar. "You're sure about that?" he's saying. "You're absolutely certain?" He looks worried, anxious, as he paces. "What's going on?" I want to ask him, but instead of ushering me in, he wags his finger, warning me not to come in. Then he closes the door right in my face.

What is it he doesn't want me to know about? Even now, despite everything, this family still has secrets.

———

"DID he tell you what the phone call was about?" Max asks, fiddling with the data lead. Then he adjusts my cloth swim cap.

"No. Every time I tried asking him, he shut me down. Said it was just business. Nothing to worry about."

"I'm not happy with these readings. You're still not relaxed enough."

Max walks over to the wall-mounted TV and taps the screen, which shows my brain in real time. Most of it is in pulsing green but there are patches of blue and even ominous magenta.

"I want all this to be green," says Max, tapping the monitor with his Biro. "Let's try again. This time, give me your very happiest memory."

———

THEN

JAMIE WANTS *to go out again on Thursday night. He's cleared it with Pavel, he says. The restaurant he's chosen to take me to is on a Covent Garden side street. It's down some steps and a roar of noise hits us as we step down into the fug. It's a buzzy, stylish place, just like the restaurants Amy loves. Or used to. She hasn't been the same since her father died. A swishy, brisk waiter ushers us to our table.*

"We were lucky to get a reservation," Jamie admits once we've ordered. "It had an amazing review in the paper."

I order simple grilled sea bass with spinach and a saffron sauce. If it swims, it slims. It also tastes utterly sublime.

There's a famous actress at the next table, who's smaller and older than I remember. Her hair is stridently red and her eyes heavily kohled. Mum used to love watching her on TV.

Our shared waiter fusses about her table taking coffee orders.

"And how do you take your coffee?" he asks, turning to the actress.

"I take my coffee how I like my men," she replies, meaningfully touching his forearm.

"Sorry, madam. We don't serve gay coffee."

We both raise our eyes at this and Jamie grins; over the past month, I had forgotten his smile. It's the first time I have seen him laugh since his father died.

After that, we talk easily. Jamie tells me about his life in New York, which sounds amazing. He's lonely, though; I can hear it in his voice. That's why he wants me to be with him. It's like there's just two of us in this enclosed bubble, speaking our own secret language. I have never done drugs—well, apart from that puff on a joint in the South of France—but right now, I feel high. He just has to say some secret word, share some piece of knowledge tantalisingly out of reach, and everything will be solved.

We've scraped both our plates clean, and Jamie pours the last of a bottle of white Burgundy into my glass. I feel pleasantly sloshed. I am debating whether to be good and not have a dessert when Jamie searches in his jacket for something.

He places a velvet jewellery box on the tablecloth and the din of the restaurant falls away.

I have a horrible feeling that I know what's coming and I'm not ready for this; at the same time, warmth floods my chest and I want to say, "Yes, yes."

Nestled inside is a stonking engagement ring with an enormous opal surrounded by diamonds. I have never seen anything so beautiful in my life.

"It was my mother's," I hear him saying. "I want you to have it."

To my consternation, he's getting down on one knee right in front of this entire restaurant. Get up, get up, don't embarrass me like this. Other tables are turning around, looking on with a mixture of approval and embarrassment.

"Susan Gummer, will you marry me?"

"Yes, yes," I want to tell him, not sure whether to look at this ring or Jamie taking the knee. It's all too much for me to take in. I am flattered, overwhelmed and amazed.

I nod.

This is the happiest moment of my life.

"SUSAN, we've got to move faster. Recover your memories quicker," Max says, helping me take off the headset. "I believe you. Nobody else does. You've become a tweet, a meme, an Insta post. People know the story and they want it to end. We've got to give them a different ending."

"So, what are you going to do? Show me some more tourist ruins?"

Max thinks for a moment. The pressure's getting to him too. It's constantly there, hanging over us, the police charging me with murder, like that crow I imagined circling high over our heads the other day on our walk. Waiting for me to become carrion.

"No, I've got something else in mind. It's highly unorthodox. You have to keep this between ourselves. Here, I want to show you something."

He rattles the keys on his keyboard as I move around behind his desk. He's brought something up on his computer monitor. Estate agent details.

My scalp crawls.

It's thirteen Chester Street.

The house of horrors, where ten years ago I murdered my lover.

Not exactly as I remember it, of course. There have been some changes made, but it's still mostly the same. Max flicks through the room-view slideshow and there is the swimming pool, just as I remember it, the bedrooms and, worst of all, the marble atrium where my fiancé lay dying.

I can't get his accusing face out of my head.

"Susan, sometimes a noise or a smell can trigger a memory. More powerful than waving my fingers in front of your face. Or analysing your brainwaves. We need to apply a defibrillator to your mind. Shock you into remembering. It's kill or cure."

"You're asking for too much. Don't make me do this."

"The police are coming to arrest you. As soon as tomorrow. You heard what the police said. They have motive, means and opportunity. The evidence against you is overwhelming. To be honest, I'm running out of tricks. Nothing's working. We have to go back, back to where it happened."

He's right, of course.

We have run out of options. Amy witnessed me pushing

her brother off that balcony. Whom are they going to believe, his grieving, wheelchair-bound sister or the jilted fiancée?

Motive, means and opportunity.

Our last chance is to apply those paddles to my mind, shock me into remembering. I'm scared, picturing my body bucking on the operating table. But he's right, I have to go through with this. Kill or cure, that's what he said. Looking down at my hands, I see I've clenched my fists.

Even if it kills me.

CHAPTER THIRTY-FOUR

Neither of us says much as we drive to London in Max's car. I can hear Max thinking and I suspect we're both thinking the same thing.

"What about Pavel, the driver? What makes the police think he wasn't involved?"

"He was, in a way. He told the police he was asleep when he heard Amanda Mawdsley scream. Said it woke him up. He was the one who found you crouched over Jamie's body. He tried to stop you from running."

So that was him in my memory, those powerful arms holding me back.

In my dream, I am still running down that street, my bare feet slapping the pavement, screaming my bloody head off. Someone coming after me, somebody who wants to do me harm.

Gaining.

That must have been Pavel.

Then swerving into the middle of a deserted London street, wearing just a nightdress, clenching my fists, shouting for help. That yellow taxi light accelerating towards me.

Then nothing.

The closer we get to central London, to Chester Street itself, the more apprehensive I feel. What if I don't remember anything? Trying to remember what happened is like being stuck on a mathematical limit—you approach the solution, but you can never quite reach it.

And if it's a complete blank, then what? The police have wanted to charge me with murder for ten years. A decade for them to put their case together. Witness statements. All those photographs on Max's wall. The weight of evidence bearing down, breaking my bones, crushing me.

What surprises me about London is how little it has changed in the decade I have been asleep. Yes, some of the shopfronts are different—there are more coffee bars and charity shops—but the grey buildings are the same.

Everything looks shabbier and dingier than I remember though. But from what I've read, England has been repeatedly punched in the face, first with Brexit, then Covid. While I've been asleep, this country has had too many blows to the head.

Blow to the head.

Don't think about that.

A man I assume is the estate agent dawdles on the pavement as Max's car glides into a parking space. Electric cars—that's something else I've slept through. The estate agent hovers impatiently as we get out of Max's Tesla. That's what he calls it.

"Mr and Mrs Quane?" he asks, approaching us. I blush at this. "I've brought the details with me. We can go straight in if you like. The house is unoccupied."

The white stucco facade looms over me. I don't think I can go through with this. The pavement feels gluey and unstable as if there's nothing to hold on to.

Thirteen Chester Street. The house that still haunts me in my dreams. And here it is, that impenetrable glossy front door which stares back at me like a black mirror. My insides quail.

"Ready, darling?" Max asks, concerned.

I nod stiffly, feeling bandy-legged. I don't think I can go through with this. Max is asking for too much. The last time I stood on these steps I was slathered head to toe in my lover's blood. Then it comes back to me, that old penny smell, the stale, spicily sweet smell of blood.

Max was right.

It is happening, it's coming back.

The estate agent fiddles with the keys, and the front door still opens smoothly, ushering in the three of us.

Inside, the atrium is as vast and imposing as I remember. But looking up, the lantern roof is green with septic light, choked with algae, making the whole place feel like a dirty fish tank. It smells of damp and neglect.

"Nobody has lived here for ten years," says the estate agent, seeing our faces. "The owner has moved to the States. You know the history of the house, of course. That's reflected in the price."

By owner, he means Amanda Mawdsley, of course. Frenemy—that's another new word I've missed while I've been asleep. Yes, we weren't exactly friends, more frenemies. She still wants twenty million for it.

Max nods noncommittally and the estate agent suggests we take the gilt lift up to the attic and work our way down. I try not to think about me and Jamie making love in this very lift as we ascend. *Don't look down, Susan. Do not look at the stairs.*

My old attic flat is empty, with dirty newspapers and sagging, bilious wallpaper. There's black damp up in one corner. Then I remember the two of us laughing in bed and the warmth of his body, sitting up on my elbows to watch him stride naked into the bathroom, catching his eye in the vanity mirror.

Why does life have to turn out so badly?

Next floor down is the arcade with the main bedrooms and, standing in the empty master bedroom, I remember finding Mr Mawdsley dead in here, his eyes wide open, staring up at the ceiling. As if he'd witnessed something terrible, death crouched up in one corner, like a gargoyle.

Max looks at me anxiously, silently asking if I've remembered any new detail. Imperceptibly, I shake my head.

Everything so far I've remembered, he already knows about. This visit, it's a waste of time. This house isn't telling me anything. It's keeping its secrets. A mute witness. If these walls could talk, they're not saying anything.

Walking along the bedroom corridor, I try not to look over the balcony. Where it happened. The estate agent burbles on about how the house was renovated by a famous architect and I take Max's hand for reassurance, letting the man think we really are a married couple.

The bedside table where Amy collected her crystal paperweights is long gone, and the walk-in wardrobe, crammed with her designer dresses, empty apart from a few wire hangers. The bed where we lay side by side, like those starchy Elizabethan mothers in the painting, just some dents in the dirty carpet.

The estate agent leans over the balcony, looks down onto

the atrium, enthusing about this incredible entertaining space.

"All the marble was imported from Italy, you know," he says, and I steel myself to peek over the edge. To my relief, the statement staircase that Jamie tumbled down now has a banister and glass panels to stop you falling off.

Only something's rising, building inside me. The most intolerable pressure. A splintering migraine. That's when the memory hits me.

Like being punched in the head.

CHAPTER THIRTY-FIVE

"Are you all right?" the estate agent asks. "You look like you've seen a ghost."

"Maybe I have," I say quietly, turning to Max. Slight nod. "Darling, I don't feel well. Can we go home now?"

Max mouths the word "pregnant" to the estate agent, putting his arm around me. The estate agent, all solicitude now, walks us downstairs.

Down those very steps I have glimpsed smeared in my lover's blood. *I was there, I was really there.* A flashback with the force of being hit by that taxi. I remembered everything in such detail and it makes me feel ill.

Because I am the one who killed him.

I pushed Jamie Mawdsley down those stairs. I must have done. I saw it all. It's all true, everything the police are saying.

"Gently does it," says Max as he guides me down the staircase. *Don't think about what happened there, what you saw.*

"We can rearrange anytime you want," the estate agent

says worriedly. "You haven't seen the basement yet. There's a swimming pool and a gym and a home cinema. It's quite amazing."

"Right now, I just need to look after my wife," Max snaps. "Now, if you'll excuse me..."

We exit back out into the street. The last time I went through this door I was slathered in my lover's blood. I think I'm about to faint. It's all too overwhelming, too much for me to take in.

Playing the concerned husband, Max helps me into the passenger seat, and, through the windscreen, I watch the two of them shake hands.

So now I know.

There was no mysterious other person in the house that night. Grasping at straws, that's all we were doing. Shock me into remembering—he did that all right. It was me all along. I am the one who killed him. I'm the killer.

Maybe I woke up and heard Jamie on the phone to his other lover, his ex-fiancée in the States, telling her that she was the one he really loved. Triggering. And when I overheard that, that I was a plaything to be picked up and thrown away, just as Amy told me that night, that's what pushed me over the edge. Or Jamie.

Max gets back inside the car, looking anxious. "All right?" he asks solicitously. Outside, it begins to rain, fat raindrops racing each other down the windscreen.

Suddenly, I can't hold all of this in.

"Oh, Max," I say, putting my head in my hands. A great convulsive sob wells up. "It was me. I'm the one who did it. I was the one who killed him. I saw it all. There was nobody else."

"Breathe, Susan. Tell me what you saw. Take your time. We're here, finally. This is important," Max urges.

My heart is pounding but I try and get my breath under control. What I remember was so real, as if I was really there, looking down on everything. It's like I was watching myself, seeing it all play out from high up.

"I was standing outside Amy's bedroom on the second floor. Looking down at the atrium. My hands were on the parapet."

"You're going too fast. Tell me everything. Every tiny detail."

Max's voice sounds far away and I am back there, in the house, looking down at Jamie's body lying dead two floors below me.

One of Amy's crystal paperweights lies smashed on the open staircase. Chunks of broken glass and dots of its tiny bouquet strewn on the steps.

Invisible hands grab my neck, throttling me, squeezing every last breath out. Can't swallow, can't breathe. As if I've had a pair of balled tights stuffed down my throat.

Two flights down, Jamie lies sprawled on the marble floor. Beautiful Jamie. Blood pools around his head. His sightless eyes stare up at me. His accusing eyes say, "You're the one who did this to me, Susan. Why? WHY?"

My scream is more like a howl as I pelt down that hateful staircase as what I've done sinks in. I'm the one who pushed him over this balcony. It must have been me. It's true then, all of it. I really did murder my fiancé.

All of this plays out in silence and slow motion, as if time itself has stretched between each moment. Time is so slowed, each breath seems to take forever.

Just my pounding heart.

Reaching the ground floor, I see myself crouched over his misshapen body, his arms and legs at funny angles. The room throbs around us and my whole body is shaking. I'm going into hysterical convulsions. My pain is immense, it fills the room.

What on Earth have I done? Why did I do it, what was it that he did to me? That I still don't know.

"Oh God," I sob, staring into his face as I kneel on the floor with my head in my hands.

Jamie is dead.

It's a dull thought, a child forming a word in her mouth she can't read and doesn't understand. All I can do is sit there, my knees painfully digging into the marble, not feeling, not thinking, as the world shrinks to a pinprick around me.

"Oh God," I moan again.

Then I uselessly rub his chest, trying to bring the man I love back to life, but it's hopeless. There's just so much blood and it's everywhere, coating my hands and arms...

"You can't do this to me," I shout, shoving his chest even harder, trying to jolt him back into life. All those first aid lessons we'd had in the care home, what to do if a patient has a heart attack, and it's all useless, useless...

I look up to see Amy wheeling herself to the top of the stairs. She too can't believe what's just happened. Cradling my lover's head, I look up at her pleadingly, and—

That's the last thing I remember. After that, my memory goes as dark as a blown television set.

Max looks grimly out of his driver's side window. He won't meet my eye.

"Did you see Jamie fall though? What made you wake up in the middle of the night? It was three o'clock in the morning. Did the two of you have an argument?"

That's all still a blank, but my memory will come back. Whether I want it to or not.

"Maybe he told me he didn't love me anymore. Or he was just playing games, like last time."

I bury my head in my hands, sobbing harder. As if crying away my guilt is going to make things better.

"You'd just got engaged. This should have been the happiest night of your life. None of this makes sense. There's something still missing. There has to be a reason you pushed him down those stairs."

Suddenly, I slam both palms on the dashboard. I've had enough. His constantly making excuses for the person I really am. Why can't he accept the truth? Because I have. In a way, it's a relief. I can finally let go.

"Max, please. Let's stop pretending. I'm the one who did it. You asked me to remember and now I have. This is where it stops, okay? Take me to the police. I want to confess."

I slump back in the passenger seat, dejected. The TikTok detectives, the true crime podcasts, the Instagram feeds all proving my guilt. Everything they say about me is true. All those newspaper clippings, those bits of string on Max's wall. In the end, Max really did solve the mystery.

Only there was no mystery to solve. It was me all along.

CHAPTER THIRTY-SIX

We drive back up to Suffolk in silence. Neither of us says a word. Both of us are talked out. It's cold and foggy out tonight. Green ghosts of frozen trees loom out of the hard shoulder. Cars overtake and disappear into the wall of fog. The outlines of everything have dissolved. All the time, there's just the scraping metronome of windscreen wipers.

The pain squeezes me tighter, tighter. I just want this to be over now, accept my fate. In a way, it's a relief. It's funny but now that I know the truth, that I was the one who killed him, I can finally grieve. Nobody teaches you how to deal with grief—you're just deaf and dumb or amputated at the wrists, saying, "Look at me, look at me."

There's still something, though, we haven't talked about —the constant anxiety hanging over me.

"Max, if I go to the police, what happens then?"

"They will arrest you," he says, eyes on the road. "Probably charge you with murder. Not that they'll get very far. From what you told me, it's manslaughter at best. Something triggered you; we still don't know what. It's the dead spot where your memory's blown. Susan, I know you. You're no murderer. I've interviewed them in places like Rampton and Broadmoor. They never show remorse."

"But Amy said *she saw me*."

"Maybe you were trying to save him and lost your balance. Have you thought of that?"

"It would still be my word against hers."

Max doesn't reply.

We're both tired and hungry by the time we arrive back at the clinic. When we finally get out of the car, Bunny is waiting for us on the front steps. The clinic has been locked down for the night. Max tells her he'll make us something to eat in his flat upstairs. As clinic director, he has his own service flat on top of the staff wing.

It's a functional one-bedroom flat that looks more like a safe house than somebody's home. Everything's mushroom soup coloured. Anaglypta wallpaper and a huge, overstuffed sofa with ugly barley-twist furniture. Vague smell of damp. There's a pile of diving magazines on the coffee table and, intriguingly, a retro music centre with LPs racked against it.

"It's not much but it's home," Max says, taking my anorak. "I've never had time to do anything with it. Those LPs were all here when I moved in. Help yourself."

Max bangs about in the kitchen, opening cupboards and inspecting the fridge. Then the welcome *thop* of a wine bottle being opened.

"Here," he says, handing me a glass. "Hope you like eggs. It's all I've got."

The cheap red wine tastes like brackish velvet. Living with the Mawdsleys has spoilt me. "The condemned woman has the right to a last meal, right?" I smile weakly, sounding mawkish, even to myself.

I have never seen someone make an omelette so carefully before. Max pours the beaten egg into the frying pan and carefully drags the runnels of egg in from the sides. It's like watching an artist at work and it's fascinating.

"My grandmother taught me," he explains. "Her parents were restauranteurs in Normandy. The trick is to cook the omelette as slowly as possible."

Being this close to him makes me feel funny. He does something to me. I can't explain it. It's like he's seen right into me, knows who I am, and is still not appalled. He knows who I am and isn't frightened of me. For that reason alone, I may be falling a little in love with him. You just need one person in the world who believes in you, that's all.

"I've been thinking about your dream, the one you told me about," he says over his shoulder. "The one about playing cards. James and Amy taught you how to play a card game on holiday, yes? You don't have to be Sigmund Freud to understand what it was trying to tell you. The two of clubs is the lowest card. That's how you thought about yourself. But the card changed into a queen, remember? That was you hoping to marry Jamie."

Max slides the first omelette onto a plate and then pours the rest of the beaten egg into the pan. The waiting omelette looks fluffy and gooey and delicious and I realise how hungry I am.

"What you said about the cards having mirror images. It's what Jung called our shadow side. We all have one. The king of diamonds and the queen of diamonds were Brian Mawdsley and his daughter, right? The diamonds equal money. Only the queen of diamonds didn't have a bottom half because you felt so guilty about her accident."

"And Jamie was the jack of hearts, but his bottom half

was the jack of spades," I say, from the other room, putting knives and forks on the fold-down table.

"That's right. A jack means a young man and spades represent weapons."

I still remember placing the jack of hearts on the king of diamonds in my dream, just as Amy used to do when she was playing patience.

"What about this? You suspected that it was Jamie who murdered his father, and you confronted him. He lost his temper, and you pushed him down those stairs in self-defence. Have you thought about that?"

"But nobody saw me arguing with him. It was still murder."

We sit at the fold-down dining table eating omelettes and what's left of a bag of wet salad he found in the vegetable drawer. I can't help but think about the two of us strolling along the beach, almost arm in arm, my fantasy of us being a proper couple, the two of us really being together.

"Max, there's something I have to ask you. Let's say you're right and there's an explanation for what happened. Is there any way... I mean," I'm not quite sure what I'm trying to say, and I get tongue-tied. "If this comes to an end... if it ever ends, is there any way..."

"I know what you're about to say, Susan," Max says, putting down his knife and fork. "The answer is no. In another world, where none of this ever happened... then, perhaps. But not in this one. I can't. It wouldn't be ethical."

"But if we weren't doctor and patient..."

"What you're feeling is something we call transference. It's a common phenomenon in therapy. It's natural to develop strong feelings for your therapist, but they're part of the therapeutic process. But you're idealising me. What you're feeling isn't real."

"This isn't transference, it is real. You know me better than anyone ever has. You've seen parts of me I've never shown anybody before."

"Susan, listen. Any relationship between us would be unethical and potentially harmful, even after treatment ends. As a psychiatrist, I'm barred from having a relationship with any of my patients for at least five years once treatment is over. Personally, I think it's a line that should never be crossed." Pause. He looks at me frankly. "Even if I wanted to, and believe me, I do."

So he can feel it too.

"There's no chance for us, ever?"

"Susan, I've come to know intimate details about you through our sessions together. There's a power imbalance. There always will be. We didn't share this knowledge through you getting to know me. You've been vulnerable and shared painful memories. I'm grateful for that, truly I am. I applaud your bravery. In turn, I have an ethical obligation to protect your well-being, don't you see?"

I understand what he's saying but it still hurts. I don't think I can stand any more rejection. I wipe a tear away with the back of my hand.

"But you care about me. I can tell."

"This person you've built up in your head is just that, a construction. It's a projection, not the real me. You've magnified me, distorted me..." He chuckles, trying to make light of it. "I'm just an ordinary, not-very-good doctor out in the sticks."

I look down at my lap. "I feel so embarrassed."

Suddenly, I can't stand this any longer. I rise from the

table and cross to the record collection, to give my hands something to do. Running my finger along the crammed LPs, I find they're all jazz or classical. I'm searching for one LP in particular, just on the off-chance. Stirred by my memory of the night Jamie took me to the opera, the evening he proposed, I search for Verdi. I was going to be married. Somebody *did* love me once.

Perhaps it's maudlin but I find the very opera which he took me to, *Nabucco*, and, shrugging the LP out of its sleeve, place the old vinyl reverently on the turntable.

Suddenly, Max's flat is filled with the urgent, dramatic opening bars of "The Song of the Hebrew Slaves". Then the flutes come in, teetering as if on a razor's edge, each note like a secret that's waiting for me, so tantalisingly close, yet frustratingly out of reach.

Suddenly, I am back there.

In the Chester Street house, the night that Jamie died.

Only this time there's no blurring, no dead spots where I can't remember. I stretch out my mind's fingers, reaching as far as I can, clawing through memories, straining to get to that moment before my brain shut down.

And this time what I remember is so very different.

This is it, what I have been waiting for.

My final memory.

THEN

IT'S STILL *the night Jamie proposed. Ironically, despite Jamie asking me to marry him, tonight is the first night we haven't made love. We go to bed and lie there in the dark and*

I can hear Jamie thinking. Then I start thinking too, about that swimming pool six floors below us, the one where Amy had her accident, and standing on that diving board with my back to the water, then feeling myself going, toppling back-wards, and—

For a moment, I don't know where I am. Yes, I'm back in my attic bedroom but Jamie's side of the bed is empty. It's so dark in here, throbbing velvety blackness. It feels like the middle of the night. He's probably gone to the bathroom.

3:05

What I do know is that I need to pee myself and, sitting there in the darkness, listening to the stream hit the toilet bowl, I realise, still half-asleep, that he isn't in this bathroom either. He must be in the sitting room, then.

That's when I hear it. What sounds like raised voices coming from downstairs. Through the floor. The underwater sound of two people arguing. It must be one hell of an argument.

Unhooking my dressing gown from the back of the bath-room door, I decide to use the stairs rather than the lift. I pad down the attic steps, wondering what's going on. The shouting gets louder as I reach the bottom.

There's a chemical taste in my mouth, dread in my heart, because something bad is happening on the other side of this door. My throat constricts. It's a feeling I have, a premonition. I can't explain it.

Peering into the gallery bedroom corridor, I see Amy's bedroom door is open. Jamie's the one who's shouting. Tying my dressing gown cord, still groggy, I pad down the carpet in bare feet, wondering what on Earth's going on.

Jamie stands over his sister, dominating her, gripping both of her wheelchair arms, almost spitting in her face. Sensing me, he turns.

"Tell her, Amy. Show her," he rages.

"Jamie, stop," I cry, clenching my fists. "What are you doing?"

"I know she killed Dad. I don't know how, but I'll find out. She's the one who killed him."

He's pulling his sister out of her wheelchair, wrenching her arms. She's struggling, fending him off. The chair is going to topple over. Appalled, I stand rooted to the spot. Don't know what to do.

"Jamie, stop. You're hurting her."

"Stay out of this, Susan."

Amy screams again and this time it's loud enough to penetrate the brickwork. Not thinking, I rush towards them, grabbing one of the glass paperweights off her bedside table, a way to ward him off.

He is a man possessed.

He's going to kill her.

"Stop, stop," I shout and swing the paperweight at his head. I don't know what I'm doing. I just want to separate them. To my surprise, the paperweight makes contact. Jamie staggers back, putting his head in both hands.

"Oh God, I'm so sorry," I say, dropping the glass ball. It rolls through the open bedroom door and out onto the landing, then disappears over the staircase.

Jamie still has his head in his hands, staggering about as if he's drunk. He clutches his head as blood appears through his knuckles.

He lurches into the gallery corridor and I run to help, putting my arm around him as he grips the parapet. Blood courses down the side of his head.

"*Oh, Jamie. I'm so sorry. It was an accident.*"

He shrugs me away, not wanting to have anything to do with me. I stand there, frozen with indecision.

Suddenly, from behind us, there's a banshee scream.

Amy runs straight at us, both arms outstretched, a demented rag doll on rails. Wait, she's out of her wheelchair?

She can walk after all.

The thought dumbly spreads across my brain as she slams into Jamie with everything she's got. He disappears over the side of the balcony. One moment he's there, the next he's gone.

I feel it before I hear it. Awful wet sound.

Not quite believing what I've just witnessed, I run to the balcony and stare over the parapet. Jamie lies two flights down, his arms and legs at funny angles. A puppet with its strings cut. Too astonished to speak, I stare as my hands grip the rail. I turn to see Amy clamber back inside her wheelchair. When she sits down, it's with a look of quiet satisfaction.

All these years, all the guilt I've felt. For nothing. All along, she's the one who's been lying to me. She's lied to both of us.

Then I remember him, poor, poor Jamie, and, without thinking, I pelt down that hateful marble staircase, past where the paperweight has smashed on the steps. Before it's too late. Call an ambulance. For God's sake, call an ambulance.

Jamie lies at the bottom of the steps with his eyes open, staring accusingly at me. "Look at what you've done," he seems to be saying.

The walls contract, darkness pressing in from all four corners.

The first thing I do is try to get his heart going, pull open his pyjama top, press down with both hands, heaving away.

"*You can't do this to me,*" I grunt, trying to get his heart going. But it's hopeless. All I'm doing is getting covered in blood, my hands and arms slathered in the stuff.

I look up to see Amy wheel herself to the top of the stairs, strangely unmoved.

Going into convulsions, my whole body shakes. I can't control myself. My love, my love, what has she done to you? There's so much blood pooled everywhere, as I squat, cradling Jamie's head. For God's sake, someone call for help. Isn't somebody going to call for an ambulance?

Finally, Amy screams, "Murder! Murder!"

I am on both knees, crouched over my lover, when Pavel appears behind Amy and immediately grasps the situation. Thank God. He thunders down those steps, but instead of calling for an ambulance, he manhandles me off Jamie. Stop, stop. What are you doing? I'm not the one who killed him.

We're struggling and he grabs one of my arms behind my back, trying to pinion me. He's going to break my arm. His other arm comes round my neck, putting me in a headlock. Instinctively, I understand what's happening. She's going to frame me for murder, tell them that I was the one who did this.

Need to get out of here.

Call the police now.

I bite down on the back of his hand, right into a faded tattoo of a double-headed eagle. Taste blood. He screams and I wrest free, too slippery with my lover's blood.

Get out of this house.

Now.

I bolt for the front door, my bloody fingers grappling with the latch, smearing the metal. He's coming up fast behind me. The front door bangs open and I'm off and running, too fast for him, screaming my head off. I do a cartoon skedaddle and bolt left, bare feet slapping on pavement.

It's perishingly cold out tonight, cold enough to split stones. The street is totally empty. There's nobody awake. I run hysterically towards the junction, houses jiggling ahead of me.

Why can't anybody hear me? What's the matter with everybody?

A dog barks and an upper window light does switch on and, for a moment, I see myself as if I'm looking down on the scene. A crazy-looking woman in a bloody nightdress, running hysterically down the street. Screaming for help.

I can hear Pavel. Getting nearer. It's like one of those old horror movies Amy and I used to sit up in bed and watch together, the woman running through a forest as the monster lumbers after her. No matter how fast she runs, he lurches at the same steady pace, gaining. It's the same thing now.

Thank God the junction's coming up fast. I run out into the middle of Upper Belgrave Street, waving my arms. Only this road section is empty too and, turning, that's when I see it.

A lone taxi with its orange for-hire light on accelerating towards me. I push my hands out—maybe I'm trying to stop it, maybe I'm trying to flag it down, I don't know—but by now it's too late and—

Coppery taste in my mouth.

The driver's terrified face as I windmill over his bonnet and—

I glimpse the moon upside down as I fall through space. This is going to hurt. Something black and impenetrable rushes towards me. Then the back of my head smacks something hard.

Oblivion.

CHAPTER THIRTY-SEVEN

"I don't believe you."

It's the first time Max hasn't accepted what I've remembered.

"Max, I'm telling you. That's what I saw."

"It can't be true. It's impossible."

"How can you say that?"

"Because I've read her medical records. It would be impossible for her to walk again. In any case, that's not the Amanda Mawdsley I know. Why would she do such a thing?"

Wait, they know each other?

"Because Jamie was telling the truth, that's why. That's what I overheard in the study that day, Jamie on the phone to a doctor. How she'd learnt to walk again. And what if what Jamie said about her murdering their father was also true? Then there was their mother... We know that Amy spent time in—" I look around me "—a place like this."

"Susan, listen to me. Long-term coma victims can often

have false memories. Hallucinations that seem absolutely real."

"Are you telling me I invented this?"

"Amy told me she saw you kill Jamie."

"She *told* you?"

Max hesitates, weighing up how much to tell me. For the first time, he looks almost shifty.

"She's the one who's been paying for your care. I'm sorry, I thought you knew."

The shock is so great, I feel myself shrivel.

"How often do you speak to her?"

My mind is racing. She's the one who's been paying for me to be here. Because she wanted me locked away, on this remote islet, forgotten.

"Not talk, email."

They've been writing to each other, as well?

"How much does she know? About what I've remembered."

"Not everything. Your past. That it wasn't you who pushed her off that diving board, for a start."

I'm in such shock, I don't know where to begin. This man, the one person I trusted... Then I realise, the circle of betrayal is complete. First, I betrayed Amy, then she betrayed me—and now this.

"Max, do you realise what you've done?"

"She's my boss, Susan. When she says jump, I ask how high. Please, you have to believe me. I thought she was the grieving sister."

"Exactly how much does she know? Tell me."

"Right up until the moment Jamie proposed. I told you, I'm writing a book. It's all in my notes. She asked to read them as we went along."

I am still reeling. Amanda Mawdsley kept me locked away in this private clinic because I am the only eyewitness to murder. The one person who could send her to prison. Who could derail this American takeover worth millions...

Max is still waffling, trying to justify his betrayal. "... everyone thinks she's been a saint, paying for your care. Keeping a private hospital open for just one patient—that doesn't come cheap. One who's too fragile to be moved... unless..."

"Unless what?"

Max stands stock still, having had a thought. Then he smacks himself in the forehead with the heel of his hand.

"Oh, I've been such a fool."

"Max, what is it? What have you thought of?"

"Come with me."

The pharmacy is on the ground floor corridor. Max gropes for the light switch and its overhead strip light ripples into life. The pharmacy is crammed with every kind of prescription drug you can think of. Shelves of anti-psychotics and downers to keep patients biddable. Most of those packets must be past their use-by date by now. Max moves to an old-fashioned-looking beige computer sitting on what looks like a breakfast bar. He stands over it, logs in and the hard drive grinds into action.

"Sometimes the old technology is the best," he says.

Green numerals spread across its monitor. He taps the screen with a handy Biro searching for one entry, then finds it. An obsolete-looking dot-matrix printer squeaks into life, chunking out a perforated sheet.

Max tears off the printout and we're back on the move, taking the stairs back up to the secure unit two at a time, me nonplussed as to what's going on.

"Max, where are we going? What have you found?"

He swipes his pass against the reader and we're back on the somnolent secure ward, my home for the past ten years. Nurse Linh sits in the gloom at the nursing station. She stands up, concerned, as Max walks straight past her with me hurrying behind him.

We're back in my old room, number nine, with the turned-off vital signs monitor and the ventilator trundled against one wall. Max strides to the saline drip stand, unhooks the bag, inspects it, then shakes his head.

He stalks back to the nursing station with the half-empty saline bag hooked under one finger. Nurse Linh looks up from behind her Anglepoise, anxious, worried. If anything, she looks guilty and almost cringes. Max slams the printout down on the counter.

"What's wrong, Doctor Quane?"

"You know what's wrong," Max barks. "It says here you've been feeding Susan a hundred micrograms of oxycodeine into her saline drip. Every day. That's every day for the past nine years."

Nurse Linh looks down. She won't look at us.

"For God's sake, Linh, why? I trusted you. I can't believe I didn't spot it. Answer me."

"They paid me," she says with as much dignity as she can. Then she raises her eyes to meet his. "They said they would tell the authorities if I didn't. I don't have a visa."

"Who paid you?"

"She did. Owner. Amanda Mawdsley."

"What's going on?" I interrupt. "I don't understand."

Max turns to me, incredulous. "I thought we were trying to wake you up. We weren't. We were the ones keeping you asleep."

CHAPTER THIRTY-EIGHT

"I still don't understand. If Nurse Linh has been keeping me asleep for the past ten years, why did I wake up?"

"She got complacent and forgot. She went on holiday to Vietnam, remember? To see her family. Bunny must have switched the saline bag to the undoctored one. You weren't being drugged anymore."

Max scrapes our plates into the bin. Both of us are beyond eating and I feel absolutely drained. First, the revelation of what really happened that night ten years ago, and now this.

"What are you going to do?"

"Call the police myself. Tell them what you've remembered. That Amy was the one who murdered her brother. We've got proof there was a conspiracy to keep you asleep. Because of what you know. You're the only witness."

"But the estate agent said Amy is in New York—"

"That's for them to decide. We can only clear your name." He smiles ruefully. "Of course, I'll be out of a job too. Probably struck off for gross negligence. With its owner in prison, I'm guessing the Hallam Group will be sold for pennies. You know what Americans are like. They'll buy us on the cheap."

Despite everything, I want to tell him that it wasn't his fault, that he's been manipulated. We all have. Amanda Mawdsley got us all where she wanted. Me lying in a coma for the past ten years, for a start. I flash on the dream I had, the one where I was sitting at a table turning over playing cards. The deck was rigged. She knew which card would be played next and in what order. Amy played us all.

"We've still got to get you to a place of safety. She knows you're here. It's not safe."

He fishes his wallet out of the jacket hanging on the back of the door. Finds the detective's business card. It's gone ten o'clock by now.

"Straight to voicemail." Max sighs.

He leaves a message for DCI Horner to call him straight back.

"Do you want me to go to my room?" I ask once he's ended the call.

"Susan, you're not my patient any longer. You've recovered your memory. We've done the work. Here, you can have the bed. I'll sleep on the sofa."

"If you're sure..."

"Listen, I'm very proud of you. I know it hasn't been easy." He sighs. "Especially knowing what we now know. She's put you through hell and I have no idea why."

"You know what I did to her." Even now, I still feel cold shame.

"No, there's more to this..." He taps his index finger against his mouth, thinking. "There is one thing though. I want you to have an MRI scan. First thing tomorrow. Before the police get here. When this does go to court, they'll try and argue you had structural brain damage. She'll hire the best lawyers; I know her. She's ruthless when crossed. As you said, it's still only your word against hers."

Looking at myself in his bathroom mirror, I am bone-crushingly tired. Today has been so much to take in. Rinsing my mouth under the tap, I clean the spare toothbrush Max has given me. My hair is all over the place and my eyes are streaked with chunks of mascara. I look a fright.

Max has laid out a pair of pyjama bottoms and a tee-shirt for me to wear on the bed. Releasing my bra, I give my boobs a good scratch, grateful to be rid of it. That bed looks so inviting and the one thing I want to do is get in.

But I'm still too wired to sleep. Lying there in the dark, everything keeps going around in my mind. So, Amy got out of her wheelchair and pushed Jamie to his death. She was the one who killed him, not me. And for what? So she could run a business she'd been passed over for? But if I was in a coma for ten years, then why not have me quietly put to sleep? Because people would ask questions, that's why. It would be easily traced back to her. Better to have me just where she wanted me, neither alive nor dead. And that suited the police too. Sleeping Beauty in her glass coffin. With their prime suspect fast asleep, there was no need for any investigation.

I am not a murderer.

I deserve to be happy.

Getting out of bed, I wrap myself in Max's dressing gown and find Max still awake in the sitting room. He's sitting at the fold-down dining table, his face bluishly lit behind a laptop screen.

"Max, what are you doing? It's the middle of the night."

"Just writing up what you told me. It's the final chapter in the book. The end." He theatrically mimes typing and then closes the lid. Putting his elbows on the table, he rubs his temples. "You're right. We've got a big day tomorrow."

"You'll get cold. Come to bed."

I lead him back into his own bedroom and we cuddle up together under the warmth of his plump duvet. I don't want sex. I have slept alone in a bed like this for the last ten years and what I long for now is human touch. I just want his arms around me, the feel of another human being.

Bright winter light pierces whatever I was dreaming about. It's the next morning. Max has pulled the curtains back and placed a mug of soothing tea down on the bedside table. I feel as if I've been sandbagged, I slept so deeply. Ironically, it's the best sleep I have had for years. All those dreams of playing cards, all gone. I know the truth now and I am ready to heal.

"What time is it?" I yawn, struggling up.

"It's late. I've already spoken to the police. They're on their way. They want you to give a statement down in London."

"They know that I'm innocent, right?"

"DCI Horner is willing to listen. Of course, I'll support you."

The tea tastes malty, strong and delicious. I am also ravenously hungry. I won't be able to think straight unless I have some food. My insides are gnawing themselves. Happily, Max is in the kitchen buttering toast and Marmite as I wander through, still yawning.

"What are you going to do about Nurse Linh?" I ask as he sets the plate down in front of me.

"She's handed in her notice. Her nursing career is over,

obviously. Being bribed to drug a patient. I don't care what her circumstances were."

"She was here illegally. Amy threatened her with deportation."

"I have asked her to wait until at least the police get here. She needs to give her own statement. It'll help you. In exchange, I will give her a character reference. Despite everything, she was a good nurse. I mean, a dutiful one."

So it's Bunny who takes me for my MRI scan, telling me to leave any metal jewellery in a plastic tray.

"Look here," she says. "I need to apologise. What I read in the papers, saw on TV, I believed it. Everybody in my church did. Doctor Quane told me the truth. About what happened. I feel bad about how I behaved, shame."

She looks really upset and her large brown eyes well with tears. Only I'm not ready to forgive anyone just yet. Right now, what I feel most is anger. Because they stole my memories and now I want them back.

The MRI control room could be a sales office with its desktop PCs and whiteboards. Through the observation window, the doughnut-shaped MRI scanner waits like an alien portal.

"It's going to be noisy," Bunny warns, handing me some foam earplugs, then pulling a mesh balaclava down over my head. It's a creepy facemask, like something a burns victim might wear. I adjust the uncomfortable, sweaty headphones she hands me.

"You can listen to music if you like. Rock, pop or classical."

I choose the pop channel. Bunny leads me towards the actual MRI scanner. I put my feet up on the plastic sled and Bunny gives me a rubber bulb to hold, explaining that it sounds an alarm, which can be difficult to hear over the music and the machinery.

"Anything you feel uncomfortable with, we'll stop," she says.

Settling onto the plastic bed as it slides into the scanner, I'm pretty much deaf and blind inside this machine. My claustrophobia builds until Bunny's voice cuts in through the headset. "The scan will begin in a few minutes."

Suddenly, an ear-splittingly loud pop song comes on. It's a Sixties pop song that I remember Mum listening to on the radio, only it's the Eighties version. Somehow, lying in an MRI scanner in a remote Suffolk psychiatric hospital listening to Kylie Minogue is not how I thought my life would turn out. I call out for Bunny to turn down the song, but nothing happens.

Even through this insanely cheerful music, I can feel the magnetism of the doughnut ring, which makes me feel slightly nauseous. Sweat trickles down the nape of my neck.

Come on, come on, what's taking Bunny so long?

Once the police interview me in London, then this nightmare will be over. A nightmare I have been trying to wake up from for the past ten years. What will I do then? Sell my story, I suppose. Max has the ending to his book now. *How I Solved the Murder of James Mawdsley* by Doctor Max Quane. Start over in a different city under a new name. After all, Susan Gummer is the most infamous coma victim in the world. Then I think about the excited shrieks in a playground and picture myself as a primary school teacher, calling the children inside. That's what I've missed most, the sound of children's laughter.

I cannot stand this Eighties drum machine cacophony a moment longer. Bunny must be able to see me inside the machine. She's on the other side of the control room window. I tap the side of the headphones, to show her something's wrong. All the while, Kylie keeps on singing about how everybody's doing a brand-new dance now and come on baby, do the locomotion. I just wanted her to turn it off.

Suddenly, the bed jolts and begins to slide out again. Thank goodness, she saw me. Then it shudders to a stop, leaving just my head still hidden.

"Bunny?" I call out. "Are you there?"

Suddenly, strong hands grab my throat. They're squeezing the life out of me. Pressing down. Strangling me to death.

Can't breathe.

I frantically pump the alarm. Call for help. Whoever this is has clambered up onto the bed and lies spreadeagled on top of me, pressing down with all their weight. Crushing me to death. I'm spasming, kicking out, anything to get them off me.

...They'll stop now, they'll stop in time, they'll stop now...

My lungs burn as I frantically squeeze that bulb but nothing's happening. I'm blacking out. I can feel my senses leaving me, one by one—can't see, can't hear, can't think. The pressure becomes intolerable. Those strangling fingers bear down even harder, and I'm sinking, being pulled down into an open grave. Everything turning red, then purple, then black—

CHAPTER THIRTY-NINE

The two-tone alarm is loud. Wincingly loud. So loud it even cuts through these headphones and the earplugs.

Eee-eww, Eee-eww.

Suddenly, those hands let go and I turn onto my side, gasping. I'm coughing and retching as deep pain sets in, pain so deep it goes down to my very core.

Whoever's on top of me clambers off. I sense their heavy tread as they hurriedly run out of the room. Can't see. Head still trapped inside this scanner.

Thank God I'm still alive. I want to shout for help, but my vocal cords are so raw. They're on fire. Finally, I sense somebody else run into the room as I lie there, coughing and heaving.

"You all right?" Bunny shouts over the alarm. "What happened? What have they done to you?"

Still can't speak. She's standing over me but I can hardly hear her over this din. It's so loud, it's trilling my eardrums. Then the alarm shuts off as abruptly as it started.

I lie there, heaving. Can't get enough air into my lungs.

It's like they're two rubber sacs that have been sliced through with a scalpel. They won't fill. I'm lying there, wretchedly gasping.

I have never been so thankful to be alive.

"Who was that? Did you see their face?"

Can't speak, coughing too hard. Bunny touches me and my first thought is, it was you, you're the one who did this. It could only have been you. There's only three of us now in this godforsaken clinic, so who else could it have been? I'm picturing her large hands around my throat. Then I think about Hussein, the caretaker. What about him? Could he be the one who's just tried to strangle me?

She helps me up and guides me into the control room. There's an overturned swivel chair on the floor and Bunny rights it. I sit down to get my breathing under control. My kneecaps turn to water as I realise what's just happened.

Somebody tried to kill me.

"I came in and saw that man through the glass," Bunny says. "I sounded the alarm. When he ran out, he pushed me out of the way."

Hence the overturned chair. "What did he look like?" I rasp. My throat is on fire. I'm thinking about Hussein, what do they know about him? Who is he really?

"He was wearing a—" she flutters her fingers, searching for the word. "—a balaclava. Dark clothes."

The only two men in this hospital are Hussein and Doctor Max, and it couldn't be him, could it? Then another thought. Doctor Max is already in Amanda Mawdsley's pay, so why not?

Half an hour later and I am back in Max's office with my hands around another mug of tea. It's strongly laced with soothing honey. The three of us are watching what happened in the MRI scanner on his laptop. The CCTV footage is black-and-white and ghostly but sure enough, Bunny leaves the room and for a few minutes nothing happens until this stranger, this masked face, runs in and clambers on top of me, strangling me to death. Then he's disturbed, runs out, barging my nurse out of his way.

Whoever it is, it's not Hussein. The build is different. My assailant is well built, more like a rugby player or a builder; Hussein is plump and has a slight waddle when he walks. And it's clearly not Max either, it's someone else entirely.

Max and Bunny look down at me with concern, as if each sip will restore me to health.

Bunny has already inspected my throat. There's bruising and red marks where my attacker's fingers gripped but I'll live.

"Better?" asks Max.

I nod gratefully.

It's only now, though, that the shock sets in. My God, I could have died. Somebody wanted to kill me. Of course, it was her, Amy. Or set up by her. The puppet mistress pulling strings from New York.

"I got through to DCI Horner," says Max. "The police are on their way."

"What time are they getting here?" I rasp. My throat is so hoarse, I can only whisper.

"They just said sometime this morning."

"What happens after I give my statement?"

I try clearing my throat. My voice sounds so raw.

"They'll bring you straight back. They want to interview you at Scotland Yard. It's going to be a long round trip, I'm afraid."

Feeling less shaky, all we can do now is wait. It's like Max and I are in a railway station, sitting in armchairs, waiting for the police to get here. You feel as if you should be doing something but really there's nothing to do. Finally, Bunny knocks and puts her head around the door.

"They're here. He's waiting for you downstairs."

The detective standing in the front hall is not DCI Horner, however. He's sent one of his plainclothes officers, who's putting his wallet away as I come down the stairs. The policeman wears a thick jumper, black combat trousers and Doctor Martens boots, while a lanyard peeks out from under his ski jacket. Brown hair, rimless glasses. He's heavily built, easily a match for whoever attacked me this morning. Let them try getting to me now.

"You made good time. I only spoke to your boss a couple of hours ago," Max says, putting his arm around me.

The detective nods but says nothing.

"Take good care of this precious cargo. We want her back in one piece."

The detective gives a toothy grin at this.

Max takes the Met Police officer aside and explains what happened this morning. The detective looks worried and keeps on nodding, glancing concerned at me.

Outside, Hussein waits in the golf buggy to drive us to the quay. Could it have been him, though? I am glad it's not just going to be the two of us on the golf cart. The policeman gets in behind us, facing the other direction. Max and Bunny stand on the front steps between stone pillars like proud parents seeing their daughter off to school.

Our buggy sets off over the bridge and down the long straight road to the quay. It's another cold January morning with a piercingly clear sky.

The clinic launch waits for us below the gantry and Hussein, who's also going to pilot the boat, helps me down into it.

Sunlight ripples in the water like quicksilver as we cast off, and there is the faint screech of gulls. It's a truly beautiful morning.

The detective still doesn't say anything, just smiles encouragingly. I look over the side of the boat at the churning brown water and feel the gentle tug of the launch.

It's only a few minutes across.

The detective's unmarked blue Skoda is parked up on the quay. Dinghies are moored all the way along and you can hear wires tocking against their masts.

The Met Police detective holds his backseat car door open for me and I settle in. It's going to take us more than two hours to drive down to London, so I might as well get comfortable.

We set off through the quaint and charming village of Orford, where you get the sense that nothing bad could ever happen. Handsome redbrick houses and a village square with a bustling farmers' market, an imposing church, in fact, picture-postcard Englishness.

Outside these car windows it's a bright blue winter day. One last good day before the bad weather sets in again. You forget just how beautiful the English countryside can be. Or at least I have. I've been asleep for the past ten years.

We're heading out of Orford back to London when another police car screams past, heading back to the village with its blues and twos going. Thank God. They must have caught him.

"What are they saying on the radio? Have they found someone?"

The detective glances back but says nothing.

We've only been driving for about ten minutes and I'm taking in the thick forest on our left when, surprisingly, we swerve off the main road.

"Where are we going?"

The detective still doesn't answer. I'm getting alarmed. Something doesn't feel right. Our eyes meet in the rear-view mirror and there's something about them I recognise.

I know those eyes.

He might have dyed his hair and be wearing wire-frame spectacles, but the eyes don't change.

He shifts up a gear and I glance down at his fist over the gearstick and glimpse a faded tattoo of a double-headed eagle. That's when I remember.

This same hand.

The night they framed me for murder.

Grabbing my shoulder, stopping me from going anywhere.

CHAPTER FORTY

We're accelerating down a forest track thumping through gutted dirt. The engine protests as Pavel shifts up a gear. The forest outside the car window bounces crazily as we lurch from pothole to pothole.

I'm yanking on the door handle, trying to get out. He's got me prisoner inside this police car. Wait, it's not a police car and he's not a policeman.

"Let me out," I shout over the engine.

Keep trying the door.

Pavel says nothing.

It's locked with the child-lock engaged.

I turn and take one last desperate look out of the back seat at the track we've just come down. He's not taking me back to London at all—we're heading deeper into this forest.

Where he's going to kill me.

It was his hands around my throat this morning. The alarm interrupted him and now he's come back to finish the job. I feel sick with dread as Pavel swings off this remote logging road and pulls up at the entrance to thick forest.

Can't move. Can't think. I sit frozen on that back seat, with a sense of numbing hopelessness.

What if I just don't get out of this car? He can't make me. Then I picture him dragging me out by my hair, giving me a hefty kick to make sure I get the message.

Pavel kills the engine and leans across the passenger seat to open the glove box. He pulls out an ugly black handgun and turns. My whole life zeroes in on the black O of that gun's muzzle pointed straight at me.

I'm a good person, I've never done anything wrong in my life, just one teenage mistake and—

To my surprise, Pavel gets out of the car and locks me in. The passenger safety locks thunk shut. I sit there, rigid with terror, listening to the hydraulic suck of him opening the boot. A moan of fear escapes my lips. The door safety locks click open and he flicks the gun, gesturing for me to get out. What else can I do? I slide across the backseat.

Getting out of his car, standing there in this perfectly still forest, I see what he's lifted out from the trunk.

A spade.

My legs feel strangely disconnected from my body. Going to vomit. Standing beside the car, the dirt clearing rushes up to meet me, yet everything stays exactly where it is.

"You don't have to do this. I won't tell anybody."

For one desperate moment, I look around. Surely there must be someone nearby. A happy family out for a ramble. Some walkers. But there's nobody. There's nothing around us but woods. He gestures with the gun and the message is clear. Get moving. Just the crunch of pine needles underfoot and, overhead, the pitiless blue sky.

Ahead of us, the entrance to the woods gapes like a dark

open mouth. The wind moves through those tree tops and all I can think is, what a humiliating way for me to die.

For a moment, I'm back in the Chester Street kitchen with Pavel's feet up on the table, a toothpick in his mouth while he takes it easy. He liked me once. Well, enough to feel me up. I remember eyeing that knife, wanting to press it against his neck. Too late now. But I can still use that, get him to stop this and—

"Pavel, please. Nobody needs to know I even saw you," I gabble, not making any sense, even to myself.

Pavel smiles slightly, as if he's pleased to have been remembered, despite everything.

"Pavel, why? This is murder. You don't want murder on your hands."

"You kill Mister Jamie. Miss Amy saw you. She wants justice."

"It wasn't me, it was her. For God's sake, you must believe me."

"Too late," he says in his thick accent. "You lie. You always liar."

We've reached the dark entrance and once I enter this forest, there's no coming back. I feel so dizzy that I stop and lean against a grey naked pine trunk. He's going to shoot me in there. Or worse. Pavel takes me by the arm like a waiter showing me to my table and really, I have no choice.

The forest is dense with pine trees. We've only gone a small distance when we come to a patch of open ground and that's when I see it. Why he's brought a spade.

A freshly dug grave.

There must be something I can say, something which could make him stop, but my mind's a complete blank. I picture the two of us from high above. Looking down, there's nobody around for miles. I will kneel and then he'll put the gun to the back of my head. A pistol shot and then I'll topple into his pit. A secret that's dead and buried.

Pavel throws the spade down and then digs something out of his trouser pocket. It's a plastic tie and he orders me to put my hands behind my back. He yanks it hard and the plastic bites into my wrists.

Please don't do this. You don't have to do this.

How many times has he heard somebody say that to him?

Don't.

That's when I hear it. We both do. Somewhere farther off, a man calling for his dog. Thank God, I'm saved. If I just scream loud enough, he'll hear me and—Pavel stops, listening hard. We both stand there, not moving. He puts his finger to his lips. Even the trees seem to hold their breath.

Whoever it was must have moved away because finally, Pavel nods. Orders me to kneel. I do as I'm told, as if being cooperative is somehow going to save me. Already, it's an inevitability. Again, I flash on him putting that gun to the back of my head, a gunshot, the sudden cawing of crows.

Kneeling there, the cold of the gun barrel touches the back of my head and I whimper.

That's when I spot it.

Lying half buried in dead pine needles, a long silver whistle on a necklace. A child's toy. It's beyond just where I can reach it, but if I throw myself forward— "Pavel, I don't feel well."

I launch myself down sideways, landing on the dirt. He's standing behind me, my body shielding the treasure. He can't see it. I slough forward, just enough for my lips to brush the whistle, snaffle it into my mouth and blow with everything I've got—

Only nothing happens.

Realising that I'm up to something, Pavel grabs me by the collar, yanks me back up. Ow, that hurt. The whistle drops from my mouth. Spotting it, Pavel walks around, still holding the gun, and picks it up.

He studies it, grins, then throws it away. With it goes my last bit of hope. He nods for me to drop to my knees.

Pavel grips the gun in both hands, racking the slide with a snap. He stands over me and points the gun at my head. It's almost touching my temple. A tear runs down my cheek. I close my eyes.

Do it. Do it now.

CHAPTER FORTY-ONE

A hefty blur of fur and muscle *whumps* past me, shaking the dirt. Heavy and powerful. It barrels into Pavel, knocking him off-balance. It's a beast—no, a bear. The shaggy monster lands on Pavel and they both topple into the pit.

Scrambling up off my knees, I peer into the pit. The two of them are wrestling in the shallow grave. Only it's not a bear, it's a dog. A monstrous hound, a bull mastiff or something. Its ugly slobber-flecked jaws snap and bite at his face. He's pinned down. Can't move. The dog's got his teeth into him, shaking Pavel like a rag doll. That whistle, it wasn't a toy, it was a dog whistle.

Suddenly, there's a gunshot. The sound explodes inside my head. The hound drops across him, pinning him down. "Please, help me," he begs, nearly crying with pain. He's badly gored. His black jeans are dark with blood. I limp closer, hands tied behind my back, the way you would approach a dangerous animal.

Run.

Just get the hell out of here.

"Please. Need hospital," he croaks.

I turn and stumble away from him. Got to get away. Flee deeper into this forest. Find help.

Branches joggle as I run towards them. If anything, this thicket is getting denser. These trees are an obstacle course I've got to get through. I've no idea where I'm going. All I can hear is the sound of my own ragged, smoking breath. It's wincingly cold.

I lurch towards trees, stumbling head-forward. I don't know even where I'm going, I'm wailing so hard. I zigzag through those pine trees with my hands behind my back, terrified I'm going to brain myself any moment.

There's what looks like a path, and I follow it, glancing back over my shoulder. Can't help it. I trip over something and land on packed frozen mud. Hard. Traffic lights. Red, orange, then green. They talk about seeing stars, and a halo of blue dots literally spins above my head. I scramble up again, jeans torn, taste of dirt and blood in my mouth.

It's more of a sandy path now and the trees are thinning out. Daylight ahead of me. Abruptly, I run out of a treeline and into a field taken up with a half-built housing estate. The houses are just breeze-block squares with scaffolding. But there must be plenty of builders around.

"Help! Somebody help me!"

I can only limp now towards the nearest unfinished house. My calves feel as if they're bleeding. The construction site is strewn with cement mixers and wheelbarrows and piles of sand. There's even a digger. Of course, it's a Saturday and there's nobody around.

Running up a timber plank, I hide in the first house I can get to. Inside, it's dirty and cold and smells of cement. Bare grey walls. Peer over one of those square open windows.

Nobody coming. Just wind stirring the trees. The plastic tie bites into my wrists, cutting off the circulation. My hands are throbbing. Even if I found a weapon, a shovel or a left-behind hammer, I couldn't use it. This breezeblock house is empty.

Instead, I sidle between houses along planks over mud, limping towards the churned-up site exit. The village road stretches up past this newly built housing estate towards what looks like a pub.

The pub, though, is closed when I reach its front door. Hands tied, I bang my head against it with frustration.

They're not open yet.

Wait, lights are on in the back.

There's a side passage beside the redbrick building and I lurch past empty beer bottle crates. Yes, there's a kitchen door open onto the backyard.

"Can I help you?" asks a surprised bar worker as I push my way in through a beaded metal fly screen.

"Please, I need to use your phone."

She can see the state I'm in. A bearded man in chef's whites appears, drying his hands on a tea towel.

"Everything all right?" he asks warily.

"There's a man back there. He tried to kill me." I gulp, turning my back to show them my bound hands.

"Bloody hell," the chef says.

"Steve, call the police," says the woman.

No, not the police. Pavel knew he had to get to me before the police arrived. Max hadn't yet told Amy any of this, unless of course it was Max himself who tipped her off. Mentally, I shake my head. No, I don't want to go there. He wouldn't do that, *would he?* What Amy said, about everybody betraying each other in the end, comes back to me.

Even now, I refuse to believe it. Which means someone close to DCI Horner tipped her off. Or maybe Horner himself did.

First, they try to cut the tie with a pair of kitchen scissors but it's too tough. Then the chef comes back with a Stanley knife. The tie snaps off and I circle my sore wrists as the waitress leads me into the pub saloon. That's when my legs go from beneath me, and I sit down in the empty bar as the full enormity of what's happened sinks in.

It was Pavel who tried to strangle me in the MRI scanner. He still believes I was the one who killed Jamie, not Amy. All these years, she's been dripping her poison into his ear. So why not do me in before now? Because I was safely asleep, that's why. Now I can tell my story.

The chef walks through from the kitchen holding his mobile phone. "They've put me on hold," he mouths.

I want to call somebody but who? The only telephone number I can remember is Mum's and I picture our old-fashioned dial phone standing on its spindly hall table. The woman behind the bar lends me her mobile and Mum answers on the fifth ring.

"Mum, it's me, Susan."

My hands tremble as I hold the iPhone.

"Susan, is that you? Where are you?"

"Mum, I need to come home." Her voice sounds so good and my face is crumbling. Home, the place of comfort and safety. The one place where they can't get to you. "Please, I need to see you."

The chef is wandering around in a tight circle like a dog about to squat down. I tell him to hang up. I'll get a taxi to the nearest police station myself.

"That's in Woodbridge," the waitress tells me.

"This man who did this to you? Do you know him?" the chef asks in a soft Norfolk accent.

Yes, I do. He's another servant in the house where I worked, who thinks I murdered his master. He's been put up to this by his grieving sister. It's complicated.

"Never seen him before," I lie.

"How did you get away? Where is he now?"

"He took me into a forest. The one above the new housing estate. He tied my hands behind my back, but I ran away. A dog attacked him. He's badly hurt."

"How did he kidnap you?"

He pretended to be a policeman and kidnapped me from a secure psychiatric unit on Orford Ness. I'm an escaped mental patient. Like I said, it's complicated.

I'm not sure that telling them I've escaped from a mental hospital, and that they've got the most notorious murder suspect in the world sitting right here in their pub, is going to help.

"I was hitchhiking to London," I say meekly. "He offered me a lift."

"Bloody bastard."

"It's the Suffolk Beast," chirps the barmaid. "That's who it is."

The chef turns on his heels and stalks back into the kitchen, only to reappear with a fearsome-looking meat cleaver.

"Steve, don't," the barmaid calls out but it's too late. He's already gone out the side door.

It takes another half hour for the minicab to turn up outside the pub.

"They're here," she says, looking out the window.

Steve the chef reappears just as I'm putting on my ski jacket. He shakes his head.

"Well, whoever it was has gone. I found that poor dog though. In a grave. He must have shot it at point-blank range. Bloody bastard."

"I told you."

Gratefully, I lever myself into the back of the taxi. My body feels like a side of beef that's been thrown downstairs. Everything hurts. I manage to wave to my new friends watching concerned from the pub doorway. The minicab driver turns and asks me where to.

"Woodbridge Police Station, right?"

"No, Leamington Spa," I tell him.

He rubs his chin. "That's a six-hour round trip, that is."

"Don't worry, I have money."

That's not true. I hope to God that Mum has cash at the other end because I don't have any. We sit there with the engine running while the driver clears the trip with control. The chef and the barmaid stand in the doorway, wondering what's going on. I give them a reassuring wave.

The afternoon sky turns the colour of lead as we drive through the flatlands of Suffolk and then the Cambridgeshire fens. I even manage to close my eyes, I'm so tired. I must have slept for longer than I thought because the next thing I hear is the driver telling me we've arrived.

"Wait here," I tell him, levering myself out of the back-seat. I feel giddy and nauseous. Mum's cul-de-sac has not changed in ten years. Well, maybe it's got shabbier. There's a sagging Land Rover that's being taken apart in next door's driveway and the other bungalows need repainting. I walk up our garden path as the taxi idles and ring on our doorbell.

A figure appears on the other side of the front door through whorled glass.

Mum stands looking myopically up at me. We hug as I cross the threshold. She's so thin under her cardigan. Right now, I have never been so pleased to see anyone in my life.

"Mum, I need money for the taxi."

"We've been so worried," she says, turning and shuffling towards her sitting room. "I'll go and get my handbag."

Who's the we she's talking about?

I follow her in. Our house smells just as I remember it, a particular cloying rose air freshener smell which reminds me of childhood. Home, home and happy to be here. Safe at last.

As I round the corner, there's a man seated on our living room sofa. For a moment, I flinch. Can't help myself. No, it can't be. Pavel couldn't have followed me here. He was bleeding out.

Only it's Doctor Max.

CHAPTER FORTY-TWO

"My God, Susan. I thought I'd never see you again," he says, stepping towards me.

"Max, I don't understand. I mean, how did—"

"I took a guess. You've only ever had one visitor. I phoned your mother, and she said, yes, you'd been—"

He breaks off, overcome by emotion. We both are. He moves around the coffee table, and we embrace fiercely. Neither of us can contain ourselves any longer. He buries his face in my hair as we hold tight, and the warmth in my heart spreads through my body. For a moment, we pull apart and he looks at me questioningly, and yes, I want him to, and then we're kissing deeply.

"It's so good to see you," he says thickly, holding my hair.

I think we're both getting tearful.

"The police arrived shortly after you left. They didn't know anything about this other officer. That's when I realised. They had the car number plate on CCTV. When he parked on the quay. A dog walker found the car in Rendlesham Forest."

"What about Pavel? Is he under arrest?"

Max looks at me blankly.

I tell him that it was Amy's major-domo who kidnapped me in his car, marching me into the forest at gunpoint. Pavel being gored by the dog and then making a run for it. Max listens grimly.

"She told him I was the one who killed Jamie. He believes her. Natural justice, he called it."

"Attempted murder, more like. Twice. We've still got to get you somewhere safe. DCI Horner is waiting for you."

"No, not the police."

"What do you mean?"

"Think about it. How did Pavel know the police were coming for me? You hadn't told Amy. It must be somebody on the inside. Someone tipped them off."

"Surely you don't think that detective's part of it. He's been trying to arrest you for years."

"Not him, no," I concede, "but somebody close to him."

Max grimaces but nods. "Maybe you're right. We really are on our own. Look, he can't have got far. Not if he's as badly hurt as you say. We'll tell the police to watch the hospitals. Anyway, you're the one I'm worried about, not him."

He touches my face again, examining me, and it hurts. I wince as he adjusts my head. Then he prises my lips open with his fingers. Very romantic.

Without speaking, I sit down in Dad's old armchair and push up my right jean leg. My shin is as black as a rotten banana and my leg throbs like a pump.

"That looks bad. I don't like the look of your tooth either. You should go to A&E. I'll tell the police to take you to hospital."

"I told you, no police."

"Where then? We need to get you somewhere safe."

I look at him ruefully. "How about a padded cell in a mental hospital? Even I can't hurt myself in there."

It hurts to try and smile. Mum comes back in shakily holding a tea tray with three mugs on it. Max stands up to take them from her.

"We've got to leave, I'm afraid, Mrs Gummer," he says, handing me a mug of soothing tea.

"But I'm making you lunch. You must have something to eat."

She's right. My stomach is gnawing itself. The last thing I ate was that slice of toast this morning and my thinking's getting woolly, my thoughts spacing further and further apart, I'm so bone tired.

Our little kitchen smells of fried bacon as we sit at our cramped table. Mum brings out a Pyrex dish from the oven and sets it down on the counter. You can see Dad's patch of vegetable garden through our kitchen window, the allotment he was so proud of. Out of the corner of my eye, like an old family snapshot, I can picture him in his vest with his foot on a spade, digging up chard in our garden. I must have been about five years old. Before he walked out.

How many hours did I sit at this very table doing maths homework? Maths was the one subject I was any good at. Once Dad left us for his teenage barmaid, whom Mum called bitterly his fancy woman, I buried myself in maths. Numbers made sense. Answers were binary: yes or no. Maths was as precise as a decimal point, not messy like real life.

Mum takes the lid off and it's bubbling macaroni cheese.

The three of us eat stolidly, not saying much. The pasta

bake tastes unctuous and delicious and I can feel it doing me good with each mouthful.

Mum places her chicken-claw hand over mine and I'm shocked by how many liver spots she has. They weren't there a decade ago. Having a daughter accused of murder, that's taken it out of her too. I'm not the only one Amanda Mawdsley has made a victim of.

Max and I set off on the long drive back to Orford in apprehensive silence. We're past the shortest day of the year by now but it's still dark by four. Staring out of the window, I think about everything I have uncovered. All they need to do is see Amy walking again, that's all. Then they'll know I'm telling the truth.

It's dusk by the time we arrive back in Orford. Max has phoned ahead and Hussein waits for us on the quay with the clinic launch, ready to ferry us back to the island.

"How are you? Everything alright, yeah?" he asks, taking my hand as I step down into the boat.

It's cold out on the estuary tonight and Max and I huddle together for warmth. I lift my head to his and this time we kiss tenderly, without the hunger of before.

"I could be reported to the Royal College of Psychiatrists for this," he says, nuzzling closer.

"I'm not your patient anymore, remember?"

Taking the golf cart over the angular bridge, I never thought I would be pleased to see the Hallam Clinic again.

Hussein drops us off and Max says he won't be needed until morning. There's a keypad beside the front door and Max dabs the entry code. The entrance hall is eerily quiet and our steps ring out on the tessellated floor. It's Bunny's night off, he explains.

"Why don't you go up to the flat? I'll raid the kitchen for

something to eat," Max says. "I don't know about you but I could use a drink. I've got a bottle of whiskey in my office. For medicinal purposes, you understand."

"Sounds good."

"Here, take my pass."

To get to his flat, you have to walk through the staff wing and use the old-fashioned lift, which must date back to when the hotel was first built in the thirties. I pull its concertina gate across and it lurches up to the top floor, where it arrives with a hefty bump. A stiff drink, something to eat, and then an early night sound good to me. Everything hurts. I'm exhausted down to my bone marrow.

I sense it before I feel it.

Something hard and fast coming up behind me. White heat explodes in my head. I pivot on my heels, crashing headlong to the floor.

Darkness rushes up to meet me.

That's the last thing I feel.

CHAPTER FORTY-THREE

Grey shapes moving around, garbled underwater voices. Rising pressure, pushing me upward. My head breaks the surface of the water and I take in one giant gasp of air. Reborn.

Sudden focus.

Only I'm not in water, I'm strapped to a wheelchair. Can't move my arms and legs. They're duct-taped to its frame. Restraints bite into my ankles and wrists.

Thumping, grey pain. An ice pick being hammered into the back of my eyeball with my head trapped in a tightening vice. From when Pavel must have clobbered me.

He stands opposite me now, propped up on a crutch.

We're back in Max's office and the doorway to his bathroom is wide open. That murder board is still up on the wall, all those newspaper clippings, photographs and bits of red string figuring out who the murderer was.

She's sitting right in front of me.

Amy.

And I'm the one who's trapped inside a wheelchair, not her.

Amy is behind Max's desk tapping away intently at the keyboard. It's the first time I have seen her in ten years. She's aged since our last encounter, the night it happened. Then again, we both have. Her features are plainer and blunter than I remember.

My throat is parched and I feel as if I've got the most dreadful hangover. The room is still revolving in figures of eight from when Pavel hit me. Going to vomit.

Then I think about Max. What have they done to him?

"How did you know? About what I remember?" I croak.

Amy gestures towards the discreet CCTV bulb up in one corner. Of course. You're watched everywhere in this place. She must have been watching us the whole time.

"They have microphones too," she says, reading my thoughts.

The room throbs and I think I'm going to be sick. The vice trapping my head gets another turn.

"There. All done," Amy says, tapping the keyboard with a theatrical flourish. "Everything deleted. All your records gone. Nobody will ever know what you remembered."

"I will," I grunt.

Amy looks thoughtful and puts her index finger to her lips, tapping her mouth.

"I don't think so."

She stands up and moves with the exaggerated ease of somebody who knows they're the one in charge. That ugly handgun Pavel used to butcher the dog sits on the desk.

"Where's Max?"

She ignores that. Instead she says, "You know, I liked you

more when you were in a coma. I didn't want any of this to happen. It was a shame you ever woke up."

"Why, Amy? Why did you hate your brother so much? He was right, wasn't he? You did kill your father."

Pavel looks surprised. This is news to him. He frowns, digesting this new piece of information.

"She killed Mister Mawdsley, Pavel," I spit. "That's what Jamie found out. She's the one who murdered her brother, not me."

That handgun is still temptingly on the desk. Is he going to take the bait, turn it on her?

"She's lying, Pavel," counters Amy. "You were there that night. You saw what happened."

"Pavel, think," I say. "You never saw me push Jamie down those stairs, did you? It was her."

Amy picks the gun up off the desk before Pavel can reach it. "She's lying, Pavel. Just do what we agreed."

She nods at Pavel, who lurches forward. A frill of fear runs through me. He's limping badly. He must have really hurt his leg.

Pavel grips the handlebars at the back of my wheelchair, kicking off the brake. Where are they taking me? For the first time, I feel truly afraid. What did she mean when she said I wouldn't remember? Are they going to put me back into a coma?

Not that, anything but that.

Pavel wheels me out into the corridor and we turn left towards the treatment rooms. It's where they do physio-therapy and hydrotherapy. That morning when Bunny first did my physio seems a long time ago. Pavel breathes hard as we navigate the maze of hospital corridors. I sense Amy following us close behind, that gun pointed at me.

"Where are we going? What are you doing?" I can't keep the fear out of my voice.

"You know, Susan, the words operating theatre come from the days when the public paid to watch operations. It was a spectacle. Do you remember that puppet theatre you found? The one at the back of the cupboard? Well, I'm afraid our little play has come to an end. It's time to put the puppets away."

Pavel rolls me to a stop outside a door I have never seen before. Opens it.

Max stands waiting for us in a bare treatment room. He's wearing his white doctor's coat again. I'm so relieved to see him, I want to cry out but he gives a slight shake of his head.

There's a gurney with a television monitor on a stand and a trolley parked beside them with medical instruments. Racked machines that look like Hi-Fi amplifiers. This room has an odd coppery smell, and it takes a moment before I realise what it is. It's the smell of fear.

Amy takes her seat through the observation glass, as if she's about to watch a play, just as she said.

The trolley with the machine on it and the gurney with restraints remind me of something. Then it comes to me. This is like one of those prison death chambers where they execute prisoners by lethal injection. No, they couldn't do that to me. Could they?

Then it dawns on me what this place really is. This is the ECT room where they used to give patients shock treatment. Inducing epilepsy. Shocking their brains with volts of electricity. Erasing their minds.

Max picks up a sealed paper package from the trolley. Rips it open. It's a plastic hypodermic syringe.

Max, no, don't do this to me. She says jump and I ask how high? That's what he said.

Pavel steps forward and takes a scalpel from the instrument tray. All I can do is sit in mute terror as he slices through the duct tape. The bodyguard helps me out of the wheelchair like I'm one of the care home patients I used to help into bed. Once again, I can only do as I'm told. There must be somebody who can stop this, I think wildly, as he manhandles me onto the gurney, holding me down.

Behind him, Max fills the hypodermic from a clear vial, taps the barrel. A dark bubble of horror wells up inside me. He stands over me as I take one last look at the ceiling with its clinical white light. The pain in his eyes tells me how sorry he is.

Max, don't do this. You don't have to do this. Please, Max, I'm begging you.

That word again.

Don't.

Pavel pins me down harder. Presses down with all his weight. I can smell his breath. Can't move. I'm wresting my head from side to side. Stop, stop.

"Okay, Susan. I'm going to inject you with this anaesthetic, and you won't feel a thing. Just a little poke."

"Amy, I won't say a word," I cry out. "I'll tell you everything I remember."

"You've got it the wrong way round," Amy interrupts over the intercom. "I don't want you to remember, I want you to forget."

CHAPTER FORTY-FOUR

A tear runs down my cheek as Max bends over me. Whimper of fear.

I am going to be imprisoned in this place forever, a forgotten patient, one of those old women you see shuffling along a hospital corridor with their head bowed, licking their lips.

Suddenly, Max punches Pavel in the throat. What's he doing? The bodyguard clutches his neck and crashes backward over the TV monitor. Sends it flying. His head smacks the floor.

Max grabs my hand, wrenching me off the gurney. Out of the corner of my eye, I glimpse Amy banging on the observation window, silently shouting. Pavel lies on the floor with his legs cycling, as if he's in an uphill bicycle race. Then he stops. The syringe sticks out of his neck at a madly inappropriate angle.

Everything goes into slow motion as we lurch for the door. The room throbs as Max busts our way out into the hospital corridor. The weird thing is that all this is happening in slow motion, yet the sound is going on in real time.

"This way," barks Max, dragging me along.

We're both fleeing down this clinic corridor. Pounding heart. My ears, a high-pitched hum. Spotting the square red fire alarm halfway along the corridor, I tell Max to stop and, understanding, he smashes the glass with his elbow. Immediately, the two-tone alarm whoops, trilling our eardrums.

Suddenly, a figure appears at the far end.

It's her.

The hospital corridor is canted and, in my delirium, seems to stretch further and further away from us. She's waving the gun, then spots us. Oh God, she's going to kill me. I stand there, rigid with terror, a deer frozen in headlights, as she takes aim with both hands. But Max yanks me along, pulling up short beside an opaque glass fire exit, bangs down its lever. We push our way outside into the biting cold.

We're back in the ornamental garden where those photographers first ambushed me. Only it's pitch black now as we grope past garden furniture. Can't see where I'm going. Suddenly, I bang my shin on a low brick wall and tadpoles of pain swim before my eyes.

Max takes my hand and we stumble over grass towards the main entrance. It's so hard to see anything. Down the drive towards the security gates. Only when we get there, they're locked. My fingers curl around the diamond-link fencing in frustration. She's coming after us. There's no way out. It's Max who gropes for the post with the security keypad. The gate swings open and we hobble over the cattle grid, careful not to break an ankle.

She's stalking us, hunting us down.

Now we're running up the articulated bridge away from

the clinic and already I'm getting a stitch. Wincing pain in my rib. We're just coming down the other side when my calf snaps like the fan belt going on a car. I yelp and pull up short. The pain is excruciating. Hissing through my teeth, I bend over, trying to get my breath back. Can't go any further.

"Leave me," I pant. "It's me she wants, not you."

"Come on, we've got to get to the beach."

"Why not the quay?" I ask, heaving. It hurts even to breathe.

"There's nobody there. Everyone goes home at night. There's that boat on the shore, remember?"

I nod, too winded to say anything else. Max takes my hand again, drags me along. There must be moonlight because I can see something. We're running up the track through desolate flatness. On our left is the ebony-black building like a windmill without sweeps; on our right, the eerie bomb pagodas silhouetted in the distance.

Max pulls me off the track and now we're scrambling over a moonscape of shingle. Haven't got the stamina. Can't do this. The shingle slopes down now and we're half jogging, half ploughing through pebbles towards the sea. The rowing boat is still there, dragged halfway up the beach.

Then comes an ominous roll of thunder. The first fat raindrops hit my face. Then the heavens really open up. We're getting drenched. Max tries to heave the rowing boat down the shingle. Only it's no good, won't shift. "We'll need oars," I shout into the wind. "Stay here."

I scramble back up the shingle, wincing with pain, towards the abandoned hut we found that afternoon. Its rotten door is still unlocked, and it sticks as I push it wider. The musty smell hits my nostrils. I feel blindly for oars propped up anywhere. Nothing. What I do find on the bench is the iron spike Max told me not to touch, the one he said would give me tetanus. Maybe there's something we could use in that locked box on the boat. A flare gun. All boats have flare guns, don't they? We could signal for help.

Jumping back down through the screed, I stagger back towards Max once I'm back on the flat. Out at sea, there's a terrific fork of lightning and moments later thunder like the sky being ripped apart.

"Here, use this," I shout over the gale. Icy rain is coming down hard now, plastering my hair, sluicing us both. Max grabs the spike and slides it through the hawser. We're on the starboard side of the boat, facing the beach.

"It's no good," he shouts. "Won't budge."

He climbs into the rowing boat and leans down with everything he's got, willing the lock to snap. *Please, just give us one bit of luck, one good thing.*

There's a crack of a pistol and Max spins, toppling backward off the side of the boat. One moment he's there, then he's gone.

My God, she's shot him.

It takes a moment for me to realise what's happened, and then I drop to the ground. Max has landed on his back in the shingle. I crawl towards him and now we're both cowering behind the boat. Amy is out there somewhere, hunting us down.

"Save yourself," Max grunts. His breathing doesn't sound right. It's like a broken pump. "Leave me."

I think he's crying. Even in this rain I can feel his shoulder is bloody. Blood feels different to water. I am not leaving him here, though. Instead, I try grasping him under the armpits and dragging him up the beach. Only he's far too heavy.

"Max, you can't stay here. You've got to get up. Remember what you said? About teenagers in the bunkers? We'll be dry in there."

Max does hobble up and I put my arm around his shoulder. Now we're like contestants in an awkward three-legged race. Any moment, I'm expecting to be shot. Supporting Max takes everything I have. My knees and arms burn. Slowly, painfully, we drag ourselves up the shingle to the start of the chain-link fence.

There's another flash of lighting—closer this time—clearly showing a patch of fence that's been ripped through. There's just enough space for us both to crawl under.

Max goes first and I hate having to make him do this. He's in such pain. The stones hurt my elbows and knees as I crawl after him.

We're only about fifty feet away from the bomb-testing pagoda when I hear Amy's voice. She's shouting something but it's lost in the storm. *Don't listen to her. All you have to do is put one foot in front of another. That's all you have to do, Susan. You can do that, can't you? But what are you going to do if there's nowhere to hide? What will you do then?*

The black square of the first bunker is even darker than the night. It glowers over us. I un-shoulder Max, leaving him propped up against an outside wall. Another lightning flash. Right overhead this time. I can't help but touch his shoulder again and this time he cries with pain. I can still feel his blood even in this downpour. He's bleeding out. I feel so helpless but there's nothing I can do for him.

The iron bomb shelter door is heavy, but it does give a little as I strain with both hands. Thank God it's unlocked. I heave it wider, my arms being wrenched out of their sockets.

Finally, there's just enough room for us both to squeeze through.

This place has a damp, cobwebby feel and the brickwork crumbles as I brush it with my fingers. My hand gropes along the wall for a light switch and, to my relief, the lights do switch on.

The dark corridor is strung with wartime green overhead lamps. Some of the lights have fused and there are puddles and rubbish underfoot. Dripping water runs down the walls. Smell of staleness and decay.

Putting my arm around Max again, I pull him along. There's a much larger warehouse beyond this entrance corridor. Its once-white walls are infected with greenish mould, mysterious electrical cabling looped along them. The open roof is a rusty armature of metal that looks as though it could collapse any moment. Vegetation is pulling this abandoned building back down into the earth.

There's some sort of glassed-in office that looks down over the warehouse. The kind you see in a factory. You get to it up a step ladder. We could barricade ourselves in there. It must have a phone.

I decide to climb the ladder first, hauling Max up with me. The rungs of the ladder are so cold, my fingers stick to them. I try pulling Max up but he's so heavy, a dead weight. "Max, you've got to help me," I plead. Rung by rung, with Max using his good arm, the two of us heave ourselves up. It's hard going, and he's wrenching my arm out of its socket, but we're getting there. Rubber cables and electricity wires run down the wall behind the ladder. "Danger! High voltage!" reads the sign. There's a moment when I feel Max slipping but no, I've got him.

Finally, we make it to the top and heave ourselves onto

the platform, gasping. The office door bangs open as I haul Max inside, steering him into a wheeled chair.

We're in a control room. Only it's very old-fashioned. The control panel has knobs and meters, the kind which pulse with a needle. Behind us a wall is racked with computer equipment, only they look like hi-fi separates. Everything is covered in dust and probably hasn't been switched on in years. This whole place feels like a time capsule from the Cold War.

"There must be a phone in this place," I say. "We can call for help."

Looking down into the warehouse, I see now that it's dominated by what looks like a circular amphitheatre. A metal arm stands in the middle of it like a clock with one hand.

"I think it's a centrifuge," gasps Max, reading my mind. "They strapped payloads to it and spun them round."

That's when I hear it.

At first, I don't understand where it's coming from and I shush Max with my hand. Then he hears it too. We look at each other in astonishment.

The sound of a ringing telephone.

CHAPTER FORTY-FIVE

Where's it coming from?

Looking down through the control room glass, it takes a moment for me to spot it.

An old-fashioned wall phone on the far side of this centrifuge wall. The kind of heavy Bakelite phone they used during the war. My ears strain listening to it ring. If there's a phone, that means we can call for help.

Max and I look at each other, both thinking the same thing.

"Barricade yourself in. Put a chair under the door."

The telephone bell gets more insistent in the empty warehouse as I clamber back down. One slip on these slick rungs and I could break my neck. I jump down the last few feet onto packed dirt.

Keep ringing, keep ringing.

The wall phone is on the far side of the circular amphitheatre, which is dominated by an iron pole like something used to train for jousting. On its end, an ugly mace.

The horizontal pole stands at chest height and I have to duck under it to answer the ringing telephone.

Only when I get to it, the black telephone has no dial. Incoming calls only. There's no way to call out.

"Hello," I say, nearly dropping the heavy Bakelite receiver in my panic. Its cord is a twisted War Office braid. There's nobody on the other end. Just static and atmospheric pops and squeaks.

"Hello? Hello?"

I even frantically jab those cradle buttons, as if that's going to make any difference.

Shit.

Turning, I see Amy standing at the coliseum entrance. She's holding her mobile phone against her ear and pointing Pavel's gun in the other. She's drenched too. Her black hair hangs down over her face making her look like a wraith in one of those Japanese horror movies we used to watch together.

"I never wanted any of this to happen," she calls out. "This is all your fault. You should have stayed asleep."

"Amy, please. We've got to get Max to hospital. Too many people know. It's over."

Will she realise that I'm bluffing? Nobody knows where we are now—Max never telephoned I'd been found, and that was all my fault. I was the one who told him not to.

"Jamie never loved you, not really. I did it for you, Susan. He would have got bored of you like he did the others."

"How much blood do you have on your hands? Your father, your brother..." I'm about to say her mother too but stop myself, "...and for what, money? How many houses can you have? How much food can you eat?"

"You're the guilty one, not me. You left me a cripple the

moment it suited you. Do you think that's what this is about? Inheriting the business?"

She sounds almost offended.

"This is where it stops, Amy."

The jousting pole starts up, slowly rotating. Glancing up, I glimpse Max in the control room, through the glass, dimly lit by instrumentation. He's trying to ward Amy away from me, stop her from getting any closer. There's the hum of machinery and a deep *whomp, whomp, whomp* as the arm picks up speed.

It's like a single helicopter rotor. There's just enough space between its mace and the wall to stop yourself from getting brained. If you breathe in, that is. One touch would be like being whacked with a baseball bat. Enough to separate your head from your shoulders.

Amy's thinking the same thing and she's edging around the wall on the other side. One clear shot, that's all she needs. Only the spinning arm won't let her.

Thump, thump, thump.

This whole room is shaking now, as if the rotor arm is wresting itself loose. Its murderous rotor moves the air, faster and faster. It's spinning so fast, it's becoming a blur.

Keep away from that mace.

Thwup, thwup, thwup.

It's like the wall of death I saw once at a fairground, motorbikes scaling a drum going round and around, faster and faster.

She's at twelve o'clock now and I'm at six o'clock and if I can just keep edging along this wall, keep my back to it, then I could throw myself through the exit.

A police siren starts up outside, getting nearer. Of course, the alarm Max sounded. Back at the clinic. Amy hears it too. For a moment, she's distracted. She tries to take aim but can't raise her arm high enough. She's trapped just like I am, the two of us circling each other.

I press myself deeper into this wall as I edge along, its rough concrete scraping the back of my head. So close now. Nearly there and—

Finally, my fingers curl around the doorframe and I throw myself onto the muddy floor, scrambling away on all fours.

When I open my eyes, yes, I've cleared the entrance— just about—and stagger up, not daring to look back. Blue lights flash on the warehouse walls. The police are here. Thank God. We're saved. *Only what if they're still in on it*, my high-pitched other voice shrieks hysterically like a cornered rat. What if they haven't come to save us at all, but to make sure Amy gets the job done?

Then, a dreadful scream—of anger? of fear? I will never know—and a sound like a meat cleaver going through a joint of beef.

Thunk.

Amy is thrown against the wall—the mace must have clipped her—and, glancing back, I see her slide back down, as if bandy-legged drunk. She's lying on the coliseum floor like a heap of old clothes.

Behind me, the metal arm is slowing down and the *thwup, thwup, thwup* of its spins is getting longer. The blue lights blind me as I lurch towards them, hanging onto the wall for dear life.

Outside it's still pelting down. A police car has pulled up outside with stabbing emergency lights. They must have come across on the landing craft. Squawk of police radios. A bulky police officer dressed in black gets out, aiming a gun straight at me.

"Armed police. On the ground. Now."

What are they doing? It's not me they want, it's her.

Instinctively, I raise my hands in the driving rain. A policewoman gets out the other side, digging into her belt for handcuffs.

My God, they're going to arrest me, not her.

"You've got the wrong person. She's inside. She tried to kill us."

The policewoman marches forward and roughly grabs me. I am so incredulous, I even allow her to pinion my arms behind my back. Suddenly, I flash on being back in that forest, my arms tied, about to be shot. It's the same thing now. Resisting arrest, I struggle until those handcuffs clamp around my wrists, biting hard. She throws me down across the car bonnet. Taste of metal.

Finally, DCI Horner, the detective who first questioned me all those years ago, gets out of the squad car. His face is half lit up with strobing blue light.

"Susan Gummer," he says. "I am arresting you for the murder of James Mawdsley."

"I'm telling you, you've got the wrong person."

The policewoman puts her hand on my shoulder and frogmarches me towards the car. Suddenly, I can't do this. This is all wrong, it's not right. She's the guilty one, not me. I mulishly refuse to go any further.

"Don't make things worse for yourself," the policewoman hisses.

Horner is reading me my rights, telling me I don't have to say anything but it may harm my defence if I don't tell them things used later in court. I'm not listening. It's her they want, not me. How can they be so blind?

They guide me into the rear of the vehicle, as if somehow banging my head is worse than being arrested for murder.

Sitting there in the back of the police car, I can't believe this is happening. This is a nightmare I want to wake up from but can't. The handcuffs dig into my wrists. All I can do is thump my forehead against the passenger seat headrest in frustration.

Stupid, stupid, stupid.

Glimpsing myself in the rear-view mirror, I see my face is dark as blood.

CHAPTER FORTY-SIX

It's my birthday today. The wrapped present with its florid bow sits on the table next to me. Not that I imagined spending my thirty-sixth birthday in this place. On remand in prison.

The woman sitting beside me, Charmaine, is a sad, obese prisoner who's in here for manslaughter. Her tattooed arms covered with drawings of the child she will never see again. Of course, Charmaine says she's innocent. We all are, in here.

We're sitting together in the library while I give her a maths lesson. She needs help with her Entry Level Maths exam. When the prison governor told me we could use the library for our lessons, I was only too happy to say yes.

This library, with its shelves of yellowed, mouldering paperbacks all bloated with damp, is the one place I feel safe. My refuge. It's all around us, the simmering threat of violence. The iron cacophony of clanging prison doors. Cooped up with another woman in our narrow Victorian prison cell twenty-three hours a day. "Okay, Charmaine, today's lesson is going to be about a very special number called pi."

I put pencil to paper and draw a circle.

"Pi is a number that helps us understand circles better. But here's the interesting thing, the digits of pi go on forever..."

What I don't tell her is that often I lie in my iron bunk at night, calculating pi in my head. It's a way to avoid thinking about what's going to happen. Because next week, I go on trial for murder.

I picture myself sitting there, in the dock with its unscalable glass walls, watching Amy give evidence. Yes, she will say, I got myself mended *after* Jamie's murder, not before. Ten years spent seeing the best consultants in New York, waiting for Susan to come out of her coma. Waiting for her to tell us the truth, to admit her guilt.

You see, Max died in the ambulance on the way to hospital. He never got to tell the police I was innocent. From her own hospital bed, Amy told them it was *me* who shot him after confessing to them that, yes, I was the one who murdered her brother. Having confessed, apparently, I needed to get rid of them both.

According to Amy, *I chased them* across the beach to the weapons-testing bunkers, where she dragged Max to safety. She was the one who set off the clinic alarm. But she was knocked unconscious by the spinning centrifuge.

Whom will the jury believe? In the end, it will come down to my word against hers. It always has done.

Or will it?

That's when I feel them, watching us. Standing in the doorway. Fagan, the butch prisoner who runs this wing and her ratty girlfriend, Scarry.

For a moment, I flash on Amy leaning insouciantly against another doorway, at school. I was teaching maths then too. Nothing really changes, does it? "What you doing?" Fagan asks.

She's got big, frosted hair like the lead singer in a heavy metal band and an ugly square jaw. She looks like Frankenstein crossed with Bonnie Tyler.

"I'm explaining pi."

"What, like an apple pie?"

Scarry hur-hurs at this, making a sound like a car that won't start. Fagan moves closer and I feel Charmaine tense up. We both do. I nervously finger the logo of my grey tracksuit bottoms.

"A little bird tells me you've been to see the governor. Is that who you are, Gummer? A pidge? Telling the governor what goes on in my wing?" Fagan tears off the page we've just been working on. She idly folds the paper in half. "Because if I hear you've been snitching, I'll fold you like this piece of paper."

Suddenly, she grabs me in a headlock, her beefy arm around my throat. She's squeezing me hard. Can't breathe. Blood roars in my head as she pulls harder. She grabs the pencil from the table and holds it up close, its point dangerously near the white of my eyeball. It's easy to imagine the tip pressing down, a slight resistance, then a soft pop as it bursts through.

"It's my last day in here," I croak. "You won't see me again, promise. I get moved tomorrow."

That's how the prison officer finds us. Walker, the one prison warder who's been kind to me, puts her head around the door. Fagan lets go and I slump forward, gasping and heaving.

"Everything alright?" Walker asks suspiciously.

"Just having a laugh," Fagan says as I sit there, coughing my lungs out.

"They're ready for you," Walker says, ignoring her. She hands over a hi-vis jacket for me to wear. Fagan and Scarry can only watch as Charmaine packs away the maths things. "Here, I'll take that," says Walker.

Out on the gantry, some of the other women nod as I walk past. A sullen addict with spider arms and a face that's been caved in from drugs mouths "cow" at me. But I ignore her and meekly follow the prison officer, holding the present to my chest like a prim pony-tailed schoolgirl.

The visitor room is in B Wing and there's an interminable unlocking and locking of gates. I've become used to bowing my head, waiting for permission to enter.

Prison officers mill around the far end of the visitor room, trying to give us prisoners some privacy. There's always a lot of crying in here, despite the air of forced jollity. You're always desperately aware of the clock ticking down.

The visitors, mostly other women, wait at little clover-leaf-shaped tables like ones you find in primary school. Any children are quiet, cowed by where they are. A few men also sit waiting and one of them nods, recognising me, but I ignore him.

Because she's here.

Sitting at the table over there.

"I suppose you've come to gloat," I say, taking my seat.

Amy says, "You're the one who invited me."

"You look well."

She does look well. Her hair is expensively cut with subtle highlights and her complexion—nourished with the most expensive skin creams, tweakments and facials—is positively glowing. At one point, looking at each other was like facing a mirror. Not any longer.

"Oh, I've got a present for you," I remember, pushing the gift-wrapped package across.

"For me?"

Amy looks suspicious but it's only what looks like a paper-wrapped book. It sits on the table between us. She glances at her Cartier watch. "I haven't got long," she says. "Whatever it is you wanted to tell me, you'd better make it quick."

"For the longest time, I needed your forgiveness. That's why I came to work for you. To be your carer. Because of what I did. I needed you to forgive me."

Amy begins to say something, but I raise my hand.

"Let me finish. You were wrong when you said I was the one who caused your accident. But what I did, not calling for help, yes, that was unforgivable. Maybe this place—" I look around "—is a kind of penance. So I wanted to thank you."

"Thank me?" Amy blinks.

I can see her thinking, *I pushed your fiancé over a balcony, framed you for murder, and now you're thanking me?*

"You get a lot of time to think in this place. Now I realise that I am the one who needs to forgive you."

"Forgive me?" Amy repeats.

"For what you did. My trial starts next week. Maybe I did deserve to be punished. But I still need to know why. I need to understand."

Amy humphs and crosses her arms.

"I see what you're doing. You're recording this, aren't you?"

"Look, no wire," I say, yanking my sweatshirt up. A prison officer calls out there's to be no touching.

"It's just you and me, Amy. Please, I don't understand."

"I don't care if you don't understand. I just wanted to hurt you. You left me for dead in that swimming pool. Of course it was you. Who else could it have been? Did you really think you were going to stop me? That I would never walk again?" She sounds incredulous. "I spent seven years seeing the best consultants in America. I can't tell you the agony I went through. The number of operations I had. Breaking my vertebrae and then resetting them. Painstakingly mending my spine. The only thing that kept me going was the thought of you, my hatred of you. You needed to suffer, just as I did."

"But why, Amy? You had all the money in the world. Plenty of people are disabled. How much food can you eat? How many toys can you have?"

"Is that what you think this is about, money?" She looks affronted. "That I killed Daddy and Jamie because poor little rich girl couldn't get what she wanted?"

She pulls a sad clown face and then mimes crying with her balled fists. Suddenly, she leans forward.

"You really want to know the truth? I'll tell you the truth." What she's about to say has been pent up. It's something she's been saving to tell me for years. "It was all about Daddy. It's always been about Daddy. I must have been about eleven when it began. He used to come into my room and sit on my bed. Often, he'd be drunk. Tell me how much he loved me. Then he'd touch my leg... You can imagine the rest. Eventually, I told him that if he ever touched me again, I would kill him."

I think I'm going to be sick. To think that I revered this

man, even thought of him as my father. And all the while, he was nothing but a—

My mouth goes quite dry. "Did he, I mean—"

Amy shakes her head. "Not until later. I told Mummy on a skiing holiday when I was fifteen. Told her what Daddy had done to me. She wouldn't believe me. We had a terrible row. She skied off, distraught. She was so upset, she lost her balance. Collided with that tree. That's why I felt so guilty. Because if it hadn't been for me, she would still be alive today."

I've gone quite cold as she tells me this. It's all come too late. Why is she telling me this now? All of this could have been undone, could have been stopped—

"You should have gone to the police."

"Who would they believe, the business tycoon, the friend of presidents and prime ministers, or his teenage daughter, who'd already been sectioned?"

"You could have told your brother."

"Jamie?" She almost spits his name. "He was just as bad. He did nothing. I did tell him, when we were on holiday together in France. You were there too. He wouldn't believe me. Wouldn't believe that this man, his beloved father, was nothing but a child rapist."

"Oh my God."

I put my hand to my mouth, I'm so shocked.

"Then I realised nobody was going to do anything. I had to take things into my own hands."

"And then the accident happened," I say, completing her sentence.

"Yes, that's when the accident happened. Once I was trapped at home, there was no escape. He started coming into my room again. Clamped his hand over my mouth when he did it. Told me I belonged to him now. Then it came to me." Her voice gets dreamy. "We never finished playing the game. I would make Jamie fall in love with you and then, just when you were at your happiest, I would destroy you. Take everything away. Just as you had done to me."

Her eyes have gone quite black, and her voice is far away, as if she's in some kind of hypnotic trance. Whoever this is, it is not Amy.

"But Jamie found out the truth about you learning to walk again." I hardly dare ask, "Did you plan to have that taxi run me over?"

She snaps back from wherever she went to. "No, that was an accident. At first, I thought the police would ask questions. Then I realised this was even better. The police had their scapegoat. You were just where I wanted you to be —poised between life and death."

"Only I woke up."

"Yes, that was unfortunate."

She sits back, satisfied. Maybe this has been some kind of catharsis for her too. Then she remembers the present on the table, reaches forward, greedily. Suddenly, I don't want her to open it.

"No, Amy, wait—"

Too late.

She slides her finger under the Sellotaped wrapping, lifts out the book and stares at it. A handsome author photograph of Doctor Max looks back from the dust jacket. Amy goes quite pale as she realises what this means.

My solicitor brought me the hardback yesterday. The publisher wants to rush the book out before the trial. Max's case notes and my recovered memories, side by side, just as we talked about, right up to the moment when Amy shoved her brother over that balcony. Yes, it's all there in print. Her guilt, my innocence. My final memory. Funny, they call these early copies a proof.

Amy looks appalled as she clutches the hardback. The plainclothes police officers sitting all around us stand up as one. DCI Horner peels himself away from the wall and walks towards us. Amy tries to stand but DCI Horner pushes her back down.

I put my hand out to stop him. "No, wait. You don't understand."

"Amanda Mawdsley, I am arresting you for the murder of your brother, James Mawdsley."

Oh my God, I've got it all wrong. All this time, I've been wrong about everything.

CHAPTER FORTY-SEVEN

It's the last good day of summer. That first week of September when England is so beautiful, it catches at the back of your throat.

The white open boat is waiting beside the wooden jetty. Hussein helps me down and it appears I am the only passenger this morning.

"Hello. How are you? Everything alright, yeah?"

"It's good to see you too, Hussein. How are things?"

They released me from prison nine months ago. The irony is that I did end up back in my childhood bedroom, not having anywhere else to go. Except this time the phone constantly rang in Mum's hall—badgering reporters, news programmes wanting interviews, publishers making offers for me to write my own book. The true version of what really happened.

Now I just want to forget. Strange for someone who was so desperate to remember. Not that I am bitter. I just feel regret for all the things I haven't done, all those experiences I never had. Maybe I'll have to change my name and start again in a different town. It's difficult when everyone knows you as the Sleeping Beauty Killer. I don't want that on my headstone.

The boat casts off from the jetty and we chug across the short grey stretch of water. Back to the islet. Like the ferryman crossing the river Styx, except Hussein carries the living across to the dead. A breeze picks up, ruffling the water, and I pull my parka tighter, a reminder that winter is coming. The ferryman takes my hand and helps me up onto the opposite jetty.

"Last boat leaves at five," he reminds me.

"Don't worry, I'll be back well before then."

Then the long walk along the track that runs the span of the islet. Bullrushes on my left stir in the breeze, whispering names. All those who have gone. Mr Mawdsley, dead of an overdose. Goodbye, Jamie. I loved you so much. And then poor Max.

On my right is another path that leads down to the sea, past the abandoned weapons-testing shelters choked with vegetation, sinking back into nature. Those strange ebony-black lookout posts as alien as tripod robots. Then the shingle where Max and I fled along the beach, Max toppling backward off the side of the boat, and the crack of a handgun, scrambling up the shingle, weeping with fear.

Don't think about that.

You never want to think about that.

The clinic appears over the next rise, the incongruous Art Deco building with its tiered balconies and portholes, as if an ocean liner from the golden age of transatlantic travel has drydocked on the island.

I take the lonely path right up to the front door. If anything, the clinic is in an even worse state than I remember. Its stucco is peeling, and gangrenous moss has crawled up the columns beside the front entrance.

It's Birgita who answers the door, Nurse Bunny. The American deal went through with the Hallam Group being bought on the cheap, leaving Nurse Bunny in charge of just one patient.

"Look here, you shouldn't have come," she says. "I'm surprised they gave you permission."

"I have a letter."

She unfolds the handed-over letter with its NHS letterhead and studies it. To be honest, I am surprised they gave me permission too. It was my lawyer who told me, forwarding the sealed handwritten note he'd received. That note burned a hole in my pocket all day long because I was too afraid to open it. Because I recognised her handwriting.

What did she want? Why had she written to me?

Unhappily satisfied, Bunny hands back the letter. She reluctantly gives way and I step into the hall with its familiar institutional smells. Walking back through these corridors, I can see everything has changed yet nothing has. Last time I was here, Max and I were fleeing for our lives. His ex-wife and daughter refused to speak to me at his funeral, as if it was all my fault.

"There's to be no camera or mobile, no recording equipment of any kind. Do you understand?"

"I won't cause any trouble, I promise. She was the one who asked to see me."

Amy never said one word during her trial. She never repeated what she told me in that prison visitor room. Instead, she sat flanked in the dock by two women police officers, protected behind thick sheets of toughened glass. A lattice of florescent squares in the Old Bailey ceiling. The drop-down seats with their green cloth covers.

For days we listened to a succession of police, forensics experts and psychiatrists. Amy sat catatonic throughout the trial. Psychiatrists agreed that the shock of being on trial for double murder had sent her into what they called a fugue state.

It caused a sensation when I appeared as a witness for the defence, not the prosecution. I kept my eyes fixed on her all the time I gave evidence, willing Amy to speak. Once again, it was my word against hers. Except I was trying to justify what she did. Tell them of the years of abuse she suffered at the hands of her father. I spent hours in that witness box, a crumbled tissue in my clenched fist, tearfully describing the night of Jamie's murder. Seeing Amy stand up from her wheelchair. That moment I was never meant to witness.

That's why I've come here. To make one final act of atonement. Tell her how sorry I am.

The varnished banister feels sticky under my palm from all those patients trooping down for meals. Bunny climbs the worn stone steps ahead of me.

We reach the topmost high-security floor, the one where they kept the most at-risk patients. My home for ten years. Bunny presses her ID against the reader and the door clicks open, what I used to call the airlock.

The corridor has not changed but of course, the nursing station is empty. Past the bathroom where I had that blissful first shower. Patient bedrooms on the left.

Of course, they've put her in my old room, number nine. Of course they have.

Bunny puts her face to the porthole and then nods for

me to take a peek. Amy sits primly in a chair, staring out of the top-floor attic window. There are still iron bars across it, flecked from where the paint has chipped, as if someone has gnawed at them with their teeth. She is white-faced and hunched as if she's cold, and her hands, palms turned upward, lie lifeless in her lap. Gulls wheel beyond the glass but she doesn't notice them.

Bunny knocks softly and then pushes open the door.

With an effort, Amy lifts her head and turns to look at us. She's plainer than I remember, and her lips are thin and disapproving. Her hair has been cut short in an unbecoming bob. Most of all, her features have been blunted, as if she's gone through trauma.

We both have.

"Hello, Amy."

She turns her head a little way, frowning, like a person who's heard someone calling from a long way off, trying to remember. Our eyes meet but there's nothing. If Amy recognises me, she certainly doesn't show it. She gets up slowly from her chair and stands as submissively as a schoolgirl waiting to have her hands inspected for dirty fingernails.

She's become a child again.

Amy gives a timid, hopeful smile and asks, "Do I know you?"

Whatever prompted her to write to me, why she needed to see me in person, well, that moment has been and gone. She doesn't recognise me. Everything I wanted to tell her, how I've got a public campaign going, trying to get her sentence quashed, all of that gets forgotten.

"My name is Susan. We were friends... once. I wanted to see how you are." Then, remembering, "Oh, I brought you a present."

Another one. This time I rummage in my shoulder bag for the bottle of her favourite perfume I'd brought, Leather Rosa by Angela Flanders.

"Not allowed," says Bunny, intercepting my gift.

We stand there, Amy quizzical and hopeful. It's almost heartbreaking.

All I can think to say is, "Are you happy here?"

"Oh yes." She smiles. I had forgotten her rather beautiful smile. "Everyone is so kind to me."

Pause.

"You really have no idea who I am, do you?"

I flash on Doctor Max asking me almost that same question—what, nearly a year and a half ago? Amy shrugs and almost simpers. It's pitiful. She really does want to help. Nurse Bunny shifts her weight to another foot, indicating that we're done here. "You see," she seems to be saying.

Just as I make up my mind to go, Amy darts forward, plucking at my elbow. I flinch.

"Can I ask you a question, Susan?"

"Of course," I say, turning.

It's the same question I asked Doctor Max in this very room.

"Can you tell me who I really am?"

THANK YOU FOR READING

Did you enjoy reading *The Woman in Room 9*? Please consider leaving a review on Amazon. Your review will help other readers to discover the novel.

ABOUT THE AUTHOR

Tim Adler is an author and journalist who has written for the *Financial Times, The Times* and the *Daily Telegraph* among others.

His debut psychological thriller *Slow Bleed* went to number #1 in the Amazon Kindle psychological thriller chart.

Tim has had three nonfiction books published to date, the most recent of which was reviewed by *The Sunday Times* as "compulsively readable", while the *Daily Mail* called it "dazzling".

In 2024, he was nominated for the Crime Writers' Association Margery Allingham Short Mystery Prize. He is also a graduate of the Curtis Brown Creative novel writing course.

You can find Tim on his website:
www.timadlerauthor.com

Printed in Dunstable, United Kingdom